B"H

Peter Gimpel

turning back
the river speaks

a Polymorphic Novel

of

Music, Mischief & Murder

Red Heifer Press

Turning Back the River Speaks: A Polymorphic Novel of Music, Mischief and Murder, by Peter Gimpel

ISBN 978-0-9855199-5-7

First edition. Copyright © 2022 by Peter C. Gimpel

Published in the United States of America by
Red Heifer Press
410 Oakwood Court
Tehachapi, California 93561-1943

Cover art: Reverse image of Rockfish, by Utagawa Hiroshige.
Cover and Book Design by Red Heifer Press.
Graphic artwork by Charles Vaught.
Printed in the United States of America.

The paper used in this publication meets the minimum requirements of American National Standard of InformationSciences—Permanence of Paper for Printed Library Materials. ANSI/NISO Z39.48-1992.

Acknowledgment

My grateful thanks to pianist-composer
Edward Dimitri Kennaway, a dear and esteemed friend,
for generously and expertly setting the musical notes
in Chapter 17.

What is a Polymorphic Novel?

The polymorphic novel is a literary genre I developed in my novel, *The Carnevalis of Eusebius Asch* (Red Heifer Press, 1999). The genre was inspired by Hermann Hesse's literary masterpiece, *Magister Ludi or the Bead Game*. The genre is to be understood as a narrative version of the ritualized board game described by Hesse in *Magister Ludi*. The central thesis of that great novel is the search for a universal art form encompassing all the arts and sciences and combining them into an organic whole. The Bead Game consists in identifying and applying the interdisciplinary principles capable of organizing, correlating and unifying its divers themes and ideas.

As played among masters, the Game can open great intellectual and spiritual vistas; however, it can only be studied and appreciated in a cloistered society (Castalia) devoted to a mastery of its symbolic language and of the store of erudition from which it draws. As the protagonist of *Magister Ludi* discovers, such artistic and intellectual elitism relegates the Game and its devotees to an effete existence removed from humanity, its needs and its concerns. The solution, however, is not to discard the more esoteric refinements of civilization, but to awaken the masses to a full appreciation of its gifts. That is the definition of Humanism. First, feed, clothe and house the masses; then give them the tools to explore, understand and enjoy.

In the narrative form represented by the polymorphic novel, the Game's reliance on a massive handbook of symbols and formulas is obviated by the ordinary capacity of language to transmit knowledge and explain ideas. While the operative elements of the narrative must be reasonably grounded in theory and fact to be taken seriously, the correlations would be valueless to art if not embedded in a creative framework capable of stimulating and sustaining the vicarious emotional involvement and intellectual and aesthetic interest of the participating reader. Thus the elements of a polymorphic novel may be set forth as follows:

iv

1. An engaging, compelling, and entertaining story.

2   A serious, original treatment of social, political, scientific, philosophical, musical, mathematical, and suchlike problems of general interest and appeal.

3. A unifying structure in which seemingly disparate themes (see No. 2, above) are shown to be related in such a way as to reveal a central message, theme, or lesson that in turn "interprets" the story (No. 1, above).

4. A structural method of narration that makes use of innovative metanarrative and metastatic techniques, whereby meaning is self-explained through the unfolding of part from part and the relation of all the parts to each other and to the whole.

5. The reader's active critical and imaginative engagement. Hesse envisioned the Bead Game as a gradated, creative ritual marked off by sessions of meditation and analysis.

Thus, the structure and content of a polymorphic novel can be quite different from those of a conventional novel. While some of its features may resemble aspects of other learned novels, the polymorphic genre seeks not to pelt the reader with facts, figures and theories, but to engage and guide him or her through an intuitive process of discovery, critical thought, insight and catharsis.

A pretty girl is like a melody
that haunts you night and day

— Irving Berlin

turning back the river
speaks

ז

Arabesque

There is an ancient Jewish tradition that when a soul passes into the next world, it must immerse in a river called Dinur. When the soul emerges from the water, it will have lost all recollection of its life on earth. Some say that there are fish in this river, and that they remember everything. To this, some retort that they must be *gefilte* fish. Others say that they are the same fish who eat the morsels of stale bread thrown into rivers and ponds on Rosh Hashanah. The morsels represent the sins we cast off in the ritual of *Tashlich.*

The Ancient Greeks had their own river of forgetfulness. Its name, Lethe, reappears in the Greek word for truth—αληθεία (*alētheia*): the alpha privative (α-) placed before the word for "forgetting" turns it into "what can't be forgotten". The implication is that, to the Ancient Greeks, only Truth was worth remembering.
There is no recognized privative function for the corresponding Hebrew letter א (aleph), but words like אמת (*emeth* – Truth, literally, "deathless") and אשם *(asham* - guilt, literally "loss of name") might preserve traces of an archaic aleph privative, possibly derived from the Hebrew אין (ayin – "is not").

Souls can be forgetful in this life, too, of course, without help from the Dinur or its Greek counterpart, but such forgetfulness is usually not absolute, whereas it is so in the world of spirit. Faded memories can come alive, misplaced objects turn up in unlikely places, a forgotten name or face or sequence of events can be fished out from the depths of what seems like total oblivion.

11

But there are also times when the Dinur overflows its banks, or a strong wind whips up a spray from its glacial surface, and tiny drops of the hypnotic fluid fall to earth to cause some poor shlemiel to forget something so completely, so profoundly, that he will walk around for days as if searching for a missing piece of his own life. He may remember the circumstances, he may remember the time, the place, the weather, the scenery, lighting, mood, even the direction of the wind; but he will never remember what actually happened—the thing itself—only that he has forgotten it. It has been decreed from Above that this particular memory of his shall be stored not in the treasury of his own brain, but in some far-away vault impenetrable to him—for all we know, in someone else's brain. There is much talk today, in legal and scientific journals, of people remembering things that never happened to them.

Jewish tradition does not say whether what has been erased down here will be restored Up There, or whether the knowledge washed away by the celestial lymph will leave uncovered some other knowledge that otherwise would remain forever obscured. Or perhaps there is another river—a River of Remembering, whose sliding waters counteract the first, and likewise spill over from time to time to help some frantic and befuddled individual remember the address where he was supposed to meet the young woman who is actually predestined to become his wife.

My father, Yasha Yashanoshan, one of the great pianists of the 20th century, told me a story from his childhood, and I retell it here, though it may detract from the biography of him that I am always promising myself to write. It was soon after the outbreak of war—the First World War—that the Russian forces occupied (September 3, 1914) the Polish-Austrian city of Lemberg, where my father was born and raised. To be precise, Lemberg was only the Austrian name; the Polish and Russian name was Lwow, and now that the city has been incorporated into the territory of the independent Republic of Ukraine, it is known as Lviv. Does that matter? There were a hundred thousand Jews living in Lemberg, and in Lviv there are virtually none. In any case, Lemberg/Lwow is where my father lived with his mother and father and two brothers in a second-storey

12

rear apartment that looked out over the headquarters of the City Police.

The year was 1915, and it must have been springtime. The Russians had commandeered the Police Headquarters and were using the yard and building as a detention camp for Austrian prisoners of war. From their living room windows, my father and his older brother would entertain the prisoners below with concerts performed on the family upright, my grandfather occasionally joining in with his clarinet. From the same windows they could also watch in horror when prisoners were marched out to the high wall below that separated the yard from the apartment house. Mercifully, the condemned were hidden from view by the high wall, as was the firing squad with their pointing rifles, but the shots were heard and never forgotten.

One day, a commotion was heard in the yard, and word spread that soldiers were searching house to house for two escaped prisoners. Late that night, there was a quiet knocking at my grandparents' door. My grandfather, Reb Aharon (that is how I think of him, but his secular name was Adolph, and he was known to family and friends as "Dolu"), opened cautiously, and there stood two weary and disheveled men. One of them, holding a piano-tuner's kit, spoke deferentially in a broken German thick with Hungarian accents.

"Please forgive the disturbance. We are the men the Russians are looking for. We escaped this morning from prison camp. We have been in hiding all day. Our plan is to rejoin our unit encamped outside the city, but first we wanted to thank you, on behalf of ourselves and our fellow prisoners, for your kindness, for giving us food and music. This is greatly appreciated by everyone. Thank you."

In fact, my grandparents (may their blood be avenged!), were ardent Austrian patriots (thanks to the Jew-friendly disposition of the Emperor Franz-Josef), and had organized a neighborhood drive to collect food for the prisoners. My grandmother would prepare soup in a large cauldron—the kind used for boiling laundry, while Grandfather would lean out of the window and throw paper-wrapped sandwiches down into the thicket of waiting hands. Uncle

Lolek, my father's older brother (may his blood be avenged!) would trundle the steaming pot downstairs, and, with the help of a ladder, a big ladle, and a pair of Russian guards won over with a few groschen and cigarettes, would splash the soup into the prisoners' uplifted tins.

"My friend doesn't speak German or Polish," continued the piano tuner, "but he would like me to ask if it would be alright for him to play something for you on the piano by way of gratitude." The man—the silent one—sat down to the piano and played something that made a deep impression on my father, something that he had never heard before. It was obvious that the man was an accomplished pianist, and my father, then a boy of nine, lay on the floor on his stomach, chin in hands, listening in rapt concentration. When the conscript finished the piece, there were murmurs of "Bravo!" and "Thank you!" and "Good luck!" and warm grasping of hands.

My father, of course, wanted to know the name of the piece and the composer, but the soldier did not understand the boy's questions, and the men were in a hurry to leave. So, with packets of food pressed into their hands for the journey, the men took their leave without my father learning the identity of the wonderful piece that had so enchanted him and now haunted him.

Weeks passed, and a card arrived with the news that the two friends had arrived safely at the front. My father renewed his search for the mystery piece, leafing through his father's music library album by album but finding nothing. Eventually, the boy's attention was absorbed by some other interest and the mysterious music passed into the background of his consciousness.

As the months went by, however, my father came across a set of albums of collected piano pieces. It was an anthology of different composers, and when my father told me the story, he still remembered that the anthology was entitled *Gesang und Klang*— "Song and Sound." He opened the volume at random, and there on the page before his eyes lay spread the longed-for music. It was Debussy's Arabesque No. 1, in E Major. Excited over his discovery, the little boy ran to the kitchen shouting, "Mammi, Mammi! Look, I found the piece the soldier played for us! Come, I want to play it for you!" At that very moment, told my father, there was a knocking at the door. My grandfather opened, and there stood the postman with the mail. There was a card from the front. My grandfather read it in silence, turned pale, and then read it again quietly to his family, his voice trembling. "I am very sad to tell you that my friend _____ died yesterday on the field of honor." The note was signed by the piano tuner.

I am not sure why I have retold this story here. Is it really pertinent? Its true import seems to overwhelm the subject I have chosen to investigate, unless that import be that there is a level upon which nothing—even an unknown soldier—is ever forgotten—particularly those things which bind one soul, one mind, to another.

What pricks my curiosity, however, is that, already as a child, my father had a phenomenal musical memory: so it would have been uncharacteristic of him not to remember the Arabesque, or at least enough of it to identify it in his mind. Perhaps his frustration derived not from forgetting, but from not knowing. Who composed this wonderful piece? What is it called? How can I acquire it so that I may study it and play it myself?

But there is also a music that we are not permitted to remember until the moment is fitting and right. Anyway, on a deeper level, the story is not irrelevant. Not knowing the name is analogous to not remembering the music, for without the name, one cannot possess the thing. For my father, whose love for music was passionate, deep and devoted, it must have been like finding oneself in impromptu conversation with a beautiful and charming girl, exchanging shy glances with her, dancing with her for a few moments and then having her taken away by an indignant chaperon without so much as learning her name or phone number. (This actually happened to the parents of an old friend of mine!)

My uncle, the great violinist Boris Yashanoshan, had an experience of exactly the opposite kind. He had been going through a large trunk of his music, looking for a piece that he needed for an approaching concert, when he came across a chamber work by Ernst Toch. Struck by the whimsical-sounding title of "Pensive Serenade", he put it back in the pile intending to examine it later, and resumed his search. However, when he reopened the trunk to retrieve the "Pensive Serenade", he couldn't find it. Annoyed with himself, he went through the pile several times in vain, finally concluding that he must have imagined the whole thing. When he told me this story, however, he noted with residual perplexity that the title was very much like something Toch himself would have invented.

Many years later, when, alas, this same trunk came into my unworthy possession, I inventoried the whole collection, and had to laugh a rather pensive laugh when Toch's "Pensive Serenade" turned up in my hands. So my uncle possessed the name, but, in practical terms, not the music. That was obscured from him by a cloud of concealment—another errant phenomenon from the Upper Realms. Indeed, Ernst Toch, one of the great composers of the Twentieth Century, was obscured from the world by a similar cloud, and much of his musical production still remains undeservedly neglected.

As for myself, as the saying goes, I have forgotten more than I ever learned. However, I can remember three occasions when I, too, was sprinkled by the waters of Dinur. I am also quite familiar with the Clouds of Concealment, which I have studied carefully from both inside and out. To relate these encounters, however, I must first travel back to my student days in Italy, where I was studying the classical languages and literatures at the Università degli Studi di Perugia.

2

The Refinisher

After four years of attending classes and sitting for examinations at the university, I was at last accepted as a doctoral candidate by Aristotele Pilastri, my revered professor of Greek Literature. Exhausted and homesick I decided to return to my home in Smokey Hollow, where I could research my thesis at the HBU Library in close proximity to my aging mother and father. When I had completed my basic research and drafted the introductory chapters, I returned to Perugia to resume the life of exile I had interrupted the year before.

Soon after my arrival, I had an audience with the Professor. The purpose of our meeting was to discuss the work I had done in Smokes, which I had mailed to him shortly before my departure. The result of that conference, which began quite ominously, was that the Professor told me get someone else for a thesis adviser—perhaps Prof. T., who held the chair of *"Etnologia"* (Cultural Anthropology); but that he, Professor Pilastri, when he assigned a thesis on a certain subject, expected the student to carry out the assignment exactly and not go off on his own tangent and work on something else.

The truth was perhaps a little more complicated. Professor Pilastri had assigned me a thesis title, *"De mimis graecis alexandrino tempore conscriptis,"—On the Greek Mimes* (popular theatre pieces) *Composed During the Alexandrian Period*. He had handed me a list of fragmentary texts culled from the Oxyrrhyncus Papyri. All he had said was, "Start with these." I had duly sent him from

Smokes my translation, philological analysis and description of the passages he had assigned me. However, I had prefaced my philological treatment with an introductory essay on the origins and development of Greek popular theatre (*mimos*) and its relation to Greek tragedy, comedy and the satyr play. My research had erupted rather unexpectedly into an original theory of drama that drew heavily from Lévy-Bruhl and Lévi-Strauss and challenged certain well-established premises. In the heat of that fateful confrontation, it did not occur to me that Pilastri had probably blown up long before reaching the philological portion of my manuscript, and thus had most likely never seen the work I had done at his behest. Until the belated arrival of that moment of illumination, I wandered dazed and desolate through the streets of Perugia, unable to make sense of the years I had spent mastering Italian, teaching myself Greek, obtaining the Italian high school diploma—all for the purpose of realizing my dream of becoming a great classical scholar like my revered teacher.

At some indeterminate moment during these desperate peregrinations, I felt a tug at the sleeve of my wool jacket, and I turned around to see Ugo Marinelli staring at me with an expression of quizzical concern.

"*Stai bene?*" he asked, "Are you alright? I greeted you, but you walked right past me. How long have you been back?"

"*O Ciao, S'or Ugo! Non L'ho visto.* I didn't see you. I'm sorry. Yes, I confess I'm a bit down. How have you been? I got back a couple of weeks ago."

"I received your card. Thank you. I should have answered, but you know I'm not good with correspondence."

I had suspected for some time that S'or Ugo could neither read nor write. From time to time he would bring a letter or postcard with him to Trattoria "Da Serenella," the restaurant we both patronized on a near daily basis, and ask me to read it aloud. He would tender this request in the manner of one who had received through the mails a literary pearl or an astonishing piece of news, and who wanted not merely to share it with me but to grant me the pleasure of reading it out loud. As I read to him, he would sit there beaming, to all appearances savoring the retelling of a story he had already heard several times; and when I finished reading what was, as often as not, little more than a "thinking of you, wishing you well," he would say, "Well, what do you think?" as though the only reason he had had me read the thing was to know my opinion of it.

Ugo Marinelli was tall, gaunt, and soft-spoken, a man of few words, of gentle demeanor and mild expression. His hair lay smooth and gray. He would have been quite pleasing in appearance if not for some missing teeth, whose vacancies he attempted conceal when speaking. This, as I have intimated, was not very often. The first time I met S'or Ugo was at "Da Serenella" in Via dei Cartolari, where we were introduced by my then girlfriend, an attractive blonde Danish widow, a bit older than my nineteen years. The two of them already had a chatting acquaintance, and in my youthful insecurity I adopted an attitude of wary coolness which did not appear to offend him. I began to take him more seriously, though, when, three or four years later, the girlfriend long gone, I discovered that Ugo was well known to my close friend, Mario Martini, professor of Filosofia Morale at the *università,* and to his twin brother, Carlo, a professor of art history. "*È un tipo straordinario,*" they said, "a remarkable fellow. He is always asking about the great painters."

In spite of the boost to my esteem for Ugo, our encounters rarely went beyond the conventional exchanges, and on the rare occasions when we dined together, the conversation consisted of his rather simple-minded questions about America and my laborious attempts to answer them without seeming to condescend. Ugo managed nearly always to steer the talk away from himself. I gleaned that he was married and had a family from whom he was to some degree estranged. It was not clear where he slept, although it was obvious that he did not take his meals at home. Before I departed for the States, Ugo had asked me to send him an occasional postcard. He had given me his address as Via Bontempi, No. 19. I sent him one postcard from "The Valley", but received no reply. When I got back to Perugia I was in no particular hurry to seek him out. "Serenella's" had in the meantime closed, and our respective eating places no longer coincided.

"*Perché sei giù?* Why are you down?" inquired Ugo, solicitously.

"It's a long story," I said.

"Have you eaten?"

"*No. Non ho molto appetito.*"

"Come with me. I'm going to the *Mensa Popolare*."

The *Mensa Popolare* was new to me, so I went along more out of curiosity than hunger or desire for company. S'or Ugo led me past the Fontana Maggiore and through the Maestà delle Volte to a little street that slanted steeply down to the Via dei Priori. We stopped in front of a stone *portale* that I had slouched past many times on my way to San Filippo Neri, an old, neglected church that, perhaps in punishment for some carnal sin committed there, had been damned to projecting old Hercules movies onto a dingy bed sheet for a couple of hundred Lire.

Strange, but as I remembered it after so many years, this *portale* was in another street altogether—Via del Pinturicchio, to be exact, which skirted the northern edge of the city. In my memory the *portale* led to a garden atop the city wall that rose high over a deep valley. My friends assure me, however, that the *Mensa* was in Via Fratti, across from that miserably depressing cinema, near the center of town and far from any vistas of rolling valleys and hills. As a matter of fact, the entrance led into a graveled courtyard enclosed on all sides by apartment houses, but open to the sky. Perhaps there were rows of potted cypresses, suggesting to my imagination panoramas inaccessible to the eye. It seems however, that I have remembered everything but the location and the view with tolerable accuracy.

The *Mensa* was a kind of outdoor soup kitchen for students, workers and the poor. Subsidized by the *Comune di Perugia*, it offered bland, simple fare for a few Lire—about sixty cents' worth for a plate of pastasciutta or minestrone, to be followed by a little meat and vegetables. A small flask of sourish wine of local provenance was included. Manual laborers, university students, beggars, all sat side by side on wooden benches at long picnic-style tables. The sparse talk was the usual animated socialist patter—the corruption and impotence of the state, the oppression of *operaio* and *paesano*.

Ugo and I listened to them more than we spoke to each other, but in response to his questions, I told him what had happened between me and Professor Pilastri. Ugo appeared to listen attentively, his eyes thoughtfully downcast.

"*Hai da fare dopo il pranzo?* Are you doing anything after dinner?" he asked, as though I had been telling him nothing of any consequence.

I said I had no special plans. "Why?" I added.

"I want to show you something."

"What?" I inquired.

"You'll see."

Payment was on entry, so when we were done eating, we just got up and left. It was a nice little walk from Via Fratti to Ugo's workshop in Via Bontempi, uphill, downhill, and silent. On the way, we stopped at a *bar-caffè* and sipped an espresso which Ugo offered and paid for.

Via Bontempi was one of those dark streets barely wide enough for two *Cinquecentos* to pass each other in opposite directions, a downhill slope of ancient stone apartment houses that followed the curve of the road in an uninterrupted façade. We stood soon enough in front of number 19, which, if I remember, was not very far down the hill. The doorway was set back in a shallow alcove formed by a brick-lined arch, and through it we descended a short flight of stone steps into a kind of vaulted cellar. The atmosphere was rich with the smell of varnish and turpentine, and by the dim light I could barely make out the shadowy forms of chairs, tables, wardrobes piled on top of each other in an eerie jumble.

Ugo switched on the electric light over his work bench, which was set against the wall facing the street. The bench was favored by what daylight trickled from a lone, street-level window set high up in the plastered stone wall. I couldn't see where Ugo practised his craft because the gloomy light did not reveal sufficient space for carrying on a refinishing business, but it was clear what Ugo was doing at night. The workbench was laden with artist materials—pots of tubes and brushes, palettes, pencils, rulers. Art books were piled high at one end, on chairs, on a small table, on the floor. A half-painted canvas leaned against a makeshift easel rigged out of a tall chair and sections of wooden board. Facing it, like one decrepit lady drinking tea with another, was an old wooden armchair with half-gutted upholstery.

As I squinted at the painting on the easel, Ugo clicked on a reading lamp, directing the illumination onto the canvas. The painted half was not quite finished, but already alive, copied from an open book perched upon the adjacent easel (a real one). The blank portion of the canvas was mapped out with a precisely ruled network of squares etched onto a coating of white underpainting. The open page, too, on closer examination, proved to be overlaid with neat little squares, each having its corresponding counterpart on the canvas.

"*Rafaello?*"

"*Sì. Che ne pensi?* What do you think of it?" It was more of a statement than a question.

"You did this? *Accidenti!* It's quite wonderful."

"Isn't it? You know, he lived just a few streets away."

I continued to admire the canvas, my eyes ferrying me back and forth from canvas to open volume.

"Do you have any finished paintings?"

Without replying, Ugo reached under the worktable and pulled out canvases one after the other. I was speechless. They were all remarkably well done—two or three of them masterfully. Tiziano, Giotto, Giorgione, il Perugino, Mantegna, da Messina, Masaccio, della Francesca, Michelangiolo, Van Eyck. The Bacchus of Caravaggio glimmered at me through the surrounding darkness, its own dramatic shadows mingling imperceptibly with the chiaroscuro of the workshop. The copy had all the divine smugness of secret knowledge possessed by the original. A cry of joyful recognition escaped my lips as I caught a glimpse of Bronzino's scandalous Cosimo de' Medici posing as Orpheus at the gates of Hades, the beautiful head detached by shadow and foreshadow from the muscular curves of the massive *corpo*, the viol bow iconically phallic in the amorous poet's hand.

Other canvases—his first attempts, he assured me—exhibited a less authoritative line and something of the amateur in coloration and shading, yet they still impressed me as worthy achievements. The furniture refinisher reached again under the magic bench and drew out canvas after canvas. It was breathtaking. Each was done with meticulous attention to the tiniest detail—color, shading, precision of drawing. Square by square, frame by frame. How many years had he been doing this, night after night, into the early hours of the morning? Giorgione, Tintoretto, Reni. Ugo obviously favored the Italians, was inclined to dramatic scenes and portraits, and appeared to confine his attention to the *Rinascimento* and the *Seicento*. Almost all the copies were reductions, he pointed out, smaller than the original sizes, which he knew by heart and reeled out to me one by one as we went through the stacks. He could not afford to work with life-size canvases.

"*È una meraviglia, S'or Ugo, una meraviglia!*"

"*Aspetta un attimo,*" he uttered. "Wait a second." With an air of suppressed pride, he went behind the chair piled high with art books and gingerly lifted out a frame that had been leaning face toward the wall. He turned it carefully, removed the art book from the easel and set the canvas down in its place. It was a masterpiece—from a painting that I had never set eyes on before, a battle scene, gleaming with silver armor, flashes of drawn swords, clamorous with shouts of war and wound, and dark with dust and clouds of omen.

"*È magnifico! Che cosa è?*"

"It is of Rembrandt—the battle for Jerusalem."

"But it is truly magnificent!"

"*Davvero?*"

"Yes, truly! You have the original—I mean the reproduction?"

"*Ecco qua.*" Ugo fished out the album from one of the piles and opened it to the pages. As I looked back and forth, it was as though the original was before me and the photo reproduction taken from there. And yet, there was something that I could not put into words, overwhelmed as I was by the mass of detail.

"Do you notice anything different?" inquired Ugo.

"I do, but I am not sure what."

"Keep looking."

It took me a while, but after a pause, I spoke up. "What happened to the rest of the picture? The photo is cut off on the left." In fact, the reproduction shown in the album ended in the full mix of combat, with the horse in the foreground cut off in the middle.

"There is nothing wrong with the photo," said Ugo quietly. Indeed, this was one of Rembrandt's remarkable innovations in the area of composition: until then, the borders of a painting were little more than an imaginary frame, directing the eye to the center of composition. In this painting, however, the canvas arbitrarily cut off the action, as in a snapshot, as if to say that the scene was really much larger and that the artist would have painted more if his canvas had been big enough. The power of this technique was astounding.

"You added something!"

"Look here." Ugo came closer and pointed a stained index finger at a panicked horse with rolling eyes and frothing mouth that, except for the rump and the pluming tail, found no counterpart in the photo. In fact, everything to the left of the hindquarters had been invented by the copyist, but with such skill and style and seamless construction that one could not tell that it was not the hand of the master himself. Ugo had expanded the original by a third of its width. And he had done so without compromising one iota of the integrity of Rembrandt's composition!

"*Ugo, sei un maestro!*"

He ignored my outburst and continued to point out with his finger several noteworthy accomplishments of his brush.

"*S'or Ugo*," I persisted. "You could open up an atelier. What need have you to be a *verniciatore?*"

"What need have I to be an artist?" he retorted. "If my *mestiere* must give me heartache, it is better I get it from refinishing furniture than from painting pictures. If my art were to give me grief instead of enjoyment and solace, what would I have left?"

It was a question that left room for no answer. What would he have left? His wife, his children, if he had any, were estranged from him, had rejected him in jealousy of his passion, or else had tried to stifle it and had pushed him further and further away until he had shut himself out. For all I knew, there was a cot tucked away in some dark corner of the shop and he slept there among the paintings, the furniture and the fumes. It was a wonder the man could see straight let alone reason like a human being (I was by now beginning to feel somewhat woozy). And if he did not sleep there, where did he sleep? A tiny room somewhere with a bed, a wobbly table and a chair and no window for an artist to look out of. Or did he go home to a resentful woman who gave him silence, cold, recrimination?

That evening, I ate alone in my room and for the first time had trouble justifying my ambitions. What was the point of it all? Ugo had spoken well. Was it wise to break one's head against one wall after another, sacrifice one's comfort and the company of one's loved ones in order to turn one's passion into heartache? For what? For prestige? Whenever I had been introduced to someone back home in the Valley of Smokes and told them I was studying Latin and Greek, it was the end of the conversation. For money? *Non farmi ridere!* For pleasure? *Ma va!* I remembered the glee radiating through the halls of the Classics Department at HBU, from whence I had fled all the way to Italy.

Yes, Ugo was right. It would have been more sensible to go into the hardware business and consort with Homer and Virgil and Dante by night. I could have done just that only a month prior, when a family acquaintance invited me into his firm. He wanted to train me to take over his shop in place of his sons, who he knew would run it into the ground. I turned him down, as graciously as one can a desperate old man who begs you to accept what is most precious to him and means nothing to you.

Around ten o'clock I put on my jacket and went out, walked up the hill to the town center, knowing quite well that at that hour the streets would already be deserted and the cafés empty and shuttered. I could never understand how, with thousands of university students, the Perusine night life could be so entirely lacking—or, given the lack, how others like me did not feel the need to walk off their sorrows and longings before going to bed.

The night was cold and damp, and Corso Vannucci was swaddled in thick fog. From the Fontana Maggiore one couldn't see as far as the Arco dei Priori. In this cloud of saturated concealment, I walked from one end of the Corso to the other—from the Duomo to the Giardini Pubblici and from the Giardini Pubblici to the Duomo—I don't know how many times. Despite my depression, I could not help thinking of Hermann Hesse's little poem, *Seltsam in der Nebel zu wandern.*

> *Strange to wander in the fog,*
> *Every person is alone.*

I had come to Italy hoping to study the classics "on location," had taught myself Greek while learning to speak Italian, gone back to high school (the *Liceo Classico*) in order to earn the diploma that would enable me to enroll at the *università*, discovered a professor of Greek literature whom I admired, loved, and respected, had got him to be my thesis adviser, and had written an eighty-page introduction that promised to put Greek drama in a new perspective—only to be dismissed by my teacher because I had given him more than he had asked for. I had put a great distance between myself—an only child—and my mother and father, causing them and myself to endure long, agonizing periods of separation, had suffered years of loneliness, deprivation and anxiety. For what? For heartache? Lo! I had already achieved that.

Was I now to change my academic "major" to *Etnologia*—Cultural Anthropology—a field I certainly found fascinating but for which I felt no special passion? Throw up all my good work and place myself under the whimsy of another professor—one for whom I felt no special scholarly attraction? Or was it time to throw in the towel, admit defeat and return in disgrace to the Valley of Shmucks, and beg old Mr. Carter to teach me Nuts and Bolts? Or should I attempt to complete my studies in that strange land where I had, years before, dared to begin them? I had despised the pomposity and the condescension, the isolationism, the ideological bankruptcy of a system that offered degrees in the humanities that were virtually useless outside of the academic environment, the pathetic and disingenuous attempts of the faculty to make classical philology appear "relevant" to modern society and popular taste.

Whichever way I looked at it, I found the prospect repugnant and humiliating. I was starting to feel cold, dry and faint, yet I could not stop turning the matter over in my head—as I could not stop turning the Corso under my feet.

For all that, the thought of Ugo the Refinisher kept returning to my overstimulated brain. I recalled Thomas Grey's beautiful verses,

Perhaps in this neglected spot is laid
Some heart once pregnant with celestial fire

for surely he would die one day and no one would remember his passion for the great masters; the paintings that gave him so many uncountable hours of exaltation and pride would be thrown into the garbage, and he himself, and all that made him an artist, laid to rest in a grave commensurate with his humble status, under a stone that made no mention of his talent or his dreams. I, too, my thoughts went on, would be buried one day, unwept, bereft of accomplishments or honor. And so on.

I don't know how long I might have continued in the same vein, but—it must have been a few minutes past eleven, for I remember hearing the tower bells toll the hour, as they tolled in Thomas Grey's beautiful Elegy—when my obsession was interrupted by what seemed like the wafting sound of distant music.

Music, at that dark and empty conjunction of time and space, was completely anomalous, because the streets of Perugia-Centro were officially quiet at that hour of night. At first I thought someone must have turned on the stereo with the windows open. However, as I walked, the sound seemed to be coming from many directions. This would not have been remarkable in the summertime, when you could walk down Via dei Priori at nine o'clock and listen to *Il Carosello* or *Canzonissima* as you went: there was only one television channel, everybody was watching it, and all the windows were open. But now it was winter and people were barricaded in their apartments for the night. Windows and shutters were sealed against the cold and the fog, and the broadcasts were long over.

On impulse I stopped still in my tracks, intent on pinpointing where the sounds were coming from. The notes were getting louder and closer, and I thought they made a marching tune, but couldn't be sure. Yes, it certainly was a march—a one-two, one-two, one-two. Perhaps it was an auto driving up to town with the radio blasting, or maybe one of those little Fiats with loudspeakers that the political parties dispatch through the city at election time with music and propaganda blaring. But why so late? And besides, the music was too clear, too high-fidelity, unspoiled by the Doppler effect so characteristic of those detestable vehicles.

There was something surreal about it, and a little frightening, too. There I stood, completely alone under the town clock in the center of a dead city, bathed in heavy mist, and enveloped in march music that seemed now to be coming from the direction of Piazza Matteotti, from the post office on the other side of a block of old shops and apartment buildings. The music was quite loud now, and always closer and closer, yet I still could see nothing, although I was staring— confused and vaguely apprehensive—straight at the blind spot where all the fanfare was coming from.

Suddenly, right where I am looking, the clouds part like a curtain and out of the fog, rank by rank, in full uniform, banners trailing, bursts a full brass band marching green and red and white, trumpets, trombones, horns and bombardons—thirty or forty men—all in perfect step, all blowing and farting and tooting like a summer's day at the races.

I watched in disbelief as the apparition passed before me without so much as a single sidelong glance at their lone spectator, watched mutely as row after row greyed out into swirls of fog just as they turned the corner into Via Mazzini. As the last tuba disintegrated into the mists, I had a sudden urge to run after them, to catch up with them, march along with them, talk to them, ask them who they were, what they were doing, where they had come from, where they were going—but I couldn't move. Something held me back. Perhaps it occurred to me that if I followed them, I might never find my way back. I stood rooted to the spot, doubting my own senses. No one else had stirred. Not a soul had come out into the street, not a window was cracked.

I remained standing there as long as I could hear the music. It was not exactly a beautiful tune, but a rousing one, jaunty, full of determination and boisterous good feeling, like a warm, congratulatory slap on the back. When the last notes had faded away into silence, I was surprised to hear my own voice sing-shouting after them words heard long ago sung to a different tune,

> *Now you may think that this is the end,*
> *Well it is, but to show that I'm a liar,*
> *I'm going to sing it again,*
> *But this time I'm going to sing a little higher!*

And then I burst out laughing like a fool, hearing my laughter echo like ghostly hiccups all the way down the deserted Corso.

Yet the most remarkable part of this whole story—perhaps the only reason I have remembered it—is that when I did try to sing that spectral march to myself—to test myself, I think, to reassure myself that I had not been dreaming—I could not remember a note! It was as though someone had erased a tape recording. There was nothing there, nothing that I could dredge up from the river of forgetfulness other than *Stars and Stripes Forever*. I had been hearing the other tune repeatedly for several minutes, until it seemed quite familiar— in fact as though it had been drilled into my head. Yet, as I have said: nothing.

Later that night I wrote a letter to Professor Pilastri in which I attempted to reconstruct what had happened between us. On my return to Smokes I had completed my assignment and had gone on to write a general introduction that I hoped would lay a theoretical foundation for the work the Professor had given me and for the further assignments that were implied by it. I had posted the material to the Professor's residence in Rome, just as he had requested. In my cover letter I had asked him to let me know if he objected to my plan, and he had not replied. I had telephoned him from Smokes and he assured me he had received my papers and would discuss them with me on my return, but that he was pleased with my work and with my enthusiasm. In the letter, I was now drafting, I explained that in the absence of more specific instructions I felt it my duty to make the best of the excellent research facilities at my disposal, but averred that I stood ready to rewrite my dissertation in any way he desired, and that I had meant no offense by submitting my own ideas for his approval.

The next morning, I took a train to Rome, where Professor Pilastri had retired for the weekend. It was a long bus ride to the Professor's apartment house in a quiet, modern suburb. I dialed him up on the intercom, told him I was downstairs, explained to him that I had come directly from Stazione Termini to clarify the situation, adding that I was carrying a letter for him, and that if he didn't allow me to complete my dissertation with him I would give everything up and return to America. Without inviting me up, he bade me deposit the letter in his mailbox, promised to read it carefully and said he would see me in his office at the *Facoltà di Lettere* the following week. Many things happened to me in Italy that were worthy of *Alice in Wonderland*, but this remains the only time I ever traveled two hundred kilometers to speak to someone over the house intercom. However, when one carries a letter to be delivered *SGM*— ("*Sue Gentili Mani,*")—directly into the hands of the recipient, one becomes like the postman. One must be ready for anything, even the bite of a *barone*—a powerful "baron" in the Italian university system.

Without going into further details, the matter was resolved. It took me three more years to complete my thesis, which I did according to my original plan and with the Professor's knowledge and permission. At the disputation, Professor Pilastri, instead of defending my thesis, attacked it, cross-examining me ineffectually on minor details, while Professor Pizzuti, who was supposed to be my cross-examiner, defended it staunchly and sincerely. He subsequently offered me an entry-level job in his department, which I most reluctantly declined, being long overdue back in Smokey Hollow to look after my aging parents.

I never learned the provenance of the unearthly procession that paraded before me that night, or the name of that jaunty tune they were playing. I had never heard it before, and, so far as I can tell, I never heard it again, and if I ever do hear it again, it probably won't matter much if I recognize it or not. But when I returned to Perugia early the morning after that remarkable visit to the lobby of my illustrious professor's apartment house, I found the streets festooned with banners, and brass bands were everywhere.

3

Carosello

I have been musing about clouds of concealment and rivers of forgetfulness, not about my short career as a classical philologist. And yet, that seems to be the direction in which my ramblings are flowing in spite of myself. For I had another encounter, similar in some ways to the one I have just described, a couple of years after my return to the Rim, where I had finally obtained a research position at John Wayne University. Strange to be wandering in these memories after so many years—things not forgotten, but as if grafted onto another life once but no longer mine! As if I had forgotten that this was I.

Strolling along the beachfront on Pincer Island one night—it was late summer, when the evenings along the coast can be rather cool and wet—my thoughts were as black as they were that night on Corso Vannucci, when they were similarly arrested by a distant music. The concrete promenade was empty of people and the glass faces of the beach houses, designed more for peering into than looking out of, were uniformly dark. A cold haze, not a fog, hung in the air and chilled the skin. The beach was so deserted that if I had not been absorbed in my own gloom I might have felt some apprehension about continuing my solitary walk. But perhaps I have got ahead of myself.

The story really started several months earlier—I can't be more precise—which means that later on I will have to double back in time in order to complete the telling and tie the loose ends together. I was invited to dinner by my friend, the Greek scholar and poet Sokrates Naumachou. Both he and his wife Annie were graduate students—and my only true friends—at JW, the only campus in the New World that thought well enough of my foreign degree, or cared little enough about it, to hire me. To say that I was a fish out of water in "La Concha" (short for Conchacancha County) would be both to underestimate my powers of adaptive survival and to trivialize the psychological cost of existing in a culture without history, without memory, and without a vision of the future not conceptually limited to clean energy, 3-D TV, and interstellar space travel. The suburban inhabitants of this Swiftian land were devoted to the idea of leisure. Tennis, golf, surfing, sailing, hot tubs and horses. The business end of this storybook existence was serviced by an economic underclass of Mexicans, Hondurans, Salvadorans, Guatemaltecas, *et al.,* whose urban lives, habits, needs, works, and thoughts were virtually inexistent to campus consciousness. Neither were the higher intellectual interests readily admitted to in Nirvana, and I had made the early and repeated mistake of not dissembling mine.

I had been feeling particularly downtrodden for an unusually long stretch when my friend Sokrates limped up to me where I was sitting on the edge of the concrete planter in the middle of Humphreys Court. The poet sat down beside me and speaking in low, conspiratorial tones modulated by his rumbling, thick Greek accent, said, "Look here, Louis. I have something to tell you. I have obtained a small koantity of excellent grass, and Annie and I are saving some joints for you."

"That's very kind. You know I don't smoke."

"Louis, you must try. I can't bear to see you like this. Try it. You will enjoy it and the world will look a little bit more friendly."

"Where did you get it?"

"Where do you think?"

There was a rumor that Heinz Strauss, the Project director, had recently flown his little Cessna into Mexico and had returned with an especially fine and generous assortment of prohibited vegetable matter.

"I'm not interested."

"Look. Annie and I have been wanting to invite you to our house for a good Grik meal. Annie is a very good cook. Her *souvlaki* is truly marvellouse. She has ordered a chocolate cake from an excellent bakery and I have a couple of nice bottles of Zinfandel. You will come, you will eat, you will say *ghiasou,* you will listen to some Schubert, and you will take a few puffs of some good green grass, and . . ."

"And the grass will seem greener . . .?"

". . . and you will be a different person. There is a little room with a bed just for you if you get sleepy."

"It sounds like you have thought of everything. Is there also a girl in the bed?"

"Sure, but only if you bring one."

The marijuana was only a hypothesis, and the girl a pipedream, but that was no reason to turn down a good dinner with two friends. We set the date for the coming Friday, and that Friday I left work early to give myself time to get properly spruced, in case the hypothesis proved correct and the dream real.

The freeway was already clogged. By the time I got to Richfield Beach I barely had time to shower and shave and put on a nice suit. It was almost seven when I got back into my car and headed toward campus, where Sokrates and Annie lived in Student Housing. On the way, I stopped at a Somervilles on Bali Hai near Volcanic Highway to pick up some flowers and a bottle of scotch.

Looking for the shortest line, I came briefly face to face with a stunning young woman who took her place not far behind me. Before I had time to even consider whether to try my luck, to my utter amazement, she said "Hi!" with a surprised smile, as though we knew each other. Not recognizing her, I smiled back and said "Hi!"

Just then, it was my turn at the cash register, so I turned away. While writing the check, however, I racked my brains, desperate to remember where I knew her from. Did I in fact know her? Had we met before? Should I ask? If we had met, she would surely feel hurt once she realized that I had no idea who she was. She couldn't have been more than eighteen. She was so beautiful it would have been truly unforgivable of me not to remember. And what if she was mistaken? That would also have been embarrassing for her. And then, I was late for my dinner invitation. There was no time to converse with her or even to sort out my thoughts. I turned to wave goodbye, but she was occupied with her purchase, and I thought there was a look of disappointment about her lovely face.

As I walked to my car, I already regretted my foolishness. I tried to console myself by rationalizing that if I started up with her I would not find it in me to break away, and so would keep my friends waiting in vain at a table that was set and laden especially for me.

Driving down the highway, I still saw her face in front of me. "You're an idiot!" I said aloud. "You could have invited her to the party. At least you might have got her phone number!" To this reproach I had nothing to reply, and we drove the rest of the way in sullen silence.

Sokrates welcomed me at the door, Annie from the kitchen, both happy and excited. "Annie has prepared an exkuisit dinner, a bankuet! What? You came alone?"

"It's funny you should mention it." I told them about my experience at the supermarket.

"Louie! I can't understand you. If it had been me, I would have kept the Naumachous waiting all night."

"If you were me, you would not have invited me in the first place."

The dinner was wonderful, but I must have been a letdown to my would-be benefactors. The emjay did little for me. The cake felt foreign in my mouth, as though someone else were chewing it. The Schubert G-major quartet, ever a direct path for me to Sweetness and Light, sounded annoyingly inconsequential to my preempted ears. Nevertheless, I fell into a benign coma from which I was aloofly conscious of everything that was said and done. Eventually, Sokrates led me, swaying and stumbling to the little side room where he had his private study. I was barely able to remove my shoes before collapsing into the promised bed and a deep, healing sleep under a cloudlike eiderdown. The next morning, I awoke late, but calm, refreshed, and grateful. After a cup of coffee with my friends, I drove home to LA to spend the rest of the weekend with my parents.

As time passed, I would occasionally think of the girl in the supermarket. In that pensive state, I could remember her face very well, but not being able to place her, I became persuaded by and by that the whole thing had been a mistake. I put the incident out of my mind, and eventually her memory faded into the background. I never saw her again, though for a time I did consider changing super-markets in the hope of meeting her again. Somervilles, however, was inconveniently distant from where I lived.

I don't remember how much time passed—days, weeks, months? Yes, it must have been several months—perhaps a year and a half. But one day—I am not exactly sure through what association—I thought of my previous apartment, the one I moved into when I first took the job at John Wayne. It was a little studio apartment in one of those pretentious Rococo Beach colonies that advertise "luxury" accommodations at economy prices. A large and sinuous swimming pool, an enormous public jacuzzi and a social director were supposed to compensate for the unsociable atmosphere and the rather tacky furnishings. The best thing about the apartment was the right side of the balcony, from where I had a narrow view of the ocean. The left side afforded me an excellent perspective of my neighbor's balcony, which was occasionally improved by a very attractive brunette who, on the rare occasions when our paths crossed in the hallway, would acknowledge my greeting, if at all, with a perfunctory "Hi." One of the few times I saw her on the balcony, she was entertaining a man whom I am anachronistically ashamed to say I recognized as a notorious porn star. Or perhaps it was he who was entertaining her. I must say that it was quite a challenge, at Driftwood Cove, to know who were one's actual neighbors.

I would come home to my driftwoodsy paradise exhausted and depressed from another day of cogitative deprivation at JW, change into my swimming trunks, and slide into the jacuzzi for ten or fifteen minutes, swim a few laps in the pool, and return to my apartment sufficiently restored to cook dinner, watch a rerun, and go to bed. In "The Richfield," where I was now living, there was no pool and no jacuzzi, and while my neighbors were friendlier and their visitors more conventional, I missed the hot tub and my late afternoon swim. My best conjecture is that, thinking of the jacuzzi, I remembered something that I had wanted very much to edit out of my memory.

One Sunday afternoon at Driftwood, after cleaning my bachelor quarters and having gone down for a swim, I noted with dismay that a certain couple whom I preferred to avoid had taken possession of the pool. He, a burly executive type, white haired and heavy, she, fortyish, blonde, buxom, and given to emitting hysterical shrieks of exaggerated fun. The two of them disporting like a pair of walruses. He, chasing her through the water, and, she, when caught, tossed into the air, with a splash, upon re-entry, worthy of a Mercury space capsule. So instead, I slid into the jacuzzi, in spite of the fact that it was already occupied at one end by a cluster of people standing waist-deep in the water, drinking cocktails and chatting. I had hardly immersed myself when I noticed that between me and the social set was a very beautiful young blonde who did not appear to be too involved with the others. I looked at her with friendly admiration, and she smiled at me, so I said, "Hi! Do you mind if I ask your name?" She was about to answer—may actually have answered "Christine," when a trim looking man with short, curly blond hair turned to me and said in a rather loud voice,

"Oh no you don't! Do you mind? I'm her father."

"I beg your pardon? I was just saying hello."

"No you weren't. You were hitting on her. She's sixteen years old, and men are always hitting on her. Just back off and mind your own business."

I was so stupefied by this uncivil outburst that I just stood there speechless for several seconds, then looked down into the water, considering whether to stay in or get out. I felt my face turn bright red, then deathly white. I glanced over at the girl just long enough to see her cringing in shame, and climbed out without another word, put on my bathrobe, and left. Well over a year had passed since that incident, but I still remembered her face, bright, sweet, innocent and completely uncaring of how beautiful she was.

It was the same face. Thirty years later, I still remember it. Why did I not remember it then? The features were a little more refined, perhaps, the eyes a little deeper, perhaps, but just as sweet and bright and, if possible, even more beautiful than when I first saw her. In those eighteen months or more she had become a woman, and men, so many men, had pursued her, phoned her, invited her out to parties, dinners, dances, movies, yachts, yet she still remembered me, wanted to talk to me, wanted to know who I was. I felt a great sadness for her, and also for me.

I moved out of Driftwood Cove Apartments soon after the fiasco in the jacuzzi, but that very same night, feeling angry, humiliated, wounded, and desperately alone, I drove down to Pincer Island hungry for the sight of anonymous bipedal life. Instead, the island was desolate. And as I was saying, my thoughts were arrested by a distant music. The melody, even from a distance, was melancholy and beautiful, and this time, its origin seemed to be straight ahead of me and stationary, the notes gaining clarity and volume as I walked. The tune became more enchanting with every step. It was in a minor key, in three-quarter time, yes, definitely a waltz, and as I got closer, it took on an Italian character, though I could not identify it—an aria, perhaps, from one of the lesser operatic masterpieces. Nor, at first, could I identify the instrument that was producing the organ-like strains. But as I drew nearer to the source—still hidden from sight—I recognized the wheezy timbre of a calliope, a carousel organ. In fact, as I rounded a bend in the walkway, a small merry-go-round came into view, brightly lit, complete with revolving flags and slowly churning horses.

It was a frame from a Fellini movie, but, to tell the truth, I was too enthralled by the music to pay much attention to the weirdness of the scene. The place was empty, not a soul around, just the darkened row of glass showcases, the dark night, the invisible ocean hissing across the sand, and before me, the carousel rotating in lighted solitude like a daydreaming child. I walked up to it in amazement. The horses, beautifully carved and painted, described a poignant sine wave around a mirrored column that sprinkled petals of light onto the surrounding pavement.

A shadow moved among the machinery that made the thing go.

"Hello?" I said.

"Hey!" grunted the form.

"How much for a ride?"

"I'm packing up. Going home. 'Slate."

"I'm your only customer. How long would it take?"

"Sorry."

"What about tomorrow night?"

"Gig's over. Morning it's all going back in the truck."

"What was that song you were playing?"

"No idea. Comes with the package."

The form was busy, did not want to be disturbed, so I let it be. There was no point in walking further. I turned around and walked back, the air conspicuously silent.

As I might have expected, I could not recall a single note. It was a great disappointment for me. I had been seized by a great desire—a need, in a way—to ride one of those prancing horses. I wanted to create a memory for the future, to be able to remember myself riding that hallucinatory orbit in utter solitude. It would have been like writing a poem. Even more, I wanted to know the name of that waltz, who wrote it, where it came from, where to find it—so I could make it mine, so it would always be mine. If only I had been paying more attention to that little carousel and its music! It was as if that little song contained a secret—a special knowledge, perhaps the reason we are here, so that if one knew the secret of the song, one could die in peace, knowing that everything is just and justice, if sad, is perfect.

Shlemielke, Shlemielke, how many are the fragments of your scattered life, how like those tumbling flakes of light strewn into the night by the spinning glass! How tenuous and tangled the thread that holds them all together! What is it made of, that thread that holds everything together? What is the thread that holds *you* together? What is this waltz that you are dancing? How many wonderful things you have attempted, how much energy expended, what a strange road you have travelled!

There was another music that I forgot, but that was many years later. First, I want to say something about what I was doing at John Wayne, because that too is related to remembering, and to music also, but to a music of a different kind, and one that I have never forgotten.

4

Remember to Forget!

When most people commit something to writing, they think it is to preserve something—a thought, a feeling, a proof or syllogism, a record, a piece of testimony—in short, they do it as an aid to memory. I have a different idea. To me, it seems that when people write something down it is to give themselves leave to forget it. Perhaps that is what the Torah means when God commands Moses our Teacher to document the war against Amalek:

Write this for a memorial in the book, and rehearse it in the ears of Joshua: for I will utterly blot out the remembrance of Amalek from under heaven.

For how else are we to understand the contradictory commands in Deuteronomy 25:17-19:

Remember what Amalek did unto thee by the way as ye came forth out of Egypt; how he met thee by the way, and smote the hindmost of thee, all that were enfeebled in thy rear, when thou wast faint and weary; and he feared not God. Therefore, it shall be, when the Lord thy God hath given thee rest from all thine enemies round about, in the land which the Lord thy God giveth thee for an inheritance to possess it, that thou shalt blot out the remembrance of Amalek from under heaven; thou shalt not forget.

Isn't that why the great Sages of the Mishnah wrote down the interpretations of the Law, which until then had always been transmitted exclusively by word of mouth?

Well, perhaps not exactly, but in a way, yes. Rabbi Yehudah the Prince realized that with the destruction of the Holy Temple of Jerusalem—the center of Jewish religious life—with the collapse of the Bar Kochba Rebellion and the slaughter of thousands of great scholars and teachers among the general carnage, with the destruction of hundreds of academies of Jewish learning, the entire infrastructure upon which the Oral Tradition had rested for more than a thousand years was shattered. The Oral Tradition was the foundation, indeed the essence, of Jewish faith, society and nationhood. Now that the means of transmitting that Tradition to the coming generation had been virtually obliterated, its great store of knowledge would have to be committed to writing, so that Jewish civilization, in spite of the inevitable forgetting, would not perish. Indeed, once the Mishnah was completed, the Jewish Nation was freed from an obligation that had become impossible to perform. In a sense, where the transmission must fail, they were free to forget, because in the Mishnah they now had the means to reconstruct the entire edifice of the living Law—as was later proved by the Gemarah, which did in fact reconstruct it.

Of course, Yehudah the Prince knew that there would always exist among the survivors of past and coming cataclysms at least a small core of teachers devoted to the Law and expert in interpreting and applying it, to oversee and guide the resumption of its transmission. But from now on, reasoned Rabbi Yehudah, the foundation of Jewish society and nationhood would be the written record. This alone could preserve and perpetuate an oral tradition that by itself no longer had sufficient momentum to propel itself forward. Rabbi Yehudah also foresaw that for many years to come, the vast majority of the Jewish Nation—the toilers of the glebe, the pounders of the road, the merchants of the sea, the hundreds of thousands of enslaved, would wallow in ignorance of their laws, yet would speak with reverence of their Torah and Talmud as their eternal possessions. These things, foresaw the holy Sage, would be enough, until the coming of Messiah, to keep the Jewish Nation alive.

A similar situation, *mutatis mutandis*, exists in our own time in the West, where, with a kind of poetic justice, the cultural momentum of the Greco-Roman tradition, formerly revived and transformed by the Renaissance into the great tradition of Christian Humanism, has faltered and run out of steam. The direct cause was not siege, slaughter and physical destruction (though the catastrophe of two world wars certainly contributed to its ultimate collapse), but "progressive" irradiations of thought and politics that sought new forms and formulae—new methods of living, working and teaching, of generating and distributing wealth and knowledge.

A primary factor in this cultural revolution was the education of the masses, whose place in society had been elevated from that of mere morlocks working the factories, the mines, and the soil, to positions of responsibility, influence and policy-making. The teaching of Latin and Greek language and literature, along with their appendages of classical art and archeology, ancient history, rhetoric and philosophy, had always, since the Renaissance, formed the pedagogical backbone of the educated (and ruling) classes. Now that political power was no longer the prerogative of the classically educated, those disciplines seemed to the newly and democratically empowered superfluous—indeed, elitist and reactionary. Formerly, students impervious to the charms and illuminations of Greek and Roman literature could console themselves that by mastering Homer and Virgil they would be rewarded with positions of privilege and influence in society. For later generations, however, the drudgery of conjugations and declensions remained, but the rewards now lay in learning to use and control the increasingly complex intricacies of technology, production, marketing, construction, transportation, medicine, science, accounting, and the law.

For a time, those who had a vested interest in perpetuating the classical curriculum—principally the corps of classically trained teachers who taught in the public high schools—insisted that Latin and Greek were still essential from a practical, if not intrinsic, point of view: learning to understand and appreciate Demosthenes and Cicero in the original was, they claimed, helpful to the study and practice of law, governance, and medicine. They improved one's capacity—so ran the argument—for analytical thinking, for ethical consciousness, for esthetic and stylistic refinement, and for mastering the modern languages—including one's own—and the art of persuasion.

It was all true, of course, admitted the consensus of educators, but wouldn't it make more sense to teach those skills through courses more relevant to contemporary life and society? What does all this dead culture teach us about current events and crises? How will it help us find jobs? How will it increase our earning power? "Aha! I see you know Latin and Greek! You're hired!" What sense in Cicero to a student who grew up without books in the home and who still reads with difficulty? Why decrease that student's chances of academic success by requiring him to jump this antiquated hurdle?

The bureaucracy of public education, run mainly by politicians and fed by a demagogical antagonism toward the classical curriculum and the fossilized social class it had come to symbolize, had little trouble agreeing. To champion academic reform was an easy ticket to re-election and to promotion within the administrative hierarchy. At first, Greek and Latin were demoted to "electives;" then they were relegated to the snobbish eastern prep schools. Sweets to the sweet.

With the evaporation of Latin and Greek from the secondary schools, the main portion of the job market was lost to university graduates with M.A.s and Ph.D.s in the classical disciplines. Graduate students already in the Classics pipeline were increasingly turned back upon the universities in their quest for employment. A glut of applicants resulted, along with a dearth of teaching positions.

This situation was severely aggravated by economic strictures. The "space race," the Vietnam War, the computer revolution, corporate planning, as well as a deli menu of softer courses designed for the Gerberized, Pablumated palate of Baby-Boomers drew students and funds away not only from Classics, but from all the humanities. What remained to Latin and Greek was tainted almost beyond recognition by a desperately hip commercialism (Classics in Cinema) or the latest dictates of political correctness. Black Pride (purported African origins of Greek civilization), Women's Liberation, (Matriarchy and Greek Myth), Gay Pride (Homo-

44

sexuality in Greece and Rome), Multiculturalism (Ethnic Diversity in the Hellenistic World), Gender Studies (Gender Studies) and, in a category all its own, Christian Fundamentalism ("Read the Scriptures in the Original Language!")—all invited callow youth to dabble in Classics for any reasons but those that gave classical civilization its unique and enduring identity and character. Even literary theory, with the ascendancy of Deconstruction, was mobilized by Marxist-leaning or Marxist-affecting language departments to attack the very values their students might have hoped to absorb from the literature and history of the ancient Greek and Roman civilizations.

At the peak of this crisis, hundreds of applicants with higher degrees emerged for every job that opened up in Classics. Inevitably, hundreds of scholars schooled in the intellectual and spiritual refinements of higher civilization began to claw and tear at each other like animals. The tenure-track positions were the most dangerous. Classics departments were filled with petty politicking, slander, diabolical machinations. Fisticuffs between tenured professors whose normal spectrum of deportment ranged from courtly to snippety were not unheard of.

Naturally, the quality of teaching in the university Classics departments deteriorated. For the most part, it wasn't only that undergraduates had to be taught the elementary Latin and Greek they would have mastered in the high schools of another era; or that they had almost no background in ancient history and culture; or that the syllabus of Greek and Latin literatures was broken up into separate "quarter" courses in single authors or single works ("Ovid's *Metamorphoses*," "Virgil's *Aeneid*,"), and taught as though those ancient authors wrote in a state of complete insulation from their society, their history, and each other; or that the undergraduate courses were now imparted principally by associate and adjunct professors, while the tenured luminaries disdained contact with all but the few graduate students left standing.

No! It was that the whole concept of western civilization as an integral, interrelated and meaningful body of knowledge and values transmitted, evolved from, and inspired by antiquity had already been lost to that generation. Whereas previous levies of teachers had been proficient in all areas of classical studies and capable of teaching any one of them, professors were now hired in consideration of their "specialization." One who had done her thesis or published articles on the Greek orators would not be hired to teach Homer or the lyric poets. If in the course of teaching a work by Demosthenes a comparison with Homer or Pindar became relevant, the Demosthenes professor would restrain himself in ostentatious deference to the pertinent instructor, so as to avoid a jealous scene, a snide remark, or a glimpse into his or her own incompetence. More and more often, the insights to be drawn from an intimate knowledge of the entire field were passed over, not from courtesy, but from ignorance. The breadth of knowledge that had once inspired students to read and study widely on their own and that used to give resonance and meaning to a lecture on Plautus or Menander had now narrowed to a trickle, while lessons in Caesar or Thucydides became tedious exercises in translation.

The quality of research followed the same trajectory. The refined art of reconstructing and interpreting the ancient texts—once the very foundation of all the human sciences and the basis of western culture—became the esoteric discipline of a few crabby eccentrics who despised and feared one another and avoided their own students. Investigation into the sources, inspiration, meaning, function and cultural and historical ramifications of a text degenerated into the production of conjectural minutiae.

History itself, perennially treated by Americans with quasi-Epicurean disdain, became a compartmentalized guided tour of names, dates, battles and policies, an institutionalized desiccation of the fervent quest to understand, correlate, and assimilate.

Of course, the phenomena cursorily described here were not confined to Classics, but invested all aspects of American civilization. A general fragmentation of society into separate cubicles of specialized, often antagonistic expertise, interests, cultures and subcultures, lacking any competent framework, forum or network for resolving or even registering its conflicts and contradictions.

The driving forces behind such turmoil are not hard to articulate, nor are they altogether unworthy of praise. More was involved here than just secular pragmatism. It had much to do with the revolutionary mythology of the country, the pride in cutting loose from Old World moorings, the pioneer heritage of inventing one's own world from the ground up with raw materials abundantly supplied by the local environment; a genuine disgust with the old order, with any order, and an idealistic longing for something pure, fair and just. Of course there was also the demagogic posturing and catering of politicians, bureaucrats, corporations and the media to the young consumers of "The New This" and "The New That," and the touted disavowal of things, forms and ideas old and dead.

But, incontrovertibly, it had to do with trying to reverse three centuries of racial injustice and discrimination, with "affirmative action," with policies sincerely but condescendingly promulgated to invite economically disadvantaged ethnic minorities to sink or swim in the mainstream by lowering the water level. With all the millions spent by state and local government on digging intellectual wading pools, how many remedial school-and-library campuses were actually designed and built for the dwellers of the ghettos, the barrios, and the reservations? More pertinently: how many marginalized communities were empowered to design and build them?

Alas, the disoriented Angel of this vast and awesome continent still pines for the lost intimacy once shared with its indigenous inhabitants, the wind still longs for the lost tongues it once wafted across the plains. But the American Spirit historically resisted the sweep of foreign tides, and, what it failed to throw back upon distant shores, converted, reformed and refashioned into something new and not wholly self-conscious. There was, too, the Roarkian notion that re-inventing the wheel might not be such a bad idea and might result in something better than the wheel. There was the new religion of Science and its messianic liturgy of technological innovation as the solution to all problems; the growing ascendancy of the visual media—TV and movies—over books; and the intrusion of vacuous "entertainment" into the intellectual vacuum. It had to do with the rise in the standard of living and the rising expectations of leisure and

47

physical comfort, with the apotheosis of wealth and its ostentation as the ultimate measure of all things, and along with that, the emphasis on procuring the money to obtain, maintain, and enjoy those things.

Ultimately, however, the phenomenon also fed on itself, for with the loss of interest in classical civilization was also lost a certain interest in, and appreciation for, the human being as individual, hence for the great civilizations in which the idea of the individual took shape. A loss reflected in the explosion of standardized "personality" tests cannily designed to facilitate the hiring or selection of applicants by "type" rather than by personal ability, character and history. This system in turn found its complement in a plethora of standardized tests purporting to assess the scholastic or professional potential of prospective students and employees, but actually measuring their conformance (or ability to conform) to a real or idealized national mean or "profile". The techniques, patterns, and clues to the desired answers to such exams could be acquired, by those who coveted them and could afford the not inconsiderable expense, through special courses designed by virtually the same people who cooked up the tests!

A perhaps unforeseen though not unforeseeable consequence of this system was to weed out or deter an incalculable number of gifted, qualified and motivated non-conforming thinkers, scholars and teachers from institutions of learning and policy. Its legacy was the replacement of intellectual vitality by a prepackaged ideological homogeneity, with palpable detriment to academic freedom, and, more generally, to the ability to think critically, independently and thoroughly. A new national culture was born, distinguished by light ships of knowledge sailing rudderless on great seas of ignorance, by a superficial, shortsighted and smugly self-satisfied approach to virtually everything, and by a credulity that left it increasingly prone to disinformation, propaganda, and popular trend.

Over the years, the degradation of humanistic teaching bred a succession of administrative and political leaders and cadres charged with crucial governmental, educational and military responsibility, but incapable of any vibrant sentiment for or concept of civilization, humanity, or the nation as a whole—or of thinking a matter, a decision, a policy, through to its foreseeable consequences. Three or four generations have passed now since political leaders were able to inspire or engineer any such sentiment or policy.

On the personal level, a crisis of individuality could be discerned among the youth of both sexes in an atavistic explosion of tattoos, body piercings, outlandish haircuts and dress—all sported with the intent of marking the wearer as a unique sausage in a long chain of anonymous links. Socially, it was attested by aggressively intrusive "music" that everywhere drowned out what was left of meaningful conversation, by the emergence of Political Correctness (another form of standardized thinking and speaking) as a noxiously ersatz measure of intellectual and moral fiber; and by an epidemic addiction to the pernicious illusion of power and control offered by videogame consoles.

Interpersonally, it manifested as a growing alienation—an inability fostered by those same videogames—to relate to one's fellow men and women as living, thinking, feeling beings with whom it might be possible to interact in other than hostile, reactive, manipulative or otherwise preprogrammed ways. But at the time of which I am writing, this last symptom had not yet blossomed into indiscriminate mass shootings and stabbings.

Whatever the causes, Americans who do not altogether despise it tend to conceive of "culture" as a kind of stage in a movie studio where the plots and the lines are always the same, but the costumes rotate according to the epoch. University students are admitted giddy into this walk-in warehouse of period props and outfits with complete license to try on whatever awakens their fancy. It goes without saying that advanced math, science, engineering and music are legitimate vocational interests, but most undergraduate courses are offered as mere shmattes on a second-hand clothes rack, or a smorgasbord at a UNICEF fundraiser.

All this is hilariously satirized in a novel by Evelyn Waugh, who intuited the phenomenon more than a half-century ago, and more savagely by Vladimir Nabokov, who observed it first-hand. Perhaps neither of them could have foreseen the day when the very term "university" would be usurped by a massive corporate industry pandering basic job skills to immigrants and former dropouts at disproportionate profit to itself.

And why not, one might ask? Haven't the authentic universities of the land made billions from passing off as their own a curriculum that only a century earlier was offered at taxpayer expense in the public high schools?

You might suppose, after what I have said about Rabbi Yehudah the Prince and the compiling of the Mishnah, that if the transmittal of classical culture was threatened by a decline in learning, it was at least safely preserved in books. But this was not so. The Nineteenth Century and the first half of the Twentieth saw great strides in the application of scientific methods to philological research, but much of it—particularly during the period between the two World Wars— was published on cheap acid paper that would quietly eat itself up along with anything printed on it. With money scarce in all the humanities, little could be spent on reprinting or microfilming books for which there was small demand. Increasingly, older volumes were cleared off the shelves of library stacks to make room for the ever rising flood of new publications of ever declining value. The ousted tomes were either sold off cheap or placed in special depositories whence they could be retrieved by special order for scholars who knew what they were looking for, but where actual browsing—the true scholar's joy and inspiration—was out of the question.

Enter Heinrich Strauss, Chairman, Department of Classics, John Wayne University, Nirvana, Conchacancha County, Kalisperia.

5

Archaica

Every war has its generals, and Professor Strauss was clearly the Chares for the occasion. A gifted linguist, fluent in English and Spanish in addition to his native German, expert in Latin composition and Greek style, Strauss was a master, above all, of academic politics and a peerless manipulator of people. To speak true, I only heard of Strauss's reputed prowess in the classical languages from himself. I never had the means to verify his claims, as the only conversation I had from him, besides departmental matters, concerned stereo loudspeakers, cars, electronic gadgets and guns. A good public speaker, well-liked by his students, who were chummy with him and called him Heinz to his face—and, depending on the context, "Noah", "57 Varieties", or "Waltz King", to his back—Professor Strauss was neither an intellectual nor what you would call a scholar. However, while he never boasted of any special talent for research (indeed, the only publications to his name were a brief article on the cannabis plant in classical antiquity and a computer-generated concordance of an obscure Greek author), Heinrich Strauss had an eye for opportunity. It is to him, perhaps more than to any other person, that *Romanitas* (in the medieval sense of Greco-Roman civilization) owes the explosive development of a whole new area of classical research—and perhaps even its very survival into the Third Millennium.

Strauss saw the decline in classical scholarship, rued the thinning of the humanistic ranks, lamented the drying up of funds, noted the shrinking opportunities for important discovery in an over-plowed field, observed first-hand the gradual physical disintegration of venerable editions of Homer, Sophocles, Plato and other ancient Greek poets and thinkers, as well as of many essential scholarly works of more recent production, and concluded that only one vessel could save the ancient traditions from the impending flood of complete destruction and decay.

Thus was born the Archaica Project, or "Noah's Ark", as it came inevitably to be called—a computer data bank of all the extant writings of Greek antiquity. Did I say that Professor Strauss had an eye for opportunity? Opportunity also had an eye for Professor Strauss. An obliging graduate student, heiress to the Pemberton millions, put up one of them as seed money. The seeds, duly tended and watered and touted, sprouted and propagated.

Not long repatriated from my long Italian sojourn, I had recently returned from a—for me—disastrous annual conference of the American Philological Association, held that year in the throes of a brutally harsh east-coast winter. I had received but one invitation to interview—from Blowhurst, a small but prestigious, ivy-clad college—and, having flown out from balmy Kalisperia for that sole purpose, I was, without exaggerating, the very last of several thousand registrants to be called. I took this slight as an homage to my Italian credentials, for as I had already learned, American professors—for reasons never explained—did not think well of Italian institutions of learning! I fully expected to be ridiculed to my face, as I had been on other, less formal occasions.

The interview took place while the hotel staff were vacuuming the empty lobby and hallways. Exhausted, irritated, and desperate to appear cheerful after three days of waiting, I performed accordingly. The interview was cold and cursory my interviewer inscrutably opaque as to why they had ever invited me.

I happened to see Strauss's advertisement in the APA Job Manual, and remembered reading about him three years earlier in the *Smoke & Mirror*. I sent him my resume and was surprised and rather overwhelmed when I received a written reply with a warm invitation to drive down and interview.

My mood was so buoyant as I floated down the freeway in my new used Chrysler Newport Custom notchback sedan that I was not seriously phased by what might have seemed a rather ominous portent. It may be difficult for my compatriots to understand the degree of detachment from the home culture produced by years of living abroad—a disadvantage which in my case was aggravated by homecoming to a foreign-born mother and father who had never been fully acculturated. I must confess, however, that I had made minimal efforts to familiarize myself with the new domestic scene, and the scene had changed drastically in the intervening years.

What happened was, having studied most of the night to prepare for my interview, I had time neither to eat nor to prepare a bag lunch before driving off that morning; so I intended quite simply to stop on the way for a quick roadside hamburger. Not long after passing the Giant Donut, I espied from the freeway the strangely cartoonish, ketchup-and-mustard-colored dog-house of a "Wienerschnitzel" establishment. The lexico-visual oxymoronic pun created by this fast-food franchise had not yet registered with me, for I had taken its name as evidence of advances achieved in the culinary sophistication of my fellow citizens during my long absence from home. "Alright," thought I. "I shall now try my luck with the 'drive-thru' version of this Viennese breaded-veal delicacy." I peeled off the freeway toward the "Wienerschnitzel," drove thru, and buzzed my order into an impertinent looking microphone.

"You want a what?" crackled the intercom, nonplussed.

"A schnitzel, mashed potatoes, a side of coleslaw, and a medium ginger ale."

"Sir, we serve hot dogs, here. Please place your order. There's a menu right next to the box."

"Box? What box?"

"The one you're talking into."

"I do see hot dogs. Isn't this the Wienerschnitzel?"

"Sir, place your order, or move on. You're holding up the line."

"Is this some kind of a joke? Am I on 'Candid Camera'?"

I don't remember the details. The stand-off ended with the crackling, disembodied voice threatening to call the police, and me driving away rattled, hungry, perplexed, and grievously disappointed in the level of American gastronomy.

In spite of my empty stomach, the next encounter went much better—in retrospect, perhaps a little too well. Professor Strauss ("Call me Heinz!"), smoothly ingratiating with his native German charm, antithetically military with his flat top and Von Moltke moustache; Professor Duchinsky ("Oh please! Daisy!"), Director of Bibliography, coyly self-deprecating. Both put me very much at ease, discoursing familiarly on the achievements and challenges of the Archaica Project.

For my part, I was very candid about my concerns that, according to the academic grapevine, the Italian *Laurea* (Laureate Degree) might not meet the posted job specifications, which I understood to be a Ph.D. "in hand or near completion." Lifting my thesis out of my brief case, I proffered it to them for examination. Daisy hefted the massive volume in her hands, and commented weightily, "You're a Ph.D.!" Then, to Strauss, she blurted, "He'd be perfect for the Philodemus bibliography!"

Catching the aside, I asked, "Why is that?" I had a vague recollection of Philodemus of Gadara, a Syrian Greek poet of the late Hellenistic era, whose philosophical writings, rolled up in carbonized *volumina* (rolls) of papyri, had been discovered among the excavations at Herculaneum. Ercolano, its modern name, was one of the ancient towns on the Bay of Naples destroyed by the eruption of Mt. Vesuvius in 79 of the Common Era.

"Most of the work being done on Philodemus is published in Italian," volunteered Professor Strauss. "With your background, it would be a cinch!" A slight trace of a German accent was still detectable in his speech. I also noticed a small lisp that shyly revealed itself when he approached a sibilant.

I also remember posing the following question: "Considering the difficulties I have encountered over my foreign degree, and in view of the fact that, were I to be hired, my term would be no longer than three years, what would be the effect on my marketability of having the Archaica Project on my resumé?" In reply, Professor Strauss assured me that not only would Archaica give me ample opportunity to perfect my Greek and broaden by knowledge of the literature, but that having the Project on my resumé would lend sufficient prestige and distinction to make me a "prime contender" for any entry-level teaching job in classics.

As the interview drew to a close, Heinz and Daisy cautioned me that State law required them to advertise the position. They promised to give me their serious consideration. Six weeks went by, and a letter arrived with a formal offer. I was elated. I telephoned to convey my acceptance. "Congratulations," Daisy said. "Drive down for a visit in the next few days, and we'll introduce you to the rest of the staff."

My term was to start in the beginning of August, which left me about four weeks to put my affairs in order and move into an apartment near campus. Heinz and Daisy, exchanging a glance, recommended an apartment complex called Driftwood Cove, in fashionable Rococo Beach, some eight or nine miles from campus— a mere *ballista* shot, by Conchacancha County standards.

ϐ

Introductions

JWU was not technically in Nirvana, though close enough, and there is no such place as Kalisperia; but if an inland empire had ever swept southward and westward in quest of a warm-water seaport, that's where its phalanxes would have paused for a Coke and a soak. Caledonia would have been more apt, but it had already been picked for the Scots, so I was left with Kalisperia. The name garnered some nods of approval and it stuck.

In those far-gone days, John Wayne was a beautiful, wide-open campus, naturally landscaped, with plenty of pines, rolling lawns, an artificial stream that bubbled over rocks and boulders, and a large number of coral trees and soulangiana magnolias long since cut down and replaced by academic sprawl. There were far-west spaces between buildings in those days, and many students commuted from class to class on bicycles or skate boards. The surrounding farmland has become a distant memory, but back then there were still cows ruminating across the highway, and I considered it a good omen that as I drew near the university access road that early August afternoon, one of those placid creatures turned her cumbersome head and hailed my approach with a prescient μ for *mneme.*

JWU was one of a network of campuses that flickered up, down and across our state like the semi-precious stones in the Urim and Thummim. Heinz, Daisy, Jason, Janoš and Edythe, the priests and priestesses of this esoteric confraternity, received me with cordial formality. Janoš ("Skippy" or "Skipchick" to his friends, the soubriquets being derived from his surname of Cipcik), "Our Resident Historian," gave me the tour.

56

Cipcik's job was not, as his title suggested, to compile a *res gestae* of Noah's Ark, but to supply the historical and literary-historical background of each of the authors whose works were to be digitized. The purpose of his labors was principally to make sure that no extant work—even if only a fragment consisting of a single word—be left out. However, Janoš Cipcik also supplied more than a patina of real erudition to a project that might otherwise have seemed purely mechanical. In my estimation, it was he, more than anyone else on the project, who made it possible for the Ark to communicate without presumption or embarrassment with the classical confraternity. He was a genuine scholar, a congenial type, with a sad face and a nervous guffaw that issued, it seemed, more from a sense of insecurity than of humor. Tall, round-shouldered and of slender build, he wore his disheveled, thinning hair long. His tonsured, monkish appearance was incongruously accentuated by his jeans and tee-shirt, which were mostly various shades of sackcloth.

Jason Crowleigh, the Assistant-Director of Noah's Ark, possessed a lean and polished bearing contradicted by a small but noticeable potbelly. He spoke in long, facile periods replete with clauses in various stages of subordination, each one marked by its own graceful gesture of the hand, the most frequent being a leisurely diving-board back flip of the dexter ending in a palms-up just below the nipple, as if to indicate a what-could-be-more-obvious-than-that? accord between mind and body. He kept about him an air of quiet dignity and privacy that contrasted pleasantly with his cowboy boots and hat and much more voluble wife.

Actually, a few weeks passed before I figured out that Jason and Edythe were marital, and considerably longer for me to learn that Edythe was Heinz's ex. Both marriages struck me as mismatched. Edythe was short, moderately obese, wired, high-pitched and bubbly, pasty and perennially dressed in a short denim skirt that exposed her chubby calves. Where Jason might utter a quiet, little chuckle, Edythe sent forth a musical burst of nervous hilarity whose initial charm waned in its Pavlovian predictability. The stimulus was most often a quip by one or the other of her successive husbands.

I mentioned to Sokrates the striking incongruity I saw in Edythe and Jason, and Sokrates reproved me. "Louis! You can't believe how stunningly beautiful she was only a few years ago! I don't know what has happened to her. She must be very ill."

Edythe's responsibilities at the Ark seemed just as incongruous. She headed the computer department that checked and corrected the data sent back from India before it was added to the main data base. It was a demanding job and a big responsibility, and she was obviously very proficient at it. Her habit of jabbering "Wirk-wirkwirkwirkwirk" in a shrill voice while breezing through the room puzzled and annoyed me. Her remonstrances could be blistering when she discovered errors in our text "prepping." Otherwise I found her amusing, and pleasantly unfathomable.

There was something else about Edythe, and to some extent she shared this idiosyncrasy with Daisy Duchinsky. I don't know exactly how to describe it, but often when she spoke, it was with a kind of self-consciousness of holding forth, as though putting quotation marks around her own words as they issued from her mouth. Edythe performed this remarkable feat by means of gestures, both vocal and physical, of exaggerated emphasis where, to my perhaps unaccustomed ears and eyes, none was necessary, so that I began to visualize her speech as materializing inside a kind of comic-strip bubble which followed her wherever she went.

Daisy achieved a similar effect, though not nearly so regularly, through her use of the plosive consonants—by delaying—long enough to light a fuse, as it were, or compress enough air—and then popping her "P"s and "B"s in an audiovisual display of pouting frustration, irritation, sarcasm, skepticism, or self-martyrdom—as the case might be. She used this mannerism like an emoticon of a later era, and because it was an exaggeration, it was more of a performance than a communication.

In a way, Daisy's habit of "displaying" suited her personality well. She had a sort of avian, or perhaps reptilian, elegance that, in spite of her stick-like figure, caused me to visualize her sunning herself on top of a stone wall like a lizard. She was tanned to a deep brown and dried to a crisp, oven-baked finish, except for the skin on her throat, which remained an unappetizing white. The displays were also an effective part of Daisy's rhetorical arsenal. She was a good lecturer, a meticulous, if unimaginative, scholar and a dedicated teacher, devoting long hours to the preparation of her lessons. I attended two or three of her annual plenary lectures on Sophocles, and they were admirable, if not memorable.

On the other hand, I suspected that she had little talent for original research. Her ideas were straight from the books, and her list of publications, not much longer than Heinz's, consisted mostly of computer-generated concordances.

Then, there was the support staff—Pamela, the receptionist from the Philippines, and Sheila the bookkeeper, both of them courteous, efficient, and ostentatiously servile. Sheila used the word "okay" a lot, but gave it an officious twang by pronouncing it "o-kye," to rhyme with "Ojai," where she had previously fudged books for one of the more tantric private high schools.

There was one other person who left a lasting impression on me because of his unusual intelligence, sensitivity and unselfconscious charm. This was John ("Sky") Mileszewsky, an undergraduate student with the face of a suffering, French poet and the air of a tribal chieftain in a gang of street urchins. A conscientious and careful worker in spite of his "habit," he would zoom into the library on his skateboard, his long auburn hair flowing behind him. He went barefoot most of the year, and religiously clad in short pants. Treated by all with special deference, he seemed especially close to Heinz, for whom he performed various household services in addition to his part-time mansions at the Ark. I will have more to say about him soon enough.

I was also introduced to Professor Winterbotham, who had acceded to the post of Chairman of the Classics Department on Strauss's abdication in favor of the Ark's helm. "Bottom" was bland and British, thought it cute to refer to the working class as "The Great Unwashed," and entertained himself, when undisturbed, by dum-dee-dumming Bach violin sonatas to the beat of an extended index finger. And then there was Bunny Pemberton, who had predictably exchanged her mask of God ("Build thee an Ark") for the slightly more modest one of Latin prof (*"Apparent rari nantes in gurgite vasto"*).

It was, to say the least, an interesting assortment of people. With the arrival of three new workers in time for the fall semester, Noah's Ark truly began to resemble a zoo, as Janoš / Skippy called it with manifest relish. Clarence Woodbine, Ph.D., an octogenarian in a thirty-four-year- old body with a monomaniacal devotion to the keyboard—piano, organ or computer, it made no difference—as well as to the music of Messaien, manifested a spinsterly intolerance for smoke of any kind, and objected violently to the proximity of Sokrates with or without his devoted cigarette.

The other two arrivals were students. Tom Cooke, mid-westerner, plumply nondescript beneath his blue-grey raincoat, pale behind his well-groomed moustaches and thick eyeglasses, introduced himself with a request for someone to help him carry his books from the parking lot to his graduate cubby hole. I volunteered, but in executing the good deed must have said something which offended him to the core of his being. He never thereafter addressed a word to me directly, notwithstanding the long hours he spent lounging in our work room, whether dozing, chatting with the others (mostly about the movies)—or venting his exasperation with Bunny Pemberton's excruciating and sparsely populated Latin seminars.

With the appearance of Steven Windfall, a touchy under-graduate, with a histrionic head of hair that made me think of a blonde, beach-boy Beethoven, I began to wonder if in America anybody normal ever studied Classics. Intense and athletic, he sported the manners and dress of an angry hippy while displaying an acolytic fervor for the philosophy of Plato and a corresponding resentment toward Skippy and me for trying to wean him off it.

"Generally speaking," I observed to Janoš as my second week of official duty drew to a close, "my European colleagues were considerably more run-of-the-mill."

"Have you met Sokrates yet?" inquired Janoš, with a twinkle in the eye that bordered on malice.

"It seems I have just met his devoted pupil," I replied, alluding to the beach boy. "He either thinks he is Plato or is studying for the part." So Janoš led me up the hall to the data-checking room to meet the poet, S.N. Naumachou, who greeted me like the old friend he was very quickly to become.

There was someone else I had noticed, a rather large man, a professorial type with a large china-bald head crazed by a few silvery wisps of hair, and a large, bulbous nose dominating a round, cheruby face that for all the seriousness of its expression, denoted a great deal of innocence about the real world.

"Who is that fellow?" I eventually enquired of Janoš, as the object of my curiosity transited the courtyard, sipping from a sky-blue coffee mug as he walked.

"What? You haven't met Professor Parthenopides? *Mea magna culpa!* Pheemy! Can you come over here for a moment?" Thus I was finally introduced to Euphemios Parthenopides, pink-faced and pudgy, the man responsible for bringing Sokrates over from Greece, a most erudite yet unpretentious scholar, with the personality of a true gentleman, an addiction to coffee, and an endearing, and—for post-structuralist John Wayne—a quaintly eccentric interest in structural linguistics.

Of course, there were other students besides Sky and Windfall, but, as might be expected, they were a small and rather nebulous group that kept pretty much to itself. Although some of them did part-time work for the Ark, they stood shy of us regulars, and offered little in the way of interest or society.

One exception was a tall, somewhat gangly maiden whose friend I became when, passing her in the hallway, I turned and said, "Mmmm! Patchouli!" and Veronica laughed. The effect was enhanced by long, dark tresses, freckles, a pair of leather sandals, blue jeans, and, hung around her slender neck, a large wooden cross which kept me, like a vampire, from getting too close. Ronie Agriopoulos was usually in the company of another born-again Christian, who dressed the same, but wore her long blonde hair in braids and pointedly avoided conversation with the men folk.

Noah's Ark, located on the ground floor of Humphreys Hall, overlooked—or would have, if it had had any windows—a sunken courtyard or patio that with a noncommittal shrug joined Humphreys with Deconstructionist Shriver Hall in the shadow of a wide bridge that rather too optimistically linked them together overhead. In fact, very little traffic actually passed between these two buildings. The denizens of each—students and faculty—seemed not to recognize each other, as though each were dark matter to the other.

One entered our complex through a ground-floor hallway that, opening onto the patio, bypassed offices allocated between the Archaica and the Classics Department, angled around, and abutted into the Archaica library. Fortunately, the library was blessed with its own outside access via patio entry to the two rooms—front and rear—of which it was comprised. The frontward, scene of my interview a few weeks earlier, boasted a polished-wood table of massive proportions and three walls of books floor to ceiling. The fourth, by which it was separated from the adjoining rear room, displayed a gallery of photos—mainly of Heinz, and Heinz posing next to various name-famous persons of the Classical World. An interior doorway led unsuspectingly to the adjoining rear space— another bibliothecarial cavern lined with shelves and punctuated with books piled high like stalagmites or scattered like step-pingstones across subterranean tabular lakes.

As noted, our ship, like the Biblical Ark, had no portholes. I found this extremely oppressive at first. Fortunately, the outer door of the last-mentioned room was usually propped open to the ceaseless wonder of passing students, many of whom exhibited a touching amazement on beholding so many tomes gathered together in one place. "What's this?" they would ask. This was the heart of the Archaica Project— the "Inner Sanctum," as Janoš liked to call it—where Janoš held court beneath his tonsure, and where I was to do my work—under his more or less benign supervision.

Notwithstanding the impressive array of ancient culture packed into my immediate surroundings, I soon discovered that opportunities for perfecting and practising my knowledge of Greek were hard to come by. Our work consisted mainly of "text-prepping"—marking up the printed volumes of text before they were shipped off to India for data entry. The "prepping" consisted of estimating the number of words contained in every text that came to hand, and identifying the structural subdivisions of each (for example: books, parts, chapters, paragraphs and printed lines of text) and tagging and numbering them with the appropriate distinguishing symbols.

It was Zen work: mechanical and stultifying, yet demanding of constant mental focus. Notoriously easy, after two or three hours, to get mixed up and mark the Paragraphs as Chapters, the Chapters as Books, the Books as Parts, and the Parts as what not. Once marked, the texts would undergo the close scrutiny of Daisy or Edythe, who, as often as not, sent them back to us to be tediously erased from beginning to end, and "prepped" again. Since we all shared the suffering, we enlivened the tedium with sporadic eruptions of conversation and periodic breaks for fresh air and coffee. When the coffee no longer made an impression, I would make a brisk circuit of the grounds to catalog living trees instead of crumbling dead ones. By the time I got home of an evening, I was too mentally wound down and emotionally wound up to reach for my Thucydides and my pencils. It was as much as my intellect could handle to warm up dinner and settle down with "Laverne & Shirley," for whom I developed a shameless attachment—perhaps due to nothing more than their silly theme song ("Shlemiel, Shlimazal").

Shlemiel, I should explain, is the Yiddish pronunciation of my Hebrew name, which is Shelumiel ("Lulu" to family and close friends). Mentioned three times in the Bible, Shelumiel, was Prince of the Tribe of Shimon when the Mishkan (Holy Tabernacle) was first set up in the desert. Why Shelumiel should have been remembered as a "shlemiel," we are told by neither Torah nor Talmud. Some say that Shelumiel was actually Zimri, Prince of the Tribe of Shimon, who was executed in flagrante by having a spear thrust up his hiney in such a manner as to dispatch by one stroke both him and his Moabite seductress. Zimri, at any rate, can be said to have acted like a shlemiel, having occasioned through his own folly the ostensible omission of his Tribe's name from Moses' Catalog of Blessings. However, according to our own family tradition, Shelumiel was a poet—and a good one—but because he sought fame and literary glory, he was punished by having his wish granted: his name becoming for all ages a byword for a careless fool and a nincompoop (a word, by the way, that very likely derives from the Latin expression, *non compos mentis*).

Evenings were lonely and depressing. My new friends at JW were too scattered and the intervening miles too numerous for the casual after-dinner get-togethers I had grown used to in Italy. The distances made even the occasional movie more trouble than it was worth. I developed a habit of drinking a beer with my dinner. The beer made me drowsy, and after washing up I was generally happy to go to bed.

One night I dreamed that my life was a tickertape and I couldn't figure out how to prep it.

7

Questions of Degree

After five or six weeks on the Ark, I felt secure enough on my sea legs to bring the question to Heinz. Would he help me establish the equivalence of my foreign degree, which, as far as I was concerned, was still very much up in the air? At the appointed hour, Pamela admitted me into Heinz's lair, another windowless cave, long and narrow like a trailer, at one end of which Heinz lounged behind his desk in a reclining chair.

"Heinz," I said. "I'm very grateful that you've hired me, and I'm relieved that my *Laurea* managed to sneak under the bar with your job specifications. But ever since I got back from Italy, I've been hearing from everyone but you and Daisy that the *Laurea* is not generally considered equivalent to a Ph.D. Is there any way I can get a formal, in-house evaluation that could serve as a precedent for the future, when I'll need to go out and look for another job? Because if I can't settle this question, at some point I might have to go back to school and enroll in a graduate program."

Heinz galvanized into action. "I understand your situation. I'll see what I can do to help. Let me make a few phone calls, and I'll let you know what I find out."

A few days later, Heinz called me into his office. JW was not equipped for the kind of evaluation I had requested. However, it appeared that there was an office at HBU up in Smokes—another campus in the university system with whom JW had several joint programs. They could do it.

"Hey, Pamela! Which campus did they say we should send Louis's credentials? Wasn't it HBU?"

"Yes," called the ever-obliging Pamela from the front office. "Dear old Bogie!"

Heinz would take the necessary steps to get the process started.

I thanked him profusely and offered to provide him with all the necessary documentation, including a copy of my dissertation, but he declined. "I already have the documents you sent me with your application. Let's start with those, and if we need to give them more, we will."

Maybe six or eight weeks went by, during which, despite Heinz's understanding of my "situation," I endured much good-natured needling from him, Daisy and Skippy, about my "obsession over a piece of paper". Finally, one morning, Heinz and I crossed paths in Humphreys Court. After we had passed each other with a smile and a nod, Heinz turned suddenly and called me back.

"Oh, Louis! I meant to tell you: your evaluation papers are here."

"Oh, really? Well, how did it go? What did they say?"

"I'd say it went pretty well. They gave you full credit as a Ph.D."

"That's fantastic!" I exclaimed, practically bursting with relief. Can I see the papers?"

"Sure, any time. You know, let me hang on to them for now, and when something opens up you want to apply for, let me know, and I'll give them to you. Okay?"

"Sure, Heinz, that's great! Thank you!" I really wanted to see those papers, but Heinz was my boss, had just done me one of the biggest favors of my life, and if he had his reasons for putting my documents in safekeeping, I was not going to impose on him. I would have trusted him with my life savings and no receipt.

Not everything was hunky-dory, of course. I had a great need in those days to trust people, especially savvy, street-smart people with power and connections. Perhaps this was a reflection of my own sense of utter helplessness in a social world whose practical mechanics I failed to understand. Or perhaps it reflected something entirely different. I don't know. Just how defective was my early warning system, if I had one, appears from the following. I had developed a small hobby of taking cuttings from the trees I visited on my daily campus walks, and one of them having taken root, a fine magnolia slip, I gave it to Heinz and Daisy with a note of gratitude. I suppose I should have found the letter that Heinz wrote back bizarre, not to say alarming, but apparently I did not. You be the judge:

Louis:

Thanks for the magnolia. You know I love plants, and you know, therefore, that I will take good care of it.

More importantly, however: thanks for the note. It meant a lot. Since you told a bit about yourself, let me tell you a bit about <u>myself</u>:

[*Good Grief!* What did I tell him?]

I <u>watch</u> people. Not like a "boss," but like someone who is concerned, and who cares. Very few of the crew members know it, but I am aware of what goes on in all of them, and what makes all of them tick. I've been watching <u>you</u> tick, too, and have been glad to see happening what you talk about in your note.

Back to you. I am particularly glad to see (and this you don't talk about in your note) that you are beginning to understand the Ark as what it is. It is the most important thing which has ever happened in our field. When you first applied for a job here, you had—I think—a totally wrong notion of our project. As a romantic, you saw it in romantic terms.

Now then: the more important something is, the harder it is. We on the Ark—rather than to walk on ethereal scholarly heights—are busting our backs on very mundane day to day things.

Yet: I don't believe that anyone else could do what we are doing. And what we are doing—in spite of our sore backs—is worth it for the sake of those who come after us.

My own job on the Ark is the least romantic of all. For the most part, it amounts to little more than hustling and hassling people. But there's another aspect to it, also: It is my job to—somehow—make people work together for something in which I, for one, believe. I could never bring this off if my own staff didn't trust and believe in me. I often wonder and worry about that.

Your note gave me a bit of reassurance. Hang in there. It's worth it.

[Signed]

Heinz

"I watch people!" My blood curdles as I reread that paragraph. Not long after moving into my one-room paradise, I noticed that a stack of some potentially compromising articles of mine seemed to have been disturbed. Suspicion was something I could not just then afford, so I attributed the anomaly to my own carelessness, and put the matter conveniently out of mind, and, not long afterwards, the articles into the trash.

The first sign I got that the honeymoon was actually over was an incident that happened between me and John Mileszewsky—Sky Miles, as we called him. After a couple of months on the job, I noticed that Sky, normally sunny and cloudless, had become somewhat withdrawn and morose. He would absent himself periodically and return reeking and in a much better mood. At times, he could be seen lighting up in plain view of any one passing through the library. Because I liked him and was afraid he might get into trouble, I took him gently aside one morning and suggested that perhaps he should be more careful about smoking in public. I said I wondered whether his habit might be aggravating, rather than helping, his depression. To the foregoing, I added that, although I knew very little about the subject, my personal physician—a well-respected M.D., had informed me (unnecessarily) that, notwithstanding popular opinion to the contrary, "grass" was indeed addictive, harmful to the faculty of memory, and often led to the use of other, more dangerous substances.

Sky thanked me for my concern, and went straight to tell Janoš. Not a half an hour went by before Janoš gripped me firmly by the arm, pulled me outside and gave me a good scolding, which included the word "Nazi"—allegedly used by Sky in describing my behavior.

A more subtle, but no less humiliating, debriefing in Daisy's office later that afternoon removed any residual doubts I might have had that Noah's Ark, at least, was a "Smoking Area". Discretion, rather than secrecy, was called for, and if I chose not to smoke, that was my business, and wisdom consisted in keeping my opinions in re to myself.

The episode left me a bit shaken, but, of necessity, Sky and I were eventually reconciled, and Skippy's assault, though perhaps not forgotten, was never spoken of again.

Other mishaps occurred from time to time, and told of my increasing anxiety and the gradual wear on my nerves. The excruciating monotony of text preparation would induce in me a torpor more powerful than any drug. I would have, on occasion, thrust under my nose errors such as could have been committed only by someone in a light coma. My negligence (augmented by someone else's—whose I can't remember) once resulted in Heinz, Daisy, Janoš and me staying until 1:00 AM to correct a whole shipment of books due to be sent off the next morning to India.

Another time, after I finished prepping the poet Meleager, the whole staff had to be mobilized to locate the lost volume of *Anthologia Graeca* containing his poems, among others, which I had shelved among the "M"s, instead of the "A"s.

I suppose on balance that as eccentric as my co-workers appeared to me, so must I have cut a rather strange figure in their estimation. Understandably, the directors were completely absorbed by their task and acutely aware of their responsibility toward the academic community which had given them its scholarly credit and support. They had little interest in my ideas for reintroducing classical instruction into the secondary school system, and must have thought it highly presumptuous of me that I invited them to a lunchtime meeting in which I sought to involve them in organizing such a program.

During a campus symposium on experimental writing, I observed that discussions of that subject always seemed to presume that experimentation meant exploration of the unconscious and the irrational, rather than of new and more refined modes of artistic expression. The moderator, a noted critic from the *New Yorker*, replied that "there is always someone who gripes that the subject of a symposium is not other than what it is." Daisy reproached me afterwards for "bad vibes" and "always trying to provoke something."

Nevertheless, I believe that on the whole I was recognized as a team player, and that my extravagances were fairly well tolerated by all. Why begrudge the placid kettle his occasional puffs and whistles? Were they not a kitchen full of pots and pans, all simmering and rattling at once?

Notwithstanding my resentment of his brusque handling of my run-in with Sky, I developed a cautious liking for Skippy. Apart from Sokrates and Professor Parthenopides, he was the closest thing to an intellectual on the premises. Extraordinarily well-read in history, with a vast store of knowledge at his mnemonic fingertips, he was almost always able to draw upon it to satisfy Daisy or Jason when they came to him with questions about this or that obscure late Greek or Roman author. In those first months, we were working on the Church Fathers and when Athanasius fell to my lot, Janoš immediately warned me, "You'll find him exceedingly anti-Semitic."

"How so?" I asked. "Will I have time to read him?"

Mercifully, Janoš was also endowed with a lively sense of humor, and often had me in stitches with his snipes, his pantomimes, and his mimickings. He could transform himself in a matter of seconds from a John Bircher redneck excoriating a broad assortment of ethnic minorities to a church choir boy singing "Uh-mazing Grace" with eyes turned heavenward.

When it came out in conversation that Janoš held no more than a Master's Degree, I was surprised. I asked him why he had never gone for a Ph.D.

"I tried," he answered with a sad smile. "I passed all my exams. All I had to do was write my thesis. I amassed a whole closet-full of shoe-boxes filled with my notes. When it came time to write the damn thing, I had so much information, I just couldn't figure out what to do with it all. I still have it. It's all sitting there in my closet. I keep thinking one day I'll go back in there, take 'em out and start writing, but ten years have gone by now, and I think I've lost my grip. I wouldn't even know where to start."

"Start with an outline. What was the subject?"

"The title was supposed to be 'The Afterlife in Post-Classical Antiquity.'"

"My goodness! That's enormous! Who ever assigned you a thesis like that?"

"Oh, my teacher. Sometimes I think it was more a prophecy than a title."

"More a curse than a prophecy: 'You want a Ph.D. from me? You'll get it in the hereafter.'"

"Yeah," he agreed, with a resigned chuckle.

"What did you do to him?"

"Rebuffed him." Here he grinned sadly, with his eyebrows raised.

One day, as I was admiring the far, purple hills from the concrete parapet of Shriver's Upper Level, Janoš, who must have seen me from below, joined me, lit a cigarette, and, leaning over by my side, fixed his gaze on the distance. "Louis," he said, "I hope you don't mind my asking. I can usually tell, but in your case, I can't seem to make up my mind." Here he gave me an intense look straight into my eyes.

I told him I wasn't, and thanked him for his candor.

"Because if you were," he added unnecessarily, "I could really go for you in a big way."

"If you were her," I parried, nodding toward the nymphet who at that moment was traversing the patio below, "I would happily take you up on that."

"The funny thing is," he said, eyeing the girl with interest, "is I can appreciate your sentiment."

It was fortunate that this clarification had taken place with so little apparent discomfort on either side, for it left our working relationship status quo. Still, his personal interest in me was a disappointment, because from that moment I knew that our relations would never go beyond the campus borders, whereas I had thought I might enjoy getting to know him socially. Perhaps in an attempt to cover my embarrassment, I asked him, with a directness intended to match his,

"You were raised Catholic?"

"Is it that obvious?"

"I was thinking of your choir-boy act. It struck me as authentic, and also charged with a certain animus. And then, your thesis on the afterlife."

"I did the altar-boy thing."

"Your parents forced you?"

"No. I went through a phase. I was very sincere."

"What turned you off?"

"Sodom and Gomorrah."

"Because you identified as homosexual?"

"You know, I wasn't clear about it then. I think it was more because of the attitude of Abraham. I found the whole thing hypocritical. God warns Abraham He's going to destroy Sodom, and Abraham knows his nephew Lot lives there, yet he does nothing to save him. Even though, I might add, Abraham had previously gone to war to rescue Lot from his kidnappers. I decided that Abraham went to war for the booty and betrayed his nephew, and then God blessed him. I guess that really stuck in my craw."

This revelation of Skipchick's was to have far-reaching consequences for me, as it led me to a fascinating musicological discovery, and, long afterward, to a religious awakening. I had read the King James Bible in my teenage years, but retained little, except the majesty of the language. I seemed to recall that Abraham had wrested a concession from God to spare Sodom if the city contained ten righteous souls. But I did not remember him putting himself out for Lot's sake. I wondered privately if Janoš identified somehow with Lot—certainly a tormented man full of moral and sexual ambiguities.

Janoš drew a long, contemplative breath of smoke from his cigarette. "I realize there's probably more to it, but in the meantime my interests shifted." He chuckled, threw away his cigarette. "Well, back to Purgatory," he announced glumly, leaving me alone with my thoughts.

Skippy's disclosure about the origins of his doctoral thesis was strangely apropos. The news broadcasts were full of the Strelesky case, and the unfortunate affair permeated all our activities for several days. If I remember correctly, this man Strelesky, convicted of murder, had served three years with exemplary conduct and had just politely declined an offer of parole, stating that although he had no immediate intention of killing anyone, he could not guarantee that he would not kill someone in the future. While the Parole Board deliberated this highly unusual case, the matter was earnestly debated on the deck of Noah's Ark.

The facts were straightforward and undisputed. Strelesky, a graduate student at a prestigious university for fully nineteen years, had spent twelve of them diligently, dutifully, and doggedly writing and rewriting his doctoral dissertation at the endless behest of his math professor and advisor. The jury had not bought the insanity defense, perhaps reasonably concluding that it was not insanity to entertain a murderous intent toward one's math professor under similar circumstances. However, the jury had enough sympathy for the defendant to convict him of only second-degree (in other words, unpremeditated) murder, despite the fact that he had shown up at the fateful thesis conference with the murder weapon (a ball-peen hammer) providently secreted in his briefcase. It became evident at the parole hearing that Strelesky had grown passing fond of prison life and its amenities, which, however meager, clearly afforded him greater security than he had ever got from academic life.

The Strelesky case became notorious for three reasons: for popularizing the term "ball peen," which had till then been unknown to all but specialized craftsmen; for exposing the hazards of graduate life to public commentary; and for unfairly making a mockery of a parole system that could not be expected to deal with a Catch-22 like Strelesky. The latter had defended himself, before sentencing, by claiming that what he had done was "logically and morally correct." Now, constrained by that same logic and morality, he staunchly refused to promise that he would not recidivate. As it turned out, at least per one hypothesis, he did kill again, albeit through no fault of his own, and in a manner that no one could have foreseen—least of all Strelesky.

8

Ipsissima

Another subject—of not quite so general interest—that kept coming up was the *"ipsissima verba* question." Several Greek authors are known to us only through a few snippets of text attributed to them by other authors who quote them in their own writings. The question was, which digital cage should those Very Small Animals, as A.A. Milne might have called them, be locked up in? Should their data be retrievable under the name of the author quoted, or the author who does the quoting, or both? The problem, simple as it might seem at first impression, actually raised an interesting philosophical issue. If we answer, "The quo-*tor*," as Heinz facetiously pronounced it, we are faced with the situation that the words are not, in fact, his own. If we answer, "The quo-*tee*," how do we know that he or she really said them? We have no text that directly attests to his authorship.

The problem is rendered even more embarrassing when there is no independent evidence that such an author ever existed. In such an event, the authenticity of the quotation becomes dependent on the supposed existence of the alleged author. Conversely, the existence of the author remains dependent on the supposed authenticity of the quote. At best, the primary question was always whether the quoted words were the *ipsissima verba* of the quoted author—"his very own words." Did he really say those words and not some other words? Was it really he (or she) who said them, and not someone else?

The sensible answer would have been to attribute the quotation to both parties and let the person retrieving the data worry about it. Instead, the entire outfit got itself "hung up" on the matter, including myself, who finally wrote, in a semiconscious stupor, a six-page memo to Heinz, advocating the creation of "two data bases, not one!"

The topics of our conversation were not always so serious. Much time was spent discussing Kalispesrian Civilization, especially that to be found in the southern sector—a subject which infallibly inspired Janoš to break into rapturous song with a raucous rendition of

Hol-ly-woood, da da da da da da da Hol-ly-woood . . . !

At the time, I was working here and there on a long satiric poem in attempted emulation of my most beloved poet. No need to say that I was out of my depth, but *Dante in Disneyland* did incorporate some fine swatches of verse. It began,

In the middle of my life's great traffic jam,
I woke to find myself on the wrong freeway.

I was working desultorily on Canto No. 6, when from the networks emanated the melancholy news that Morris, the orange-striped, sardonic feline celebrity featured in a well-known cat food commercial, had expired after a long, successful life in television. The story was immediately picked up by networks and newspapers across the country, and I found this phenomenon significant enough to include it in my poem. Deep in the entrails of Noah's Ark, however, the story continued to agglomerate uncorroborated details. According to Janoš, the VOS City Council had voted to hold a funeral procession at the Coliseum, with Morris's little casket to be drawn around the track by a troika of white Shetland ponies. Incredulous though I was, I bought it all, only becoming suspicious when Janoš threw in the bit about the golden arches to be supplied by a national hamburger franchise. My suspicions were confirmed when, reading the expression on my face, the small crowd that

75

unfortunately happened to witness the scene burst into hysterical laughter.

The incident taught me an interesting lesson: social satire is meaningless in a society that unconsciously yet ostentatiously satirizes itself by its own spontaneous behavior. I began to lose interest in *Dante in Disneyland* and, regrettably, abandoned the project soon after—but not before submitting Cantos 1 through 4 to the Campus newspaper—with what result I shall recount later.

Morris's death and transfiguration also inspired a literary discussion that ran on, intermittently, for several months. "What," I posed, "is the essential difference between a true story and a fictitious one, and is there any way to distinguish between the two without reference to external facts?" I pointed out an example that I have never been able to forget since reading—still as a student in Italy—*One Hundred Years of Solitude*, by Garcia Marquez. I had devoured it in a beautiful Italian translation that a Columbian student assured me preserved all the graceful, picturesque and childlike artifices of the original. One reads this wonderful book with the enchantment of a child listening to a fairy tale. But there is one episode that strikes one, beyond any doubt, as true, and that is the massacre at the railroad station, where the army mows down two or three thousand protesting workers. How do I know this? How did the author manage to convey this one truth in the middle of a story that, despite its supposed cultural veracity, everyone understands to be fantasy?

"That's funny," interposed Tom Cooke, turning to Janoš: "When I read it, I thought the railroad massacre was the one part of the story that was fiction."

"Brother Thomas can't deal with real slaughter," I retorted. He needs laser swords and atomic disintegrators to sterilize the actual dying part. That's why he believes in *Star Wars*. How many times have you seen it now? Fifteen?"

"I don't believe in Communist propaganda."

This was as close as Tom Cooke ever came to addressing me personally, which in itself was a kind of victory, so I ignored the remark.

"Another example: in one of his novels, Sinclair Lewis tells the story of a white bigot who discovers he has a minute amount of Negro blood in his veins through a remote ancestor, and explores how that changes his life. The story is clearly fiction, a parable; but suddenly he describes in the most naturalistic terms a certain character met at a cocktail party. It's immediately clear that the person he is describing is real. In fact, I even recognized him, because I used to know him—and what a privilege it was! However, had I not sensed that Lewis was talking about a real, live person, I would never have recognized a good man so vilely smeared with mud."

Jason: "The description happened to match your recollection, and only then did you conclude Lewis was writing about a real person."

"But wouldn't the more general category precede the more specific? If you find an unfamiliar species of butterfly, don't you recognize it first as a lepidopter? It's only after careful examination that you determine that it's a butterfly, and only then, what variety."

Jason: "If it's a variety you're already familiar with, you don't need to analyze it to understand what it is. Thereafter, if you so choose, you may generalize and say that such and such a specimen belongs to the lepidoptera family. But you knew that to begin with. No deductive or inductive process was involved."

"Well, let's go back to the first example. I've never witnessed a massacre first-hand, thank God! so what is it about Marquez's description that tells me he's describing something real?"

"Your pessimistic view of humanity," intervened Janoš. "Which I share, by the way."

Louis: "In other words, verisimilitude? Marquez's description matches my picture of what human beings do to each other?"

Jason: "I suppose you could phrase it thus."

Louis: "But isn't the whole art of writing modern fiction based on verisimilitude? So what's to distinguish the verisimilitude of fiction from the verisimilitude of truth?"

Jason: "But didn't you say before that *100 Years of Solitude* was written like a fairy tale—except for that one horrifying episode?"

"Well, yes, I did, but actually, don't you see, the massacre is described as if it, too, were a fairy tale. The soldiers kill two thousand striking workers, and by the next day, not a sign is left of what happened and nobody knows nothing."

"So are you saying that there is a point where reality and fairy tale meet, and that point is what: politics?"

Tom: "OK, I'm outta here."

Louis: "No, I don't think I'm saying that. I think what I'm saying is, maybe that just as in human affairs, there are certain telltale signs that clue you when the politicians are lying—I don't know, blinking, sweating, looking away, failing a lie-detector text . . ."

Sky: "Or growing a twelve-inch nose . . ."

". . . so in fiction there are certain signs that tell you when the author is speaking true. But what are they? There should be a special discipline devoted to that question."

"Perhaps there ought to be one for politics, too," added Jason.

"You don't need a special course. It's politics, it's a lie," said Janoš with a chuckle.

As Tom left the room, I remarked maliciously to Janoš, "Do you think he ever takes that raincoat off?"

Sky, who had been diligently marking a Greek text, suddenly looked up. "The real question," he deadpanned, "is, does he wear anything underneath?"

Another running discussion had to do with the problem of recording and preserving information for posterity. Perhaps it started when one of us—it must have been Sky—broke a long stretch of silence to observe:

"This is so weird! I mean, here we are prepping texts for data entry into a machine so complex that not one of us would be capable of taking it apart and putting it back together again, a machine whose workings I, for one, don't even understand, yet look at us! What are we all holding in our hands?"

"Pencils," came the unanimous reply.

"Pencils!" Steven Windfall confirmed. "A writing tool that is essentially unchanged since the Bronze Age!"

Janoš: "Are you suggesting that that 'Univac' over in the Physics basement has failed to revolutionize the writing industry?"

"He is saying," I interjected, "that the new technology has created a kind of dichotomy between writing and storing data—one that has never existed before."

"I don't see it as a dichotomy," corrected Sky. "I think the computer age has introduced a new intermediary between the writer and the reader. The computer geek today occupies the kind of exalted yet ridiculed position that was once upon a time held by the scribes of old. In antiquity, those who knew how to write wrote directly on—and read directly from—the very medium—stone, vellum, papyrus or parchment—that was used to preserve the recorded information.

Jason: "I see nothing new here. The writer might make his scratches with a piece of charcoal, but if he wanted to preserve it for the next generation, he gave the scratches to a stonecutter who chiseled them into stone."

Louis: "Except that, often as not, the inscription outlived so many generations that by the time it was dug up, the language it was inscribed in had long been forgotten. The message had evaporated. All that was left were the *Semata Lygra*, as Homer calls them—the 'mournful signs' of a dead civilization."

"Which raises the question," appended Janoš: "For whom are we busting our asses to preserve these texts? Will there be any one left, fifty years from now, who will give a (and here, Janoš invoked an act of airborne sexual intercourse—a favorite expression of his) about any one of these texts?"

"Will there be any one left, period?" grumbled Tom Cooke.

Jason: "Well, assuming that Classics will survive another fifty years, the problem will not be deciphering the Greek, but rather locating the technology that will be needed in coming times to retrieve it from our by then antiquated data base. In some ways, the good ol' days did have the advantage over us in data preservation. The medium was its own time capsule. If our Thucydides tape gets dug up centuries from now, the scholar who gets a hold of it is going to have a devil of a time locating the ancient equipment and the outdated programs he's going to need to read it."

Edythe: "Unless the Ark survives long enough to keep updating the format of its data."

Jason: "And if it doesn't? Someone is going to be very busy maintaining a huge warehouse with heaps on heaps of equipment from every era—a museum, really—a museum of computer technology. All this presumes, incidentally, that civilization will not take a sudden downturn—a barbarian invasion or an atom bomb, a Cultural Revolution, another Woodstock . . ."

"Today, I'm feeling much younger than my age," announced Windfall, shaking a Greek text out of his blonde curls and ambling through the open door out onto the patio.

"He walks remarkably well for a guy with a thermometer up his rectum," was Skippy's comment.

"Those are a lot of presumptions, Jason," I ventured, "but if that's the case, wouldn't it be better to spend a million or two just to reprint our crumbling texts on acid-free paper, store a few exemplars of each in a vault under vacuum, and scatter the rest to the four corners?"

Edythe: "Yes, it would, if all we wanted to do is pickle the texts that have come down to us from antiquity. But remember: the Ark is preserving these texts in machine-readable form, so that scholars can search for words or phrases or patterns of words or phrases with minimal expenditure of time."

Louis: "Well, I can certainly see the value of an index of concordances as a peripheral tool, but in all honesty, my bias says that if a machine can do the research, the machine should get the credit."

Jason: "It does! Well, not the machine per se, but the Ark. Many articles have been published that acknowledge the use made of our data base."

Louis: "That wasn't my point, exactly. But OK. We're getting away from our initial inquiry. Sky raised an interesting point: printed books store data very well, until they fall apart and it becomes time to reprint them. But they also present the data they preserve in a directly readable form. If digital data must also be transferred from one type of storage to the next in order to keep up with technological progress, what is the advantage over traditional printing of introducing a storage technology that intrudes a barrier between writer and reader? I'm asking about storage per se, not fringe benefits like machine-readability versus human readability."

Jason: "I think it's not so much a question of advantages, but rather, this is the way our civilization is developing, and that puts old fogeys like us in the nasty position of having to adapt or join the extinction list."

Louis: "Somehow, I think the extinct species—the raptors—have a better chance of being exhumed and revived than the adaptors. Can you imagine what will happen if all the significant data produced by a civilization gets preserved in machine readable form? Think of Janoš's closet!" I said, alluding to his doctoral research. "How will anyone . . ."

Janoš: "Bite your tongue, Lulukins, I haven't been in the closet for years!"

Louis: "How will anyone—man or machine—ever be able to organize it, browse through it, select worthy from unworthy, gold from dross, in order to study it against a meaningful context—let alone pass it on for the benefit and enjoyment of future generations? We are already living in an age where the amount of printed material militates against the discovery, appreciation, and productive use of works of real importance. How many times do the same stories, the same "insights," the same discoveries, the same recipes, get repackaged and published over and again? Bach's compositions were regarded as pretty much obsolete in his own day, but his manuscripts were eventually published by those who knew how to appreciate them. I wonder if this would have happened if his works had only survived in machine-readable form."

Sokrates (passing through to return a volume to the shelf): "Bach's manuscripts were discovered purely by accident . . ."

"No they weren't!" objected Clarence Woodbine, who had breezed in to retrieve a text, by pulling it anachronistically off the shelf. "That story is apocryphal. You're thinking of that old chestnut about Mendelssohn buying a fish that turned out to be wrapped in the St. Matthew Passion?"

Sokrates (laughing): "What? I never heard that!"

Louis: "Well, there is an element of providence, if you will. It took a Mendelssohn to catch the fish, so to speak, and run with it.

Bach was still remembered by some, but if not for Mendelssohn's activism, his work might have been lost forever. But computing machines don't have the ability to make critical judgments."

Janoš: "Don't blink!"

Edythe: "But what you've just said, Louis, is that, today, it doesn't make any difference in what form the works are preserved, since, whether in magnetic tape or traditional print, the enormous mass of archival material alone will prevent a critical assessment of its contents—whether by man or machine."

Louis: "No, Edythe! What I'm trying to say is that, without some way to distinguish diamonds from paste, the Bronze-Age—the Pencil-Age—method of storing useful information is more efficient: writings that are used or valued get preserved by collectors who use or value them. What's not used or valued gets buried or burned. Time, taste, need and climate do the winnowing, while works of special value and utility get copied and reprinted through the ages."

Jason: "But time is blind! Climate is blind! Critics are morons! Black holes swallow everything! We ourselves are forced to limit our data entry to one edition per author. How many plays of Sophocles and Aeschylus, how many poems of Sappho's have been lost along with the hacks? How many excellent editions of Homer and Herodotus—each representing years of painstaking labor by revered scholars—shall we have flushed down the W.C. of . . . Western Civilization, simply because the Ark can't afford to preserve them?"

Louis: "Are you suggesting that Sophocles and Aeschylus and Sappho were incapable of writing anything that wasn't worth preserving? I have a theory that the amount of manuscript in a society's waste baskets is inversely proportional to the cost of the material it's written on."

Jason: "What about the prize-winning Athenian plays that haven't come down to us? What about Naevius and Ennius?"

Louis: "So you are telling me that every National Book Award winner deserves to be embalmed for eternity?"

Sky: "And what about pornography? That gets 'used and valued by collectors!' Shall we preserve that?"

Janoš: "Heck yes (guffaw)! But the smut that's come down to us is all veiled in literary elegance or historical significance: it's got 'redeeming value'—or whatever the courts call it! Beneath the veil, it's got zero cultural meaning. 'He unpinned her *chiton*' is the same as 'He unzipped her cocktail dress.' It doesn't take philological or sociological research to figure out what he did with her after that. When *Deipnosophistae* describes a live sexual performance in a nightclub, it tells us something about social mores during Hellenistic times—namely that there were locales where such performances took place before a large, gaping audience. But what the performers actually did with each other offers no more cultural or historical interest than going into the bushes to relieve oneself."

Louis: "And hence no redeeming value? Hmmm . . . that's an interesting idea!"

Jason: "Well, it depends on whether your 'cultural meaning' test differs from Part Three of the 'Miller Test'. I'm not sure that it does—or that Parts One and Two have much life left in them."

Louis: "Why is that?"

Jason: "Because prurience and offensiveness are incompatible. What's prurient does not offend, and what's offensive is not prurient. So Parts One and Two of the test can never be simultaneously satisfied. Besides, the more society is exposed to either, the less aroused or offended it becomes. So the 'average' response is a declining standard, as well as an undefinable one. Anyway, I gravitate more to Terence's dictum that *'Humani nihil a me alienum puto.'* Nothing human is foreign to me. Nothing done by a human being lacks cultural significance!"

Janoš: "But what Louis is saying, I think, is that a data base of books lovingly collected and handed down is more effective than an all-purpose data base of such enormous proportions that it's of no use to anybody."

Jason: "But the human brain is just such a data base. Our brain cells preserve an incredible amount of information that's of no conceivable use to their owner—sealing wax and cabbages and kings—all mixed in with a great deal of significant, even vital information. Yet somehow the brain knows which drawer to open for the data it needs—and which drawers to lock and throw away the key."

Louis: "Naturally. The brain is master in its own house. It organizes its own information, hence knows how to retrieve it. Supposedly, it would take a trained psychiatrist four years to retrieve from my brain the information he needs in order to complete his analysis."

"Or she and her?" interjected Edythe.

Janoš: "From *your* brain? Lulu, I must say, you're an optimist!"

Sky: "I would never have myself analyzed professionally by a female. Why deprive the woman whom I may someday marry?"

Jason: "But Louis, there's a fundamental misconception at work here. Granted, computers don't think for themselves—yet. But the whole idea of data retrieval is that at one end there is a human in charge who has a fairly good idea of what his data base contains, and at the other end, another human—a patron—who has some idea of what he is looking for. Once the twain have met, the computer can be programmed to search for just those criteria. Don't think of a data base as an independent brain filled with generic mush. Each of its contents has a share in a definable class or definable classes, and within each class, each item is identified and pigeonholed and tagged by author, title, genre, subject, etc. A computer data bank is no different from a college library. You need a librarian, and you have to know your search criteria."

Louis: "And what if you don't? And what if you do and the cataloguer missed the tag you're searching under?"

Jason: "Then you browse—same as you would down in the stacks—until you have refined and clarified your criteria. Don't forget: the Archaica data base is huge, but it contains a complete index of its contents. A scholar who is looking for an ancient Greek author knows to come here, and not to a data base of airplane parts."

"Speaking of mush, I knew a fellow in college," interjected Woodbine, who, on hearing "Bach", had prolonged his furlough from his computer station, "whose goal in life was to record every second of his existence via microphone and cameras. He was actually writing up a grant application!"

84

Janoš: "How b'zarre! They'll probably give him the money."

Jason: "Well, it might have some scientific value if the rules of the experiment precluded him from reviewing his tapes and required him to keep a written diary of his recollections. Then you could compare the one against the other, and you would have a test of his perceptions and his memory. But you would still have to wade through the miles and miles of trivia."

Louis: "Exactly! And how would you ever have found that Bach manuscript if it had been preserved in some magnetic data base?"

Edythe (sighing): "Louis, you're right. If you don't know what you're looking for, it would take a freak accident to find it—just as it fell into Mendelssohn's hands through a freak accident! And no computers were involved!"

Woodbine (irritated): "It wasn't a freak accident!"

Janoš: "What's that Latin saying? 'Little data files have their fates?'"

Louis: "You want freakish? Dante's *Divine Comedy* would never have been found if his son had not dreamed one night that the manuscript lay buried in the back yard, under a certain tree!"

Sky (mounting his skateboard): "So what it comes down to is, do we leave it to fate, to morons, and to clairvoyants to select what goes down to posterity, or do we preserve everything and suffocate in our own garbage for the sake of a few pearls we might never find? Great choice! I'm late for French. Bye."

Naturally, while conversation proceeded in this manner, pound signs were misplaced or omitted, pages were skipped, and entire protocols inverted, thus jeopardizing the survival, let alone the machine-readability, of several Church Fathers and Late-Greek grammarians.

Edythe clashed with me often during these discussions. To her, the magnetic database was a kind of sacred temple whose every input was eternally safe from decay, corruption, and misuse. My position was that, so far as documentary evidence was concerned, books were more secure, in that their distribution over wide territories acted as a warranty of their authenticity and a safeguard against destruction. Whereas, I believed, any information stored in a central database

85

would always be vulnerable to hacking, sabotage, and technological obsolescence—loss of the knowledge and the hardware necessary to retrieve it. At such times, Edythe's comic-book bubble would burst wide open, and the text would tumble out in a long, shrill stream of indignant rebuttal, culminating in "That's just paranoid!"

One afternoon, Jason, who at heart was a literary soul given to occasional flourishes of creative musings, drifted into the library with a dreamy look in his eyes, and said: "I was thinking of our data-entry people in India sitting for days and months on end, mindlessly typing our codes—which they don't know—for Greek—which they don't understand—churning out volumes and volumes of digitized Homer, Aeschylus, Aristotle, and suddenly I had this (chuckle) vision of the Million Monkey Theorem—you know, the theorem that if you put a million monkeys in front of a million typewriters and leave them there for a million years, one of them will eventually type out a flawless facsimile of a play by Shakespeare. (Guffaw from Janoš.) I just thought I would leave you with that thought for the day."

"The Million Monkey Theorem," I remonstrated, "stands for the proposition that the universe is a random construct created by accident; but the example of the monkeys actually disproves the very proposition for which it stands."

"Oh really? How so?"

"The mere fact that a monkey could type out "A Midsummer Night's Dream" means nothing, because from a phenomenological point of view, it is still gibberish. No one in his right mind would read it, analyze it, or write literary essays about it, knowing that it issued from the fingers of a monkey. There has to be a premise of rationality behind it to make it worth your time. Similarly, a world made by pure accident would be meaningless, as would our attempts to control it or understand it. Your data-entry people in Hyderabad or wherever it is are able to do mind-deadening work because they believe that what they are doing has significance."

"Oh? And I thought they were doing it so they could pick up a pay check at end of the week and feed their hungry families!"

"Well, it would make an interesting experiment to start a rumor over there that all this finger-numbing data they are entering is only an experiment, that there really is no Archaica Project on the other side of the planet, and that what is gibberish to them is actually gibberish to everybody else, too—including us . . ."

Janoš: "Lulu! I knew sooner or later you'd catch on."

" . . . See what happens to their morale and their turnover rate. Don't you know that one of the specialties the Nazis devised to break the spirit of their concentration-camp tenants was forcing them to do meaningless work? I read a personal testimony from a Survivor who remembered being part of a work detail tasked with shoveling a huge pile of dirt, bucket by bucket, from one end of the yard to the other. As long as the prisoners believed their work had a purpose—simple as it may have been—they worked efficiently and with good will. But once the pile had been moved, they were ordered to shovel it back to its original location. At that point, the work fell apart and the prisoners were beaten or shot."

Jason: "Okay. Good point. So how does that translate to a random universe?"

"I'm suggesting that a random world could at best only outwardly resemble a rational one, but could never function productively or rationally. In other words, in a random world, you and I and Janoš and Sky would be nothing more than lifeless replicas wandering amuck in a mock-up of a university campus."

"Case closed!" chimed in Janoš, adding (with melodic accompaniment), "It's a random world, it's a random world . . . !"

Sky, who had been silent throughout this particular discussion, seemingly absorbed in his text prepping, suddenly piped up: "Hold on, Jason, don't leave just yet! This monkey wants to know what happens when we've added another twenty or thirty million words of data entry to the data base. What happens then? Does Heinz close up shop and go home?"

"Interesting question! Now listen up, greenhorn, and listen good: the Archaica Project will never die! It will go on forever. The wine is maturing even as we drink it. The longer we drink, the older and pricier it gets. We'll be sending off issues of ΜΙΚΥ ΜΑΟΥΣ comics to India before Heinz pulls the plug. And mark ye this and set it before ye as a memorial: The noblest causes of the most altruistic institutions will eventually all transform themselves into a single, shameless purpose!

Sky: "And that is?

"Self-perpetuation. Mark it as Crowleigh's Law, and put it on your mantlepiece next to Acton's, Murphy's, Peter's, and Parkinson's Laws. And now, by your leave, I'm going home to rope me a steer and draw me a beer."

And so it would go, and so the time passed, with deadly tedium pleasantly punctuated for the most part by amusing and thoughtful conversation. There was also a lot of foul language, much of it from the mouths of Heinz and Janoš, but not completely shunned by the others, either, including the ladies. It shocked me at first, as I had never heard such language in a scholarly setting, but I gradually became accustomed to their kind of speech, and even adopted it sometimes, self-consciously, in an attempt to divest myself of the somewhat puritanical reputation I had acquired, thanks to my disaffection for drugs. In this manner, the end of the academic year rolled around, and, despite one or two legendary screw-ups (some of them not at all my fault!), my contract with the Ark was renewed, much to my relief.

When I returned to the Ark the following September, after an Italian vacation spent unwisely and miserably as a guest of a mildly psychotic but very charming Ravegnana, I found that the crew had grown by one. Concetta was—ironically—Italian, blonde, vivacious, curvaceous, and surprisingly vacuous. In fact, her main credentials were that she had moved to Nirvana to marry an American businessman and had met Heinz and Daisy at a party. She did possess a Laurea in "*Pedagogia*," with some Greek and Latin, but showed no interest in pursuing a career in Classics. Her hiring did not speak well for the seaworthiness of the Ark, but now that I think about it, I can see that H & D were nervous about my trip to Italy and afraid I might not return. At the time, however, I took it as a personal vote of no confidence, and a disavowal of the standards on which I thought I had been hired.

By the time I resumed work, Concetta was as thoroughly mired in text prep as the rest of us, and after a few weeks, I began to despair of ever doing anything else. I was deep into Gregorius Nazianzenus when Skipchick materialized over my desk, clapped shut the heavy Migne volume with my hand sandwiched inside, and announced unceremoniously: "Daisy wants you in her office right away."

"What did I do now?"

"*Mirabile dictu*, nuthin'. You didn't hear it from me, but you're being put onto the Philodemus biblio."

9

Volcano

The earth remembers. Human blood, the wasted seed of man, the sufferings of slaves and animals, scorched crops, stolen treasure, the march of arrogant boots, wanton destruction. The earth is long suffering, but does not forget. There is a Midrash that says that in the end of days, the earth will complain to the Creator, seeking divine redress for being trodden by the wicked.

Meanwhile, the earth has its own remedies. Nine years virtually to the day (the 7th-8th of the Jewish month of Elul, 3839), after Titus Flavius and his Roman legions burnt down the Holy Temple of Jerusalem (8th-9th of Elul, 3830)[*] and destroyed the Holy City, on the ninth day before the *Kalendae* of the Roman calendar, a noble mountain that for nearly three hundred years had stood placid sentinel over the Bay of Naples, having sought and obtained the approval and blessing of the Creator of the universe, retched convulsively and vomited into the sky a towering column of fire, smoke, ash, gas, and pumice—destroying, burning, suffocating and burying the towns and villages of the surrounding plain, along with many thousands of their inhabitants. The eruption lasted two days—as many days as Roman soldiers overran the Temple Mount, slaughtering, wrecking, burning and looting.

---

[*]The traditional date is the 9th of Av, but Josephus gives the date as the 8th of Elul. The corresponding secular date is Sunday, August 31, (Julian), or Sunday, Sept. 2 (Gregorian) of the year 70 CE. The date for the eruption of Vesuvius—Aug. 24, 79 CE—Julian) is given by Pliny the Younger. The conversions between Hebrew and secular dates take into account the conversion of the Julian to the Gregorian calendar. The dates were obtained via Hebrew Calendar.net.

With the collapse of the fiery column, the convulsion ended with a pyroclastic tidal wave of superheated gas and solid debris that barreled down the slopes and swept over the surrounding plain like an express train at an estimated eighty miles per hour, slicing through and incinerating everything in its deadly path. As the destroyed cities baked under six to nine feet of rock, ash and lava, a heavy rainfall precipitated by the eruption soaked into the denuded, smoking mountainside. The slopes above Herculaneum gave way, and a seething river of mud overwhelmed the last steaming remains, cancelling their very location from the short memory of man.

For more than sixteen hundred years, Herculaneum lay forgotten under more than twenty meters of volcanic debris and hardened mud. For centuries, life had contended with a temperamental and irascible mountain, with tidal quakes of warring empires and migrant peoples. Life had prevailed. Civilization once again took root on the waking plains and verdant slopes—new life among rotting bones, new villages amid blood-fertile fields, a great and ancient city redivivus from many wracks and ruins. Churches, farms, villas and vineyards risen in the shadow of a fitfully sleeping giant. Peoples roused and loosed in the wake of Rome's demise had fought for possession of the Italian peninsula, the southern half wrested from hand to grasping hand like a jug of wine and exhausted to the dregs. Goths, Vandals, Ostrogoths had sacked and slaughtered, Belisarius, Totila, Narses had wrought terror and destruction, Lombard hordes had cut like a scythe through Campania with sword, disease and famine. Greeks, Arabs, Huns had plundered, Normans and Germans had conquered and been conquered, France and Spain, Spain and Austria had wrestled and ruled. The lives of countless thousands of no-name individuals had been overturned and torn apart times without end or mercy. Yet the life of the region had barely changed since Naevius wrote his epic on the Punic War. Gardens to be sown, grapes to be harvested, cows to be milked, sheep to be sheared, pigs to be brought to market, wells to be dug.

One well proved exceptionally productive. One day (the date is not recorded) the abbot of the local Franciscan cloister, heeding the cunning nod of a dowsing rod, gave direction to his monks to dig for

91

water in the orchard of their monastery. Water they found none, but at a depth of about seventy feet dug up a marble head. News of the find reached the vigilant ears of the Austrian garrison, and a certain general, Prince d'Elboeuf, ardent collector of antiquities, purchased the land and hired workers to tunnel out from the bottom of the well. More discoveries ensued: marble statuary, some bronzes, a few inscriptions, a marble plaque. They had tunneled into the vestibule of a large and imposing Roman villa.

War called the General away to more frivolous pursuits from which he never returned. The Spaniards having supplanted the Austrians, excavation languished for some years. However, in 1752, in one of the most dramatic finds in the history of Roman archaeology, workers burrowing further into the underground villa uncovered the remains of what, because of its trove of papyrus scrolls and various other indicia, is believed to have been the Greek-language library of one Lucius Calpurnius Piso Caesoninus, father-in-law to Julius Caesar, and a devoted student and patron of Philodemus, the historically noted philosopher poet whose bibliography I had just been summoned to compile.

With the discovery of that library, the obscure Epicurean suddenly acquired a new lease on immortality. Previously remembered mainly for his rather uninspiring epigrams, and for being mentioned favorably by the anti-Epicurean Cicero, Philodemus now enjoyed a celebrity quite disproportionate to his significance as a writer and thinker. Indeed, Piso's library—the only one known to have survived from Roman times—included what appeared to be the sole surviving collection—and virtually complete at that—of his philosophical writings. This aroused the concerted attention of antiquarian scholarship.

Reduced by heat and pressure to little more than elongated lumps of coal, the *Papyri Herculanenses* (PHerc.), numbering more than a thousand, had been carbonized by the hot gas and ash—the very circumstance, ironically, to which they owed their preservation, papyrus being under ordinary conditions a notoriously perishable material. Indeed, the papyrus itself, though extremely friable, was found to be amenable to slow and patient unrolling via the aid of an ingenious machine which simultaneously unrolled the sheets and pressed them onto a sticky backing before they could completely disintegrate. Even more remarkably, the sheets proved amenable to certain processes enhancing legibility where the papyrus was preserved.

After two hundred years of haphazard and sporadic excavation, the investigation of both the site—now definitely identified as Herculaneum—and the papyri was finally placed under the supervision of a central organization run by a committee of international scholars—archaeologists and papyrologists—headed by the late Marcello Gigante. The Centro Internazionale per lo Studio dei Papiri Ercolanesi was inaugurated in 1969, and besides expanding the excavation of the villa, helped stimulate the painstaking reconstruction of its contents.

As more and more of Philodemus's work was brought to the surface, the philosopher, though of minor stature as a writer and original thinker, was revealed to be a figure of considerable interest with respect to the cultural relations of his time and the history of philosophical teaching in Italy during the first years of the imperial epoch of Rome. Known through various references in his own and others' work to have been friendly with such major literary figures as Virgil, Varius, Cicero, Horace, and others, Philodemus was now realized to have been an influential exponent of the Epicurean philosophy and a prominent factor in its dissemination throughout Italy—the villa at Herculaneum being the center of that dissemination.

The fact that the library at Herculaneum outlived both Philodemus and Piso by approximately 120 years suggests that Piso, if Piso's it truly was, bequeathed it to a kind of institute or foundation for the study of Epicureanism. In so doing, Piso would have been following the example of Epicurus himself, whose little house in a garden at Athens had become a kind of university for Epicurean studies. At the very least, the existence of a comprehensive Epicurean library at Herculaneum defines that formerly seaside little town (the eruption of 79 CE dramatically extended the coastline) as an important center of philosophical research, where followers of the

Epicurean doctrines could gather for lecture and discussion while enjoying the simple pleasures described in Philodemus's little poems—the very pleasures once endorsed by the Master himself.

That the customary pleasures also included the company of *hetairai* and *epheboi*, as well as of assorted private guests attracted by little more than the opportunity to dignify their adulteries with a dusting of philosophical chatter unquestionably lent such enclaves a bad name among the more traditional elements of Roman society—a reputation, that of the Epicureans, not mitigated by their open scoffing at divine worship of any sort—including the official solemnities of state ritual and sacrifice. Doubtless, not a few Romans execrated the place and had it pegged for divine retribution of some sort.

"We're putting you in charge of the Philodemus bibliography," announced Daisy portentously, as though designating me as the avenging angel. "How much time do you think you'll need?"

The question was so patently idiotic that I nearly burst out laughing. "Well," I said, with self-imposed gravity, "how big is the bibliography?"

"That's the problem. We don't know. We are relying on you to inform us. Now, Clarissa did some work on Philodemus before she left us, so you won't be starting from scratch." Daisy reached an old shoe box down from the top of a filing cabinet and handed it over. "Here. This should help you on your way. Good luck! You'll need it."

I had been moved from the communal work area to a small storeroom off the "inner sanctum" that had been cleared of its paraphernalia over the summer. I now availed myself of my new-found privacy to open the shoe box, which upon inspection proved to contain a letter from Professor Phillip de Lacy, Clarissa's one-page bibliography, numbering about ten items, and two dead flies that I named Aïda and Radamès. Clearly, I was not being provided with much of a head start.

As I sat at my desk, a clunky, metallic affair large enough to be flattering to a low-ranking peon like me, I began to ponder the irony of my position. I might not then have been fully aware of the depth of the age-old repugnance of Judaism for Epicurean teachings; but having read Potok's *The Chosen*, I knew that the name "Apikoros" was still used by observant Jews as an epithet for a Jew who has departed from the pure path of Torah in order to embrace the temptations of the world. The reasons for their repugnance are obvious. The central point of Epicurean philosophy was a total denial of that Divine Providence which is the very essence of Jewish faith. Moreover, the pseudo-messianic component of the Epicurean School gave it a missionary impetus which made direct conflict with Jewish society inevitable. Indeed, for the quasi-atheistic Epicurean School, understanding the random nature of the universe and the irrelevance of the gods was key to liberating humanity from guilt, fear, superstition, and, ultimately, the violence that arises from man's attempted avoidance of those things. To the Jews, the Epicurean denial of any involvement of "the gods" in human affairs seemed a transparent excuse for, and an unencumbered highway to, the basest immorality.

The truth is that, while the humanitarian motivations of Epicurus himself, as well as of the higher-minded of his followers, must be acknowledged, what aroused the fervor of the masses was the low-budget party lifestyle, and the open pursuit of physical pleasure which Epicurean thought had endowed with the respectable coating of philosophical theory. It was a lifestyle and doctrine that made dangerous inroads among the Jews of Greece and Rome, many of whom had already fallen prey to the dazzling cultural heritage and heady intellectual openness of the Hellenistic world.

Curiously, the Talmud attributes the epithet *apikoros* not to the homophonic philosopher, but to the Hebrew word *hefker*, which means "free," "ownerless", or "unattached." However, it would be strange if the opprobrium attached to being labeled an "Apikoros" did not reflect many generations of bitter antagonism between Jews and Epicureans. Indeed, I speculate that it is within this social dynamic that we may discover an explanation for the supposed adoption by the Epicurean School of a piglet for a mascot and, perhaps, an apotropaic as well. For, however devoted to conviviality the Epicureans may have been, gourmandise was not one of their advertised precepts. Very plausibly, it is only in the context of our Torah-mandated aversion to pork that this supposed Epicurean mascot attains meaning. A clearer warning sign to Jews curious to explore and experiment would be hard to imagine. One could well imagine some delicate back-room diplomacy between the heads of the Epicurean institutions and their rabbinical opponents!

As interesting as it was to speculate on such matters, time—whether by hindsight or foresight—had shrouded most of what had been written by the Later Epicureans—until the Philodemus explosion. And now, I, a Jew, a descendant of Shelumiel/Zimri, Prince of Shimon, was being asked to delve into the huge mess of fragmentary publications that had erupted from the soil of Herculaneum, and organize it and catalog it for posterity! I tried to ignore the implications while savoring the irony. Had not Theopompus, a Fourth-Century BCE Greek historian, lost his mind while trying to write about Jewish Law?

Specifically, my job was to order copies of the published material (generally mere fragments of larger works not fully retrieved or identified) from various sources, examine them upon their arrival, try to establish from the accompanying commentary which philosophical tractate each fragment belonged to, classify it as such, take down the bibliographical information, including the code number of the papyrus from which the fragment had been transcribed, count or estimate the number of words contained in the published fragment, and then "prep" it for data entry. It was hardly deep intellectual labor—especially since I was expressly warned clear of any questions concerning the authorship of the fragments—but certainly more interesting than what I had been doing till then. Each new arrival had a bibliographical list of its own, which I would then peruse for mention of additional Philodemus publications to be ordered in turn.

So, the Philodemus project, slow and intermittent at first, rapidly snowballed to occupy most of my time at the Ark. And since I could not predict how many new publications would be referenced by each new publication that arrived, I had no way of estimating how long it would take to complete my compilation. Thus, whenever Janoš popped his head into my cubicle to say, "Daisy wants to know how much more time you need to complete the Philodemus Bibliography," I would struggle to come up with a rational answer to an irrational question without sounding disrespectful or condescending. If I knew how big the bibliography was going to be, then I could estimate how long it would take me to catalog it; but obviously I had no data upon which to base even the wildest "guesstimate". Gigante & Co. were spewing out new material every week. No matter how I contorted my brains to convey this simple concept in an intelligible manner, the inquiries kept coming. Eventually, it became a routine, almost like a changing of the guard, until I began to suspect that Skippy was conducting some of these periodic checks on his own initiative, just for the fun of watching me squirm. Naturally, I started to respond in kind, by concocting a spiel of some sort or other.

"Haven't you heard? Gigante has spilled the beans. It's all a hoax. The Villa dei Papiri was nothing more than a laundromat. DBA 'Lava-Lava'. All those scrolls? Nothing but laundry lists! Thousands of them! Three togas for Publius. Two for Titus. They've just uncovered a whole cache of linen breeches! Fluff-dried, pressed, and scorched to a crisp! It's going to take at least five more years to finish this biblio! You'll have to petition the NEH for a new grant."

Or, "Excuse me for a moment while I sequester myself in the Temple of Vulcan to consult my oracles." Then, reverently cracking open the old shoe box with the dead flies, Clarissa's list and De Lacy's letter, I would intone: "O spirits of Aïda and Whaddamess entombed herein through the wickedness of Pharoah, answer me now: How much more time do I need to complete the Philodemus Bibliography?"

"O Venerable Shlemiel," would reverb the old shoe box in a dark, spelunkean voice, "ask us the age of the universe, ask us how many grains of sand in the Gobi Desert, ask us how many more years before you get laid; but do not ask us how much more time you need to complete the Philodemus Bibliography. For the publications increase daily and daily the scrolls are unwound like *Charmin* and day after day more philosophy is pulled from the earth like carrots from Bugs

Bunny's backyard and there is no end to the troubles of man plus we know how long it takes you to get anything done around here" (the voice rising into an impression of one of Edythe's high-pitched snarls), "so quit wasting your time and ours and get back to work!" And, addressing Janoš in my own voice, "I'm not sure, but I think this means I still don't know."

Alright. You had to have been there. Janoš would roll his eyes and walk away muttering, "What a zoo!"

And I would mutter after him, "What a novel!"

10

A Novel?

For all of Skippy's affability, he could also be, as Bottom might have phrased it, a bit of a bore. Though perfectly virile in his work-a-day behavior, he would, when the mood struck him, lapse into self-parody in the middle of the courtyard, in full view of practically everybody. He especially enjoyed wiggling his hips and flopping his wrists at me from the entrance to the library. This he did with special gusto whenever he espied me trying to flirt with one of the rare co-eds whom the spirit moved to exchange a few words of noncommittal banter. "Yoohoo! Hi, Lulu!" he would sing out, just in case the girl had missed the spectacle. It was terribly funny at first, but also extremely embarrassing. When, on one such occasion, I asked him if it didn't bother him to disport himself in that way in front of strangers, he answered, "What strangers, Lulukins? I'm known all over campus!" I won't say that his misbehavior had much to do with my dismal lovelife, but more than one of those reluctant maidens let drop that she had thought I was Skippy's boyfriend.

It dawned on me, little by little, that, for all the tedium of text prepping and cataloging, I had been handed a silver platter with all the material I needed for a novel: scenario, characters, situations, philosophical excursions. Only the story line was missing. I got into the habit, on walking in every morning, of greeting my coworkers with "OK: so what's the plot?" Whenever we had a foul-up, and Janoš would shake his head and exclaim "What a zoo!" I would respond with "What a novel!" It was to have been a happy novel, a kind of gentle satire of American culture and mores viewed from the surrealistically leaning ivory tower of Piso. Sokrates would have us all in stitches with thickly accented tales of his adolescent adventures back home in Athens. Euphemios, cloudless blue mug in hand, would join me from time to time on the Humphreys planter to share his thoughts on an article by his friend, Roman Jakobson, or to ask for my wise Jewish advice on how he might extricate himself from his extraordinarily complicated domestic situations. Evenings, Jason would head home, "to slaughter a couple million brain cells," and bid us good night by singing "Happy trails to you." An hour later, Janoš would sigh, twist into his weathered leather jacket and declare, "Well, I've had enough of this dump. I'm too pooped to pop and too popped to poop. I'm going home. Shake a martini. Kick the cat. Squeeze the fish. Ta ta." I never took notes. There was no plot, and I couldn't think of one.

One bright morning, Heinz surprised us by offering to take Skippy and me up in his little Cessna. It looked no bigger on the runway than a bird, and I felt like one up there in the blue sky, circling the harbor, skimming the water and saluting the sailboats. Another time, he drove a bunch of us down to Sea World in his copper-colored "CAD-L-ARK." He sat me down solicitously in the front row of the orcinus orca show, where he knew very well that the Shamu of the day would give me a good soaking.

Veronica of the long dark tresses wheedled me into driving her to an evangelical revival. Sokrates came along. Neither he nor I had ever seen anything like it. Lots of preachings and healings and testimonies and Praise the Lords. Then a strange metallic hum that grew into a chiming, clattering roar. Thousands of people were shaking something in their hands, a long shiny object. "What are they doing?" Krati and I asked in bewildered unison.

"They're speaking in tongs!" answered Veronica, with complacent assurance. Something like that would happen every time I started to become warmly conscious of her simplicity, beauty, and patchouli, but there wasn't enough lumber in my forest to build a bridge over the wide river that separated us.

I don't remember who led our troupe to an electronically secured room in the basement of the Math Building. It might have been Jason or Edythe, or perhaps the inventor himself—an overgrown hedgehog of a man, bristling with all the capricious eccentricities of genius and affluence—who would preternaturally appear and disappear, from time to faraway time, like an autumn shadow. There, in a compact, grey case no bigger than your family freezer, dozed Icarus, primed and poised to chew and spew the vast quantity of Greek authors corralled and curried to be fed into it like so many hecatombs, its newly-waxed wings fanning, cooling, readying themselves for digital flight, its arcane motor humming quietly to itself, as though savoring in dream its sweet supremacy over the clunky rhinoceros of a mainframe still wallowing in its binary shitpit deep beneath University Admin.

There were also the occasional get-togethers down at Heinz-and-Daisy's house at the beach—some just for Jason, Edythe, Janoš, Sky and me, others genuine shindigs for the entire Ark and Classics as well, with Daisy's home-cooked gazpacho and paella and Heinz officiating over a plenteous barbecue. Nor was there lack of psychotropic pasturage passed around on silver-plated trays. Though Janoš referred to these affairs as "orgies," and had a lore of legendary bashes—graced by the token U.S. Congressman or two who had inscribed themselves in the annals of human debauchery—what I saw, though not unlively, was hardly indecorous, it being somewhat daunting, I would imagine, to let go all the way in front of people you work with every day. I remember nothing more scandalous than a couple of students necking in a doorway, and a pair of visiting professors from Spain with hashish hangovers as we drove them—with necessary pauses along the highway—back to their hotel.

It meant a lot to me to be included in these outings and gatherings. Though I have always been blessed with two or three close friends, I am usually shy of groups, and have been tagged for most of my life as a "loner." Not the "quiet" kind, like Strelesky, who end up killing people, but the shy and introverted type who are easily befriended by the more outgoing specimens of humanity. Perhaps more than anything else, my time aboard the Ark taught me how precious it is to be accepted and appreciated by one's colleagues, and how important to cultivate good relations at one's place of work.

I also learned first-hand how frighteningly powerful can be the pressure to conform and to assimilate. For I observed in my companions traits of character and behavior that I perceived as foreign and distasteful, yet at the same time mysteriously attractive. I had already had occasion to observe some of these traits take root in myself with a vigor that betokened a dangerously fertile ground. I am not suggesting, by any means, that I learned my misdemeanors aboard the Ark, but rather that I had already been tainted, and that it was thanks to my coworkers that I became aware of this contamination. The awareness, however, did little, by itself, to contain it, since the environment made it more comfortable to maintain it than to eradicate it.

I committed a terrible faux pas. Heinz's fiftieth birthday was approaching, and posters and ribbons were draped all over the office—including a poster of Daisy Duck, decked out in a Heinz moustache, a Heinz flat top, and Heinz dark glasses. I went to some big chain drugstore and bought a birthday card. It had a hole in it and invited the recipient to insert his finger in it. It was in the poorest possible taste—which was the whole point—and with an obscene overtone that made me feel suitably one of the guys. The big joke was, this was for the boss, and the boss was "having his way" with everybody, and we all had to love it because it was the boss. I don't remember what the connection was with the birthday theme. I showed it to Janoš, who said, "Don't give it to him." I did, and can still feel the blood freeze in my veins as I watched Heinz's face fall. It was as though I suddenly came to after a psychotic episode. I can't imagine what I was thinking. I know I apologized to him shortly afterwards, I don't remember whether in person or by letter, but I remember him being fairly gracious about it.

I don't know that there wasn't something else behind my effrontery. I had become very friendly, over the past two years, with a member of the Classics faculty, a young man who combined in a rather charming way the blue-eyed drawl of the Midwestern plains with the actively inquiring intellect of a natural-born scholar. He had been appointed to a two-year tenure track position teaching Ancient

Greek History, and had arrived at JW about the same time I had. According to "Hoss," as I called him, Heinz had brought him out to Nirvana with promises of a permanent job, provided he performed according to specs. And Hoss Cartwright performed. He published several articles, had a book accepted for publication, and was twice voted "Best Teacher of the Year" by the student body. Nonetheless, Hoss did not get tenure, and at the end of his two years was—according to Hoss—summarily fired. It was more than a career setback for Hoss. His gorgeous wife had embarked on a brilliantly successful legal career, and was unwilling to play sidekick to her husband on his prospective treks through the backwoods of campus country in search of a job. His vacant position was not filled during my remaining year at the Ark (imagine that: a university Classics Department with no Greek History!), but a new one, superfluous, was created in Greek Literature. It was my introduction to a side of Heinz Strauss that I had not previously been acquainted with, and it rankled.

Others, including Sokrates and Euphemios, were greatly distressed by the affair, and Heinz must have sensed the sharp decline in his popularity. I happened to be in Heinz's front office xeroxing a Philodemus text when I realized that Heinz was in the middle of a long soliloquy, ostensibly addressed to Sheila, about the difficulties of running a project like Noah's Ark while ministering to the needs of the Classics Department, kissing the behinds of his providers and wiping those of his students and staff. The brutal realities of administration, budgets and calendars, etc., etc. As I listened (it was hardly eavesdropping: he was right there, posing and pacing histrionically back and forth in front of Sheila's desk!), it began to sound more and more like an apologia re the Cartwright affair. I also began to feel that the speech was for my benefit more than Sheila's, though it was her name and not mine that he kept invoking.

I found the situation extremely embarrassing. If he was talking to me, then I should turn around and face him. If he was talking to Sheila, then I should not be listening, or should at least appear to be completely absorbed by my task. However, it was impossible to pretend that I could not hear everything Heinz was saying, and it struck me as a rather obvious and pathetic attempt to justify what looked increasingly like termination without cause. My malaise became intolerable, so I put the book down on top of the copy machine and exited, intending to visit the restroom and return a few minutes later when the harangue was over.

On my way back to the office, I was met by Janoš, who, he said, had been looking all over for me and needed me urgently in the library. Whatever it was, I forgot about the book left on top of the copier, and when I returned a couple of hours later to retrieve it, the book was gone, as were the pages I had already copied. By that time, Heinz had left, and no one knew what had happened to the missing items. The next day, after an anguished morning in which I searched frantically for the missing text, Heinz calls a general staff meeting, walks in, sits down, throws the missing items down on the conference table and launches into a diatribe that began:

"I found these on top of the copier in my office the other day. I don't know who left them there, and it's not important, because as far as I'm concerned, it's everybody's responsibility. The one thing I won't tolerate is carelessness and sloppiness with Archaica materials. Etc." Thus was I introduced to yet another aspect of Heinz's personality.

It was an aspect he shared, unfortunately, with Daisy Duchinsky. My relations with Daisy were much more complex than with Heinz, who, aside from the occasional tantrum, stayed easygoing and accessible. Daisy was a moody type who often voiced complaints about academic bureaucrats and bigwigs with an air of contemptuous impatience and self-mocking martyrdom conveyed by a string of consonantal pops, hisses, snarls and slurs. Lllionel Pppearson. Bbruno Sssnellll. Dddenys Pppage. I wanted her to like me, but felt that if she did it was with much effort. I grew increasingly insecure in her presence.

It sounds conceited of me to say it, but perhaps I exacerbated her own insecurities. There was a dash of envy in her attitudinal cocktail. She once paid me the compliment of sharing with me, with the sweet, excited air of a child showing off a picture of a house face and a sun face and a tree and a horse and a drippy cloud, that she had started work on an article comparing the ancient pleasure city of Sybaris—whence the words sybarite and sybaritic—with the contemporary pleasure town of Porto Madeira, where she and Heinz shared their seaside digs. The object of this paper could only have been to demonstrate that Sybaris and Porto Madeira were two chips off the same block, that the ancient Greeks were just like us, and that people were people. I was astonished that someone in Duchinsky's position would be occupying herself with what might have been the subject of a high school essay.

Unfortunately, I committed the unpardonable mistake of mentioning this to Professor Marcus, a colleague of hers from Roman History with whom I used to have friendly talks from time to time. For some reason, he asked me what I thought of Daisy's abilities as a scholar, and I answered him honestly, but without malice, contrasting her talents as a lecturer and compiler with what I sensed was an abysmal lack of imagination.

It never occurred to me then, that Professor Marcus's question might have been motivated by something more than simple curiosity. What if, for example, he were on a committee charged with allocating grant moneys for faculty research? Perhaps some unknown grant recipient at that university still owes me a big thank you. Well, if that is the case, then I suppose I still owe Daisy an apology—one that I cannot possibly make. On the other hand, perhaps the entire field of classical studies—including, ultimately, Daisy herself, is indebted to me for my indiscretion. Who can know the consequences of a careless comment? It was an unfair position to be put in. I was, nominally, "Faculty", but was kept out of the "loop" and was entirely dependent, for the what's what, on chance tidbits dropped by others. I trusted people's intentions in those days, and answered Professor Marcus in complete innocence.

It may be that news of my betrayal reached Daisy in one way or another. Or maybe not. However, some short time afterward, Hoss Cartwright warned me that Daisy was out for my scalp and was sifting through an early draft of my Philodemus bibliography with a fine-toothed comb and a jeweler's loupe. This Daisy herself confirmed the next day during a private conference, during which she appeared enraged and trembling. I had no idea what that was all about. Perhaps it was nothing more than surprise on being confronted with such a voluminous bibliography that showed no signs of nearing completion. In any case, her autopsy turned up nothing but a few inconsistencies in format, and, though with difficulty, it seemed to me, she calmed herself enough to give me grudging praise for my work as she handed it back to me.

I was about half a year into the Philodemus bibliography when the Ark received a visit from Egil Heklason, a noted Philodemus scholar from the University of Reykjavik, a large man with an intelligent face surmounted by a ludicrous mop of silver hair. Something in his manner put me instantly at ease with him, and when Daisy brought him into the library to introduce us, I blurted out, much to Daisy's horror, "Oh, I am delighted to meet you! I've just read *Egil's Saga!*"

"Oh, I'm not quite as hard-headed as that," came the cordial reply—a reference to the Icelandic hero's indestructible skull.

"I didn't think so, because I've also read your articles on Lucretius!"

"And what did you think of them?"

"I thought, 'There's a scholar who might like what I am going to say in an article about Lucretius that I am working on.'"

"Good. Then I'll expect to receive an offprint when it's ready."

"I'd be most honored."

Heinz joined us and asked me to brief Professor Heklason on the status quo of the Philodemus biblio, so in Heinz's and Daisy's presence, I showed him my dual filing system and explained to him how it worked, and showed him the library of Philodemean texts that I was in the process of assembling. He seemed favorably impressed, and the bosses looked satisfied. We then adjourned to the conference room, where we were joined by the rest of the crew, and where Professor Heklason said, "And now I would like to show you something." He pulled out from a little bag a small roll of soft cloth and tissue paper from which, to our collective amazement, he extracted a rather odd-looking piece of elongated charcoal. Actually, it looked like a badly overcooked blintz, and was about the same size. We passed it around the conference table gingerly and with reverence.

"You needn't be too much in awe," smiled the Professor. "In all likelihood it's a complete blank. There's nothing written on it."

"But how do you know it's blank until you unroll it?" queried Janoš.

"It was found in a location containing other rolls, all of which have proven blank. We use them to experiment with new methods of opening them up. I like to keep some on hand in my travels, in case I meet someone with new ideas."

"There's a guy here," I ventured, "right here on campus—in Molecular Biology—a Dr. Brown, I believe—who is supposed to be one of the foremost experts on micro-laser applications. I know one of his students. Perhaps I could try to set up a meeting for you."

"Oh really! That would be very nice!"

Dr. Brown turned out to be very accommodating. "Sure. Give him my number at the office and ask him to call me."

The following week, Professor Heklason stopped by and stuck his silver mop-head into my cubby hole to say goodbye and to thank me for introducing him to Dr. Brown. The meeting had been positive, he said. He had given Dr. Brown one of his papyrus rolls to work on. He said he hoped to return the next year, and reminded me to send him my article.

Other professors visited us from time to time, but none so engaging as Egil Heklason. We were also entertained on separate occasions by three different candidates who, competing for the new tenure-track position in Greek Literature, had been invited to lecture for the Department's occasional lunchtime symposia. I remember nothing about the first two candidates, except that the second one made by far the best impression of the three. It was the third one, to my dismay, who ended up getting the job. He was clearly an eccentric, and thus fitted in very well with the rest. He wore a droopy hat, droopy clothes and a droopy moustache, and his pipe, too, was the kind that hung down over the chin. His name was Dorian Prout, and I remember him for a very fine trick he played on me.

11

A Nasty Embruhlment

I can't imagine how, but Professor Prout must have got the idea that my presence on the Ark might somehow constitute a remote cloud on his academic horizon. The truth is that budgetary restrictions favor the short-term hiring of adjuncts and assistant professors over the tenuring of full professors. We had already seen one outstanding tenure tracker, a good friend, get the axe after putting in his two years of yeoman's service. So if Prout had apprehensions, perhaps they were not all that unreasonable for a newcomer.

Anyway, one day Prout, who rarely honored me with a glance, came up to me and said, "Louis! I hear you studied in Italy and wrote your dissertation on the Greek mime?"

I said, "Yes, that's true."

"Well, it so happens that Greek mime is one of my areas of interest, and I read Italian; so I was thinking, if you'd like to let me look over your thesis, maybe I can give you a few pointers."

I said, "I would appreciate that very much."

As I now see it, my reply must have astonished him no end, because he continued, I think, somewhat incredulously, "I've even been thinking of writing a book on the subject, and who knows, if I like your thesis, I might even cite it in my book."

"That would be very nice," I answered. "I, too, have been thinking about turning my dissertation into a book."

"So there you are: we could help each other," he says, no doubt wondering if I had ever had "Little Red Riding Hood" read to me when I was small. "You know," he added in an undertone, "nothing really major has been written on Greek mime in at least fifty years, so whichever of us comes out with a new book on the subject is probably going to be king of the mountain."

"Well, that certainly makes it all the more interesting, doesn't it? I'll be looking forward to your comments."

"And I'm curious to see whether you actually bring me your thesis before the penny drops!" thought Professor Prout under his droopy hat!

Well, I did give him my thesis. And two or three days later, I bump into him in the parking lot as we both arrive for work, and he sees me, hands me back the dissertation, and says, "By the way, I took a couple of hours last night to read your thesis, and, frankly, I must say that I was not impressed. Well, I have to teach a class in five minutes, so, be seein' ya." With this, he plants me right there, as they say in Italy, and saunters off.

Another few days go by, and Professor Parthenopides, his sky-blue coffee mug in hand, sees me sitting on the planter outside Humphreys Hall, and sits himself down beside me and says, somewhat furtively, "Louis! You gave Dorian Prout your dissertation to read?"

"Yes," I said.

"Really, you must be more careful! Do you know, I don't want to upset you, but I am afraid I must tell you: I was in the teachers' lounge at lunchtime, and I heard him speak about your dissertation in a . . . not in a nice way."

"He spoke badly about my dissertation? Yes, I know, he told me he didn't think much of it. He said he read it in two hours."

"Two hours? That's ridiculous!"

"Yes it is. Not even I could read it in two hours, and I spent three years writing it! To whom did he say bad things?"

"To everybody. There were several people in the room. Heinz, Daisy . . . several people. You must be more judicious about whom you show your dissertation. You must be careful with him in particular. It is fortunate that you discussed your thesis with me. Luckily, I, too was there, and I heard, and I was able to say some things in your favor."

"Thank you, Professor Parthenopides. I think I have learned my lesson. You are a good friend, and I am grateful to you." Distracted for a moment by a fleeting vision of Strelesky's ball-peen hammer, I smiled to notice that the sky-blue coffee mug was embellished with the words, "*Ariston ton Hydor*" in Greek letters. The phrase was from Pindar, Pheemy's favorite poet. It meant "Water is best."

"You know, Louis, I have an idea." Cloaked in a Greek accent about as thick and strong as Sokrates's, Pheemy's idea was that I should give a presentation for the Classics Lunchtime Symposia. This would give me an opportunity to vindicate myself before the faculty. I agreed, and he said he would set it up.

I do not remember much about my lecture, which is probably a good thing. I do not remember who attended, besides Professor Parthenopides, Sokrates, Janoš, Jason and Edythe and a few students, including Veronica. Heinz, Daisy, and Dorian had "other commitments." What I do remember is that, as I was summarizing Lévy-Bruhl's theory of *les participations* expounded in *The Soul of the Primitive* and explaining how I had applied it to the theory of the origins of Greek theatre, I used the term "primitive society" or "primitive mentality," whereupon Edythe jumped out of her seat and, much distraught, said in a shrill voice, "Excuse me, but you can't say that!"

"Excuse me?"

"You can't say that on a university campus."

"Say what?" I queried.

"You can't say 'primitive society.'"

"I can't? Why not?"

"Because the accepted term is 'pre-industrial'"

"Well, Lévy-Bruhl says 'primitive.' In fact, that's the title of his book. And we were discussing Lévy-Bruhl."

At this point Jason intervened diplomatically. "I think what Edythe is trying to say is that the academic community has rejected the term 'primitive' as being disparaging to certain societies, and has replaced that label with the term 'pre-industrial.'"

"Whether a society is industrial or pre-industrial has nothing to do with the subject of my presentation, which, by the way, I was in the middle of. The subject of my talk at this point was how individuals in certain societies described by Lévy-Bruhl as 'primitive', relate to their surroundings. Lévy-Bruhl's first-hand observations led him to conclude that a person living in such a society does not perceive himself—*or herself*—as separate from his or her surroundings. For Lévy-Bruhl, that particular mode of perception, which he calls 'participatory'—as opposed to 'dissociative'—is a characteristic of the human mind at a certain stage of social development. In fact, that very mode of perception, for Lévy-Bruhl, was a primary factor in distinguishing between modern societies—in which individuals perceive themselves as distinct, or 'dissociated', from the beings and objects around them—and the kind of society he calls primitive. It has nothing to do with industry, and it would be nonsensical to use the term 'pre-industrial' to distinguish between the two types of society. It's like speaking of Grandma Moses as a pre-industrial painter."

The objections continued, and we finally compromised by settling—much against my will—on the term "tribal" society, though I, as a Jew, found that expression equally disturbing, since the mentality Lévy-Bruhl described as 'primitive' emphatically did not apply to the Jews of the Bible—a tribal society nevertheless!

Edythe's disruption of my talk left me not only short of time, but badly shaken, though, naturally, I had no choice but to put as good a face on it as possible. It was—aside from that time I mistakenly held a door open for an ill-chosen date, and then innocently introduced her to friends as *Miss* So-and-so—my first real dustup with Political Correctness. I found myself wondering what a time I would have trying to explain the participatory mentality described by Lévy-Bruhl to a society of academics that consumed large quantities of illegal substances in a state of complete dissociation from the murderers, gangsters and warlords that terrorized and oppressed the largely pre-industrial societies that cultivated them.

Not long after this unfortunate incident, I overheard a discussion in the adjoining library among Prout, Janoš and Jason. There may have been others, but I don't know for sure. Prout was telling about a friend of his who had brought a skull home from Viet Nam, a souvenir from a Viet Cong soldier he had killed in the fighting. The friend had turned this memento into a lamp of some sort. I heard laughter coming through the open doorway. I think it was about this point that I started to awaken from the participatory stage and experience first-hand the incipient signs of a Lévy-Bruhlian dissociation from my social surroundings.

12

Doctor Wago

At some point during my third year on the Ark, Jason Crowleigh, the Assistant Director of the Archaica Project, disappeared. At first the top brass pretended that nothing was amiss, but people began to ask questions, and there was talk. Finally, after two evasive weeks, Heinz called a full staff meeting in the library conference room. Nearly everyone was there, from Clarence Woodbine, looking like a Secret Service operative in his white, short-sleeved shirt and necktie, to Sky Miles in his bare feet and shorts. Jason, needless to say, was absent, and Edythe, who, so far as I remember, had stuck stoically to her post during the past several days, had mercifully been excused, along with her text bubble.

As soon as all were assembled and seated, Heinz strode in briskly, sat down, closed his eyes behind his tinted glasses, leaned back in his capacious swivel chair, and assumed his usual position of informal yet no-nonsense authority.

"Some of you have been asking—and I'm sure you have all been wondering—what happened to Jason Crowleigh. There have been rumors, there has been speculation—let me just say that it's time to put a stop to all the talk before the situation gets completely out of hand. The Archaica Project is the center of attention of the entire arena of classical studies, and we—and that includes every one of you—are in the spotlight here on this campus. We are under constant scrutiny by the NEH and by Congress, not to mention the Board of Directors of John Wayne and the University Regents. We are liable to get a surprise visit from the media or a Congressional delegation at almost any time.

"Our very survival, the very future of Classics in this country, depends on our performance here at the Ark and how we are perceived by our neighbors on the outside. There are plenty of folks who believe that the funds we depend on would be better spent on filling potholes, and they would be very pleased to catch us with our pants down."

"Filling potholes," I interjected mentally, losing patience.

"We are all one big family here, and I care about each one of you. But I will not put up with any one talking about private, internal matters on the outside. Have I made myself clear? I repeat, have I made myself clear?"

A murmured chorus of "Yes," and "Clear," and "Very clear," hovered about our pale faces. Heinz adjusted his tinted glasses.

"What I am about to tell you is to be kept strictly confidential. Nearly two weeks ago, Jason and I had a disagreement over some administrative matters, and Jason walked out. As you all know, he hasn't shown up since. He hasn't contacted me. No one seems to know where he is. The subject of our disagreement is not relevant.

"Let me just say that Jason's behavior is completely un-professional, uncharacteristic, and totally unacceptable. I have known and worked with Jason Crowleigh for many years. Jason has been with this project since its inception. When I brought him in, he was an untenured, untried assistant professor at Podunk U., fresh out of grad school. Because I recognized his outstanding qualifications, I made him assistant director of one of the most important research projects in the Humanities of this century. His behavior is more than an unconscionable abandonment of his post. It is a betrayal of my personal trust and confidence, and puts at risk everything we have achieved together over the years.

"Tomorrow will be two weeks since Jason walked out on me and on you and on everything that this project stands for, and I'm letting you know that, as of tomorrow noon, if he doesn't show up, I am terminating his employment, and I can tell you that I will personally see to it that Jason Crowleigh never gets another job in academia.

"As for you, our administrative staff and our research faculty, I am counting on you to put this matter behind you and carry on as before, with all your best efforts and good work. I can assure you that I will be doing everything humanly possible to mop up the mess and get things back on track as quickly as possible. And now, if there are any questions, or if anyone has anything to say, I'll be listening and I'll do my best to answer."

I found Heinz's speech disturbing for several reasons. Heinz and Jason were very close friends, as well as next-door neighbors, and, to boot, Jason was happily married to Heinz's ex-wife. I found it hard to believe in a total rupture between the two. Even if they had quarreled, Heinz would surely know where Jason was. I had also come to know Jason as a very personable, balanced individual, and I simply could not imagine him doing anything to jeopardize the success of Noah's Ark. There was something paranoid about Heinz's reaction. If his fears were justified, what was it that he was so worried about getting out into the open? And if it got out, would it affect us, too? "Mop up the mess?" What mess? Was it really Jason who had screwed up? Or had Heinz done something and Jason found out about it and blown up? Would we lose our jobs? Or was the whole thing a sham, a little drama staged for our benefit, while Jason was off skiing in Idaho or sunning himself on some Greek island? How could one know, with these people, what was really going on? Somehow, I suspected that Janoš, Daisy and Edythe—especially Edythe—knew exactly what had happened.

With these and other half-formed thoughts shooting through my mind like cosmic rays in a cloud chamber, I raised my hand and said something like the following:

"Heinz, I'm sure everyone here appreciates how upset you are, and somehow I am sure Jason is just as upset—wherever he may be. I haven't known Jason for nearly as long as you, but I have worked with him for more than two years, and I can't imagine him saying or doing anything that could harm Noah's Ark or you. Good friends sometimes have bad fights. I don't know what the fight was about, but I don't think this needs to be a permanent break. In fact, frankly, I don't see how it can be. My suggestion would be—and I sense that I am not alone in this—that you have nothing to lose if, before you do anything drastic, you give it some time, another week or two, for things to simmer down, and for Jason to come to his senses."

There were some murmurs of approval, and one or two co-workers spoke up in much the same way. Before adjourning the meeting, Heinz had calmed down appreciably. He promised to take our suggestions under consideration.

Of course, Jason turned up the following Monday, tense, white and taciturn, but things gradually returned to normal. Heinz actually thanked me for my good advice.

I don't know if two oranges in a bowl are from the same tree, but two in the same bin usually come from the same farm and arrive in the same truck. Perhaps two or three months after the star chamber meeting in the library, Heinz called another general staff meeting, and told us that the Ark was in a financial crisis. Certain grants or donations had not come through as promised, he said—no explanation why. I conjectured that various commitments or payments had been made in reliance on the disappointed expectations. No cause for alarm, though, Heinz assured. Things like this were nothing new to academia. Heinz would break his back and his brains to see to it that we should not lose our jobs, that the main work of the Ark would continue. Yes, possibly various sidelines would have to be shut down or postponed if he didn't manage to locate alternate sources. He appealed to us to "flip through your mental Rolodexes" and see if we could come up with any prospects—wealthy persons looking for tax deductions, aspiring philanthropists looking for ways to make a name for themselves as patrons of the arts and culture, etc., etc.

The etceteras, as one might have guessed, stood for the occasional dowager with more money to bequeath than heirs who knew what to do with it. I suppose that the only reason Heinz didn't spell it out was that he needed the money now, and he didn't want to give the impression that he had time to wait for a bequest. On the other hand, there were many things that could keep one usefully occupied while waiting.

I took Heinz's appeal at face value. After the meeting, I went to his office and told him that I knew someone. It was a "long shot," I warned, as I knew that the lady was more interested in saving lives than in saving Classics, but if he was willing to drive up to Smokesville and give his little spiel, I would try to set it up. Heinz was interested.

At a distance of so many years, I wonder now what impelled me to venture out on a limb for Heinz Strauss. I won't say that I wasn't trying to kiss up to him, or that I didn't learn a few things besides Greek bibliography in my going-on three years on the Ark. After all, one only had to look at Bunny Pemberton to see how far a bent axel could roll with a little grease. On the other hand, as I was soon to realize, JW's place in my career designs was rather vague—not that I wouldn't have been genuinely proud to have helped keep Noah's Ark afloat. Indeed, it did not even occur to me at the time that the leak Noah was trying to plug might owe itself to some other cause than the one he indicated in the staff meeting. At any rate, I did not then question my motives, and even had I done so and found them to be as pure as snow and as noble as palladium, I would still feel shame and regret, today, for approaching Rachel Wago.

We drove up to Smokes in "The Ark," Heinz's big copper-colored Cadillac, so dubbed on account of his punningly personalized license plates. As we churned up the freeway with the speedometer pushing ninety and Heinz's anti-radar device frantically scouring the horizons, I told him what I knew about Dr. Wago.

Rachel Wago had made a great name for herself not only as a practising physician, but as a medical researcher, specialty endo-crinology, with several hundred scientific publications. A graduate of Buffalo College School of Medicine at a time when women doctors were still a rarity, she had come into her fortune relatively late in life, through her marriage to a well-respected Hollywood movie producer, whose untimely death had motivated her to discover that the female hormone estrogen could reduce the risk of myocardial infarction in men. As research director of the largest federally-funded medical experiment in the United States, Rachel Wago had used both her fame and her wealth to promote numerous philanthropic causes—not only by conceiving and nurturing many vital new projects, but by campaigning to raise the necessary funds to bring them to realization. I was still in high school when I had personally assisted her in one of her fund raising efforts by typing dozens and dozens of letters addressed to a broad assortment of celebrities in the arts and sciences—all of whom she appeared to know personally.

I told Heinz how, when my father was still relatively unknown in this country, Dr. Wago had sent her two young daughters to him for piano lessons, and how they, fresh-mannered, spoiled, and not hugely gifted pianistically, had formed a deep bond of mutual affection with both my parents, a bond into which were drawn also their mother and stepfather. I told him how, during the early days of the War, Dr. Wago had arranged a concert in her home for my father, a recent immigrant to the US, to play for a dazzling audience of famous names and influential people.

My briefing completed, I advised Heinz that Rachel was not in the best of health and that, while her medication sometimes made her drowsy, he should not in any way underestimate her intelligence or power of concentration.

We arrived a few minutes before the appointed time, and waited the interval inside the Ark, which bobbed comfortably at anchor in front of the Wago mansion, while Heinz, to my acute distress, raised the roof with his automotive surround-sound.

We were greeted at the door by Rosa, the trusted housekeeper, who ushered us into the spacious living room, where we commenced to busy ourselves with the screen and projector Heinz had brought along. A few minutes passed before Dr. Wago made her entrance, diminutive, graceful, and at eighty years, still with a frail beauty.

"Are you gentlemen taking me to the movies? My husband was in the movie business, you know. Hello dear, it's so wonderful to see you." I kissed her on both cheeks in fulfillment of the mute request tendered by her uptilted face, then turned to introduce Heinz, who, to my surprise, seemed nervous and a little cowed despite saying all the right things, such as "Thank you for receiving me, and I hope we have caused you no great disturbance by our coming."

"I understand you're here to make a plea for funds. I've been in the fundraising business for many years, so there's no need for apologies. Louis has told me something about your work, and I'm interested to know more. I'm all yours, Professor Strauss. Tell me all about the animals in your Ark."

"Well, we have the animals we are trying to save from the flood of time, and we have the animals who are working to save them. And if I may, Dr. Wago, I'd like to introduce you to the whole menagerie by rolling a little film we made a while ago as a way of acquainting the lay public with the work we do. So with your permission, I'll just—Louis, can you close the shutters over there, please? I'll just—thank you, Louis—I'll just flip the switch here, and . . . we're rolling!"

The screen blazed white for a moment of blank expectation, then, after a brief cinematographic countdown, resolved into a close-up of a huge Corinthian column. After several long seconds of the camera lovingly caressing its chiseled, fluted surface, the Greek column in turn metamorphosed into the exploding white and orange plume of an Apollo rocket pointing upward toward the moon. The plume became a column of smoke as the camera followed the enormous artifact on its fateful journey into the sky. The sky then darkened into a succession of still photos of space-suited astronauts bouncing around on the lunar surface and saluting an American flag that appeared to be saluting stiffly back. As the great blue jewel of earth appeared in its display case of black velvet, the voice of a well-known Shakespearian actor emanated from deep space, reciting verses from the Eighth Psalm:

When I consider the heavens, the work of Thy fingers, the moon and stars, which Thou hast ordained, what is man, that Thou art mindful of him? and the son of man, that Thou visitest him? For Thou hast made him a little lower than the angels, and hast crowned him with glory and honor. Thou madest him to have dominion over the works of Thy hands: Thou hast put all things under his feet: all sheep and oxen, yea, and the beasts of the field; the fowl of the air, and the fish of the sea, and whatsoever passeth through the paths of the seas.

These verses were accompanied, each in its appropriate place, by photographs of galaxies and nebulae and lunar craters and *maria*, of Michelangelo's Sistine Chapel, the *Annunziazione* of Piero della Francesca, and Praxiteles's laurel-garlanded athlete, ancient Greek mosaics from Southern Italy, depicting the requisite herds of the earth, air and water, and finally, the little trading ships buoyant on the choppy seas, sails abillow.

"What *is* man?" recapitulated the well-known voice. "The first people to pose this question seriously were the ancient Greeks, and that question became the focus of a civilization that lasted nearly two thousand years." And so on, the little reel rolling on with passing verbal and visual references to Homer, Plato, Sophocles, Thermopylae, the Acropolis of Athens, Alexander the Great, Greek theatres and temples, Archimedes and Greek science, paintings of great battles on sea and land, of Greek merchant ships carrying Greek jars throughout the Hellenistic world, the famous library at Alexandria, whose destruction by fire was to deprive the world of so great store of ancient culture.

The focus shifted now to democracy, a form of government the Greeks were arguably the first to invent and to put into systematized practice. This was our legacy, reminded the pompous voice, for though the Athenian Boulé and Areopagos lasted only a few decades, a Greek historian named Thucydides imprinted the eternal memory of this Golden Age of Greek politics onto the consciousness of all humanity, inspiring our own Founding Fathers in their quest for the justest form of government.

How was this gigantic legacy of knowledge, wisdom and beauty transmitted to later civilizations, and how was it to be preserved for coming generations?

It was a lot to pack into one short documentary. The film did not open Pandora's can of academic worms and economic woes, but it did show pictures of ancient papyrus fragments, ruined parchments and disintegrating books, all representing the jealous ravages of time on the relics of ancient learning and scholarship.

Now, see aerial views of John Wayne U. as the camera zooms in for a close-up of Humphreys Hall, the hidden hive where a unique colony of dedicated worker bees labors diligently to produce digital ambrosia out of antic pollen. A succession of stills of present and former research teams, bent over texts or smiling up at the camera from their computer stations, Heinz, Jason and Daisy conferring over an open notebook, Heinz shaking hands with Congressmen D and F, Janoš on a stepladder, reaching for a high-altitude volume, while Herr Professor Snell from the University of Heidelberg waits anxiously below. No appeal for money. Just a quiet statement of what Archaica has accomplished so far (a million words of data entry) and still hopes to accomplish (millions more). Contact Prof. H. Strauss, Archaica Project, Humphreys Hall, J.W.U., Nirvana, Kalisperia for further information.

I reopened the shutters, and afternoon light poured into the Wago living room, accompanied by the pit-pat of Rachel's quietly clapping hands.

"Professor Strauss: can you tell me why it is so important that this ancient culture, literature, art, be preserved? After all, hasn't contemporary civilization squeezed all the juice out of the ancient legacies—as much as it could absorb? Modern civilization owes a great debt to ancient Greece—who would deny that? But why is it necessary to invest so much time, effort and money into preserving the squeezed-out rinds of a dead civilization? I've been a physician and clinical researcher for almost sixty years, Professor Strauss, and I've read Galen, and Galen was a brilliant physician—in spite of the fact that he was wrong most of the time—and I can assure you that any contributions Galen made to the advancement of medicine were made a long time ago, and from where it stands today, medicine can get along very nicely without Galen. What makes him so important that you need my money to keep him on life support?"

Heinz Strauss furrowed his brow in deep concentration, and speaking slowly and emphatically, said:

"First of all, I appreciate your question, and it is an important one, and I'm very glad you asked it. A moment ago, you mentioned that we have a debt, and a debt must be paid. This is how we repay that debt—by preserving the product and the record of their labor, their ingenuity, their trials and struggles, their triumphs and defeats, their

120

hopes, their songs, in sum, their . . ."

"My dear Professor!" interrupted Dr. Wago. "I have two daughters. I raised them from infancy, washed them, bathed them, nursed them—well, you know, we didn't believe in breast-feeding in those days—nursed their measles and their chicken poxes, changed their diapers, sent them to school, taught them manners, paid for their higher education, watched and worried and shed tears over them till the day they married and till today. I am eighty-two years old, and my daughters are good girls. They take good care of me and worry over me. But if I live to be a hundred and twenty, they will never be able to pay me back for the love, the care, the tears and the prayers, the money, and the work I invested in their welfare and their future. And why should they? Everyone knows that we repay our parents by giving to our children. That is the way of the world, Professor Strauss, and you still haven't told me why Greek civilization must be kept alive at all costs."

Heinz, bent forward, elbows on knees, hands flopping between his legs, pondered the short expanse of parquet between his feet for a moment, then straightened himself up. "Perhaps I can answer that question by telling you a bit about myself."

"*No, no, no, Heinz, no!*" I could hear myself thinking.

"I came to this country when I was sixteen years old. We were poor, and my parents couldn't afford to send me to college, but I worked hard and I put myself through school with the help of a scholarship and a night job. As a graduate student at Princeton, I taught undergraduate courses in Latin and Greek while working toward my Ph.D. I'll make a long story short. I became full professor of Classics at John Wayne. I built their Classics department from the ground up. I was voted best teacher four years in a row. I was the American Dream personified. I had everything I wanted. Money, security, prestige, a job I loved and was good at. When the opportunity arose to start the Archaica Project, I gave up my chairmanship, took a large cut in pay, and embarked on a voyage through uncharted waters, a voyage fraught with uncertainties, obstacles—even dangers. We had to overcome the skepticism, the inertia, even the ridicule of a considerable part of the field. They said it couldn't be done. At every step we risked proving them right and making egregious fools of ourselves.

"Little by little, we won over the trust and confidence of the entire, world-wide community of Classical scholars. I have met with the most renowned and admired professors of the field. I have organized and addressed international conferences of philologists in Paris, Berlin and Athens. I've met with senators and congressmen. I've spoken to students on campuses across the U.S.A., and with computer experts all over the world. I have hired a staff of researchers second to none. I've travelled to India to organize our data entry team, and I've overseen the creation of a one-of-a-kind data base that currently comprises nearly two million words, and hundreds of ancient authors who were facing virtually certain extinction in the next hundred years. And if I can't answer your question, if I can't tell you why our work is so vital, so crucial, so essential, then I don't know how we got where we are today, how we've accomplished what we've accomplished. In fact, if I can't answer that question, then I don't know my own name or why I have come here to ask for your help."

A dead silence followed these impassioned words. "*Nu?*" I almost shouted, after an interval that grew heavy with its own implausibility. I sat stunned. My brain was screaming. "*Are you nuts? Are you ending it right there? She's waiting for the answer. What are you doing?*" Heinz was sitting back in his armchair with the tired, satisfied look of one who has just completed a difficult task well done. His eyes closed momentarily behind his light-tinted glasses. Was he alright? Was he "on" something? I didn't dare open my mouth.

Mercifully, Dr. Wago realized that, at least as far as Strauss was concerned, he was done. She said only, "Well, thank you gentlemen, I enjoyed your presentation. You've certainly given me much to think about, and I am going to give your petition my very serious consideration. Professor Strauss, it was a pleasure meeting you."

I helped Strauss pack up his paraphernalia while he thanked Rachel profusely. I was about to walk him back to his copper-colored Cadillac when the venerable doctor said, "Louis dear, don't leave yet.

I want to talk to you."

"I would love to stay, Rachel, but I drove up with the Professor."

"Don't worry. I'll have Paul drive you back."

I walked Strauss back to the curb and helped him load his equipment into the enormous trunk.

"Well, how did I do?" asked the professor, innocently.

"I think it all went very well," I lied. "I'll let you know the moment I hear anything." Heinz thanked me cordially for the introduction and waved goodbye. I watched him slide away from the curb and rocket up the block and around the corner.

"Your boss is a fool," declared Dr. Wago as I re-entered the living room. She sat primly erect in her Biedermeier chair, and pronounced her verdict as though delivering an unpleasant medical diagnosis.

"I'm afraid I have to agree with you," I replied with sadness, "though I didn't realize it until just a few minutes ago. I must say, though, Rachel, that I had the definite impression that you intimidated him."

It was true. Strauss had impressed the hell out of some of the world's most touted classical scholars, but little Rachel Wago had blown him and his Ark quite out of the water from the first moment. How well I understand this today!

"It's more than that, dear. He lacks depth. He doesn't understand his own job."

"And yet, he created the Archaica Project from scratch, and brought it to the forefront of the academic world."

"But that's how it goes in this country. Behind all good works is a lot of hoopla. And believe me, I understand hoopla. And I respect it, and people tell me I'm very good at it. I'm good at it because I know my business. I'm not convinced that anything worth the money can grow on top of the hoopla I heard this afternoon. Your professor was unable to answer a very simple, very direct question. When a human being dies, they bury him and he returns to dust. When a civilization dies, your friend wants to glue all the pieces back together and preserve it forever under formaldehyde. Why? I would like to know. Can you tell me?"

I said it was not a simple matter, but I would try.

"First of all," I began, it's not completely true that everyone who dies is buried. Some will their bodies to medicine and science, so that new generations of students can study their organs. But what is learned from their dissections and descriptions generally applies to all of humanity. When they examine the heart of a human cadaver, it's not to reconstruct the personality of the living donor or to relate to him as a living, thinking being. It's too late for that. To do that, you would have to read his letters—his books, if he wrote any, meet and interview his surviving family, friends, and enemies. The dissecting is only done to learn how the heart of the human animal is constructed and how it works. Because all healthy human hearts are built and work in virtually the same way. Am I right?"

"I follow you. Go on."

"With a dead civilization, it is just the opposite. The organs—the heart, the stomach, the brains—of every civilization are different, one civilization from the other. And by studying those organs, you can actually reconstruct the personality, the soul, the mind of each civilization as it was during every stage of its life. It's almost like making it come alive again.

"Rachel, the knowledge so acquired is precious for two reasons. In the first place, it is acquired with painstaking care and great ingenuity from a relatively few surviving relics that speak for the whole civilization. In the second place, knowledge, if carefully transmitted from living mind to mind and from one medium to another can last forever and even continue growing; whereas the relics themselves—the very relics which originally yielded the knowledge in the first place—are doomed to eventual extinction, no matter how well we try to preserve them. So that whatever we might be able to learn from the life and death of a dead civilization is ultimately entrusted to its students. In other words, the scholars are the sole and ultimate ambassadors of the lost worlds of the past. And finally, through their embassy, those lost worlds teach us something about what it means to be Homo Sapiens—each world, something unique about what it means to be human, something that only that particular civilization can teach us, because every civilization is different.

"That knowledge is precious, Rachel, because human beings need to know what it means to be human. When that knowledge is spurned, the results are potentially tragic, because it means that we lose forever something of the meaning of human potential and human fallibility. It means we are doomed to repeat ad infinitum the endless cycle of human reincarnation with all its transient magnificence and horror. If I were to take you for a walk now in Waverly Heights and we were to stop people and ask them whether schools and universities should teach ancient languages and culture, nine out of ten would say no. And if we were to ask them why not, they would say, because there's no point: people want the same thing in every age and culture: food, sex, money and power, and that's it. There's no essential difference between one civilization and the next. And we could do the same thing in Waterford or in Culverside or in Ferndale or in any city or town in the country and get the same answer. What does that say about our particular civilization? What does that tell you about the individual members of our society? What does that say about the value of a human being in our society?

"Suppose," I continued, "that you are in the process of putting up a building in your back yard—let's say a guesthouse—and your workers dig up a very fine piece of sculpture. You examine it, you admire its craftsmanship, you appreciate its particular flavor of line and of form. You ascertain that the sculpture is ancient, genuine, and has commercial value. However, it's not your personal cup of tea and you wouldn't put it in your living room. What do you do with it?"

"I would have it appraised and either sell it to a collector or at auction or donate it to a museum and take a deduction."

"And suppose nobody wanted it. Unlikely, of course, but suppose you couldn't get it off your hands. Would you destroy it or throw it out?"

"Of course not."

"Why not?"

"I don't know, dear. Tell me."

"Because it has a value independent of its monetary worth. It has the power to speak, to move people, to say something about the person who created it and the civilization to which that person

125

belonged. The mere fact that some man or woman in a bygone time created it with knowledge, with painfully acquired skill, and thought and labor and love, and with an investment, conscious or unconscious, of historical and cultural context—for which that sculpture, remember, is now a rare, if not unique, surviving spokesman—and with intent to communicate something to other people—that fact alone is enough to stay your hand from tossing it onto the garbage heap or smashing it to pieces. Why? Because you have the intelligence, the sensitivity, the education and the compassion to understand what it means to have something to say that is so important to you that you have to create something enduring to say it. Because to destroy it would be making a statement about who and what you are, and how little your own life and work means to you.

"Think about it. There was a French cleric, a Classics scholar, the Abbé Fourmont, who, in the Eighteenth Century, travelled about Greece with a crew of hired workers, smashing to bits whatever remained of the ancient sites he visited."

"Good heavens! Why?"

"No one really knows. The only reason I can think of is that he hoped to raise the commercial value of what he plundered for himself. In China, until just a few years ago, the Cultural Revolution was obliterating every shred of antiquity it could lay its hands on. Sculptures, paintings, manuscripts, countless, priceless artistic, literary and archaeological treasures . . ."

"And people."

"Yes. And people! The very people who valued those treasures, and would have preserved them. Destroyed them, merely because they were the products of a different socio-economic era. Until they finally realized that they were slandering themselves, destroying the roots of their own Revolution and undermining its future.

"When a society abandons its cultural roots, it abandons its future and consigns itself to a meaningless present. In the end, everything collapses into a hedonistic, self-centered, raw existence. 'FSMP: Food, sex, money and power.' You can see this happening right now. In a civilization where nothing has value beyond the duration of

126

physiological life, all deeper meanings are lost, morality collapses, and ultimately, life itself—human life—becomes valueless.

"Now, it so happens that Hippocrates—the author of the Hippocratic Oath—that wonderful affirmation of the value of human life—was a Greek, and that was hardly a coincidence, because the ancient Greeks were the first to formulate (if not to discover) and apply the principle that I have been trying to outline for you—that the creative works of humanity have intrinsic, enduring worth, and accordingly need to be studied, preserved, and cultivated if human life itself is to be understood and validated.

"For the same reason, it is certainly no coincidence that the Archaica Project has chosen to devote itself to the preservation of ancient Greek texts, when, hypothetically, there are many other buried civilizations it could have chosen. Because there is a special connection between our present day western civilization and ancient Greek culture. It is part of our own heritage, our own identity, our own past. It is, so to speak, in our own cultural back yard. Because, if we, as a civilization, nurture a belief in critical thought, in self-criticism, in philosophy and self-knowledge, in science and justice and good government it is the Greeks whom we are emulating. If we are still searching to define our moral and social responsibility as individual beings in an unknowable universe, it is the Greeks who started that quest and set us on the path. If we are driven consciously to seek order, beauty, justice, truth and meaning and consolation in nature, poetry, art, architecture, history, and in serving humanity, we owe that impulse to the Greeks, since it is from them that we have inherited it—not from the Chinese or the Mayans or the Aztecs or even the Jews of antiquity—as magnificent as those civilizations were.

"And that is why you, having found this fine old sculpture buried deep in your back yard, would see to it that it is carefully dug up, cleaned, protected from the elements, and made available to the experts for study and identification—and eventually for public edification. Because, whether that sculpture speaks to you personally or not, you understand the value of culture—provided, of course, that you are not one of the ninety or ninety-nine persons out of a hundred who were never endowed with the education, intelligence, and sensitivity to recognize that such an artefact has cultural value.

"And if you haven't already acquired those qualities over the course of your life, there is probably no way to give them to you in twenty minutes or half an hour. I think that may be what Professor Strauss was trying to tell you when he said that if he couldn't answer your question, then he had no right to hold the position he holds, and no right to come to you for a donation. I think he assumed all along that you knew the answer. And, frankly, I am inclined to agree with him."

"I may have known it," said Rachel, "but I needed to hear it from him before I would give him ten cents, and *he* ought to have known *that.* Anyway, you give him more credit than he deserves. You, on the other hand, have explained it most coherently and eloquently."

To tell the truth, I cannot be sure that the little speech I have just written down reflects faithfully what I said on that occasion. My views on the subject have also changed since those times, especially since I discovered—relatively late, alas—the incomparable magnificence of my own Jewish Heritage. To recreate that memorable encounter with Rachel Wago, I have had to filter out certain later-acquired phrases and expressions, as well as insert others that I am no longer completely comfortable with, such as "*our* heritage, *our* identity, and *our* past"—as applied to contemporary western civilization. I love and cherish those things, but no longer think of them as indisputably "mine." I also find it increasingly difficult to see the classical education as essential or even beneficial to western civilization, when the European community of nations, so profoundly steeped in classical and humanistic culture, presents such a disappointing spectacle to unprejudiced eyes.

Be that as it may, whatever I actually said to Rachel must have pleased her, because she continued, "I can tell you right now that the only way I will ever give money to that university down there is if they endow a chair for you. Would you consider that?"

"I beg your pardon?" Rachel's *Speak for yourself, John!* left me speechless.

"I'm offering to endow a chair for you in their Greek Department, or whatever they call it. Are you interested?"

"Rachel! Of course I'm interested. But it's not realistic, and I would never accept such a gift from you. You know I couldn't."

"Why couldn't you? Are you too much of a gentleman to take advantage of an old woman? Or are you afraid I'm not old enough to know what I'm doing, and influential enough to do it?"

"Rachel . . . Rachel!"

"Think about it, Lulu, and call me in a week."

"Of course I'll think about it, Rachel. Thank you."

Dr. Wago's offer touched me deeply, but I knew right away that even if it weren't ridiculous, I could never accept. I think now that it wasn't so much that I was too proud to let a wealthy friend buy me a professorship which by university standards was still unsupported by any signal achievement on my part, and which, by my own standards, let alone the university's, I wasn't yet qualified for. Yes, there was that. But there was more. Deep down, I knew that with a couple of exceptions I didn't respect the people I was working with, and I wouldn't have respected myself for choosing them to work with. Of course, Sokrates and Euphemios were different, but Sokrates would be going back to Greece as soon as he got his Ph.D., and Pheemy's influence, alas, for all his benevolence, was inconsequential. As far as I could see, the equation solved to years of misery in a cultural and emotional wasteland. Out of respect for Rachel, I waited the week, and then told her I could never work at JWU.

13

A Haunting Melody

Ironically, the very next day, as I was eating my sandwich on the planter outside Humphreys Hall, Daisy Duchinsky skittered briskly into the open air and with a rare smile on her sun-cured hatchet face made straight for me.

"Lllouie!" she declared in a preambulatory sort of way. "Can you tutor Latin?"

"Sure," I said. "Whom did you have in mind?"

"Veronica Agriopoulos. She's failing my course and she needs help. Will you do it?"

"Sure," I repeated, surprised. I had no idea that Ronie was having problems. "Is this for the Department?"

"It's between you and her. You make your own arrangements. And keep me informed, okay?"

There was no money in it, of course—anyone could see that Veronica was living on a broken shoestring—but I took it as a vote of confidence in my favor. It was very strange. I had just politely turned down my one delusional hope of ever getting a job at JW, and yet, at the very first sign of a possible interest on the part of the faculty, I was ready to leap at the chance. It was naive of me, but it passed through my mind that if I proved myself, it might lead to something more, perhaps to an invitation to compete for a teaching position. And anyway, Veronica and I were good friends by now, and I always enjoyed our occasional chats.

Our lessons, usually held as we sat side by side—her book

shifting from her knees to mine and back—on the customary Humphreys planter, were pleasant, and Veronica's progress encouraging. However, the Latin lessons had one other result, and one for which I was totally unprepared. One afternoon in the middle of our lesson, as I was helping Ronie translate the verse:

Amplius utque nihil, me tibi iungit amor,

More than anything, love joins me to you . . .

I felt a strange weight on my right shoulder, and turned away from the page to see, so suddenly close, Veronica leaning her head against me with abandon.

"Ronie!" I exclaimed, putting my right arm around her as I turned toward her.

"I'm fine," she answered with a tearful laugh. "It's just that I think I'm in love with you."

As Dante might just as well have written in his account of the affair of Paolo and Francesca,

Galleotto fu il libro, e chi lo scrisse . . .fu Nasone . . .

Galehaut was the book, and the gallant who wrote it . . .was Naso.

For the text which appeared to have predisposed Veronica to this confession was "Acontius's Letter to Cydippe" in Ovidius Naso's *Heroïdes,* a collection—and a rather bizarre one—of letters which mythological lovers are imagined by the poet to have mailed back and forth to each other about the deeds or misdeeds which their respective myths have told us they had done, were going to do, or were in the process of doing, in order to bring about that which fate had already decreed and countless poets retold. In the case of Acontius, the letter was a more or less routine follow-up to one of the more remarkable (and literal!) "pick-ups" in the annals of courtship.

Acontius, having espied Cydippe in the temple of Diana at Delos, and been smitten silly by her beauty, tosses in her direction an apple on which he has inscribed the words, "I swear by the sanctuary of Diana that I will wed Acontius." The girl, for whom reading is apparently still the laboriously labial exercise of a child, picks up the apple and reads it aloud, thus binding herself, according to the preposterous law of the place, to marry a complete stranger—and, one suspects, a madman to boot. And no less strange than Veronica's surrender to my unwitting declaration of love was the fact that not once during this entire episode did it occur to me that I was at that very time personally involved in a correspondence of my own, of essentially the same kind.

"Dear Ronie!" I soothed. "How can you be in love with me? You know my feelings about religion . . ."

"Oh, I've left all that behind for some time. Didn't you notice?" she asked, reproachfully wiping her tears. I tried to explain to her, as tenderly as possible, that it would be improper for us to take advantage of our tutor-pupil relationship, and that we needed to focus on bringing her Latin up to par. I imagined that I was being fraternal and affectionate. If Veronica felt disappointed, she concealed it rather well. The truth was, of course, that if I had really wanted her, neither her religion nor my tutorial ethics would have prevented me, and she must have known that as well as I. As far as any university regulations governing amorous relations between students and faculty were concerned, JW's was clearly a one-eyed code, with the good eye roving in the opposite direction.

The question that I don't understand to this day is, *why* didn't I want her? She was an attractive, sensitive girl, innocent, intelligent and outgoing, and obviously in need of companionship and love. It is true that I was still enamored of an Italian beauty I had met the year before in Smokesville, but she had suddenly interrupted her studies and returned to Ravenna, from where she wrote letters relating how she had founded a new religion and was gathering many devout followers. I suspect that if Ronie had only persisted for a couple of weeks, she would have overcome my reluctance, whatever its cause; but, perhaps to my own disappointment, she did not persist. Our lessons went back to normal, smiling and friendly. She wrote a good final exam and passed her course, for which accomplishment both she and Daisy thanked me warmly.

It is not so easy to reconstruct such complex feelings at so many years' distance, but the question is still interesting to me; and, perhaps because I have finally allowed myself to reflect upon the matter, maybe I do understand it after all. It wasn't, I conjecture, that I was not sufficiently attracted, for I had enough imagination to fantasize Veronica in that state of feminine adornment which, with a little astute coaching and a little more pocket money, she could easily have attained. It was her childlike vulnerability that both charmed me and admonished me to protect her rather than take advantage. Perhaps, too, I did not aspire to be her Professor Higgins, instructing her in the very arts to which I might fall victim. I don't know. Ravenna or no Ravenna, Veronica would have suited my situation very well. Her crush might not have been very deep— might even have had an economic component, but it was real enough to draw tears—real, rolling tears—hers for now, but how long before mine? And what! Are there no tears in penury, in utter dependency?

Amplius utque nihil, me tibi iungit amor . . .

I had been startled by the weight of her head on my shoulder. How long before I felt the weight of all her personal situation, whatever that might be? Whatever depths I had fallen to in the agony of my longings, I suspect I was instinctively too sensible to do thoughtlessly what many young men would have schemed to accomplish. Does that make me a mentsh?

Ah, Lulu, you pathetic fool, you veritable shlemiel! We shall soon see the end of result of your *mentshlichkeit*.

O thou who readest these defective pages: art thou worthy of my confidence? Shall I confess to you my sins? Shall I tell of hallucinatory journeys over the psychotic loops and tangles of ghostly freeway jungles, of the concrete midnight nightmares of the urban hinterland? Shall I describe what, alas, so many, nowadays, have stooped to describe, as though description were needed? Frantic journeys of a soul in pain, a soul possessed by a spirit of madness, a soul blinded to itself by the ache of a longing beyond its own

133

comprehension?

No, it is not good for man to be alone. But in our holy Tradition, the answer is marriage to a suitable partner before the disease takes hold; whereas around me stretched in all directions a latter-day Epicurean landscape where the piercing cry of casual encounters echoed among the artificial woods, streams and hills of apartment heaven. I believe that I was born incapable of initiating a liaison, however passing, with a woman I could not visualize—however foolishly, however desperately, however hypocritically, however briefly—as a life partner. Thus I missed many opportunities commonly regarded as less dishonorable, and exchanged one type of transgression for another. Dear Veronica! If I could bring you back, I would ask you to forgive me!

Curiously, though, it was on one of my visits to those miserable temples of vicious, unbridled sexual fantasy that a kind of missive not unlike Acontius's apple rolled into view from some dark, unwholesome corner of Hades. I had opened a "specialty" newspaper to the "personals" pages and lo! What do I see? Smiling up from the newsprint—in a state that might, for propriety's sake, be described as "pre-industrial"—were your earliest ancestors and mine as they might have appeared before their eyes were opened. The snapshot certainly opened mine. I recognized them at once, and wondered how I was going to greet them the next morning with a straight face.

14

Goose and Gander

And then, in the fall of that final year at JW, there suddenly appeared all over campus, like a plague of prophetic toadstools, a swarm of cardboard gravestones, all identically constructed, designed and surfaced with glossy paper on which was artfully printed not only the color and texture of chiseled stone, but the unconsciously funny, for an epitaph, inscription,

IF I SHOULD DIE...

The message, so far as one possibility could be said to predominate over others, was reinforced, after a suspenseful few days, by posters and leaflets distributed around campus, giving the date and location of a "Multimedia Extravaganza" of Evangelical drift and content. There followed still more days of waiting, during which Jason wondered aloud whether the promised event would really turn out to be an Evangelical rally or an estate-planning seminar, and Janoš was teased about his doctoral thesis coming back to haunt him.

The humor aside, there was a vague but growing resentment among the predominantly liberal faculty that the campus, now transformed into a cartoon cemetery, had been infiltrated by hidden spies and agents of corporate religion with the full complicity of the university administration.

"Isn't this federal grant land?" I remarked. "I thought John Wayne U. was leased from the Government." In fact, as I subsequently ascertained, a good portion of the campus lay on a former Federal Air Base.

135

"Well, that, and it's certainly State property," replied Jason. "Not only. The Ark gets federal funds, and a lot of the research that goes on around campus is federally funded. That raises an intriguing question."

"I don't get it," I complained. "The Separation Clause . . ."

"Confetti!" interjected Janoš, with a dismissive smack of the lips, followed by a sonorous chuckle. He raised his arms high and twiddled his fingers as though frittering a shower of shredded paper. I don't know which roused me more—the arrogance of the multimedians or the apathy of the students, but roused I was. More than a week had gone by, yet no cry had been raised, no attempt made, to remove the offending "stones." Was the mystique of salvation—spelled with a capital $ and enhanced with slick graphics and big print, so powerful as to lull the student population—normally a tinderbox for radical fringe causes—into catatonia? Or were the Nirvanians simply too preoccupied with their hot-tubs to be bothered? I inserted a roll of file folder labels into my typewriter and typed out two or three dozen sticky labels, each with the same legend.

The next morning, during an extended coffee break, I made the rounds of the campus, applying the products of my labor to the objects for which they were designed. By early afternoon, every "gravestone" exhibited my handiwork, and curious passersby distracted from their duteous pursuits by the oblong patch of white that newly adorned the now familiar metamonuments, might read the completed epigraph:

IF I SHOULD DIE...

KISS MY ASS GOODBYE!

It was a harmless prank, of course—though one that might have landed me in trouble with the authorities. Nevertheless, my exploit was rewarded by the approval and hilarity of colleagues, supervisors and students—with the exception of Veronica, who took me respectfully to task—and one or two besides—plus Jason, who, albeit with a smile, and for unfathomable reasons, sided with the extravaganzists.

"I wonder," he said, with his customary back-flip of the right wrist, "whether, with all respect for a little much-needed and not unprovoked humor, some principle has been injured here besides that of Separation of Church and State. I guess I am as offended as any one by the marriage of spiritual goods with Madison Avenue, not to mention the ghoulish exploitation of our exaggerated Kalisperian *timor mortis.* However, it seems to me that behind the cardboard and the plastic and the dollar signs, there is something here that merits, if not our respect, our circumspection. There is, I am suggesting, a belief in God—a Supreme Being, if you will—that, however bashful and inarticulate, presses forward to express itself in the only language with which it is familiar. And if its idiom be the barkers and broadsides of Barnum and Bailey, why then, who are we, because we are steeped in classicism and endowed with critical discernment, to sneer and snort? There is an opposing right here: on the one hand, yes, certainly, Separation of Church and State. But on the other hand, do we not have Freedom of Religion? And if that freedom is bought and paid for by corporate money, does that invalidate its underlying beliefs?"

"It's a valid point, Jason," I said, descending from his rhetorical pinnacle. "However, I am still persuaded that the underlying belief is not in God, but in Gold."

"You may be right," chuckled Jason, amiably. "I am only submitting the matter to the twilight zone of your esteemed consideration—as Rod Serling might have done." And, with a gracious bow, he exited.

Daisy, in the sole witticism from her own *ipsissimo ore* that I can remember in three years of collaboration, commented that it was the only time she had ever heard of a Jew defacing Gentile gravestones.

Before leaving, that evening, I again made the rounds of the campus to see how my labors of the morning had fared through the day. Despite the palpable absence of witnesses to my earlier tour, by late afternoon all the labels had somehow been removed (or the gravestones replaced). I drove off, musing on the sinister vigilance of wily acolytes.

I mentioned previously that I submitted the beginnings of my projected satiric poem, *Dante in Disneyland,* to the campus newspaper, *True Grit*—a title, by the way, which unsurprisingly inspired a more accurate nickname with which it rhymed. The sobriquet was not undeserved. Its staff had more than once provoked the wrath of students and officials alike for offending the sensibilities of ethnic minorities with statements subsequently defended or retracted as "humor," and for voicing political views—one could never be sure with what degree of sincerity—that had long been discredited by history. Such lapses were regularly interspersed with fustian protestations of First-Amendment freedoms and the heavy burdens of media responsibility. I regarded *True Grit* as a training ground for journalistic thuggery, and that I would risk exposing myself to their whimsy is an indication of my naïve and desperate neediness.

In retrospect, I got off cheap for my rashness. They sent back the manuscript along with an incredibly presumptuous rejection—in aspiring verse, of course—signed by a Daniel Toscano, which I took to be a pen name, but which turned out to be the actual name of an undergraduate assistant editor who had taken it upon himself, by virtue of an expertise acquired during a ten-week course entitled "Survey of Italian Literature", to defend the Master from the undesirable assaults of unworthy imitators.

I strode across Humphreys Court to the editorial offices of *True Grit,* and gave Mr. Toscano, who appeared to accept it with quiet contrition, an authentic Tuscan dish of *penne all'arrabbiata.* A week or two later, I was amazed to discover, in volume __, issue no. __ of *True Grit,* a centerfold layout of the JW campus with the headline

On The Trail With Shloomiyail at Disney U

in which the various campus departments and other prominent landmarks were characterized as rides of one sort or another. It was,

138

essentially, if not technically, plagiarism, which is, if what they say is true, the purest form of flattery. So, indignant as I was, I let it alone.

The last I saw of *True Grit,* it carried, duly blown up to fill its entire front page, a revealingly candid photograph of a pretty girl—the very same nymphet Skipchick and I had once eyed appreciatively from the battlements of Shriver Hall—her little fist clenched tightly around the handle of large and sudsy beer mug, gyrating amid a centripetal cluster of enthusiastic young men. The banner headline:

JW COED IN WET T-SHIRT CONTEST

AT HUBBA-HUBBA'S

I believe a lawsuit ensued. If so, I would not have been surprised if the editor were by then studying medicine or architecture very comfortably in faraway Paraguay or Uruguay. I am just glad that the money was not Rachel Wago's.

I left Noah's Ark shortly after that, so I never heard the upshot, and many years passed before, *causa* Veronica, I thought of that wretched paper again.

15

Papyrus

Toward January, I was pleasantly surprised to see Egil Heklason's smiling mop head peering through the doorway to my cubby hole. I jumped up and greeted him warmly.

"Has there been any progress with the laser approach?" I asked, after the conventional exchanges.

"Not really," answered the professor, "but we are discussing other possibilities. Dr. Brown seems to think the scrolls could be read without opening them, by means of an X-ray device."

"Oh, fantastic! So no writing would be lost."

"Exactly. Of course, there are many technical problems remaining to be solved, but the idea is very promising.

"By the way, I wanted to inform you that I have read the article you sent me, and I have cited it favorably in an article of mine that will appear next year in *Vichiana*."

"That's wonderful. Thank you! I think you will be in sparse company. Few have responded favorably."

"You cannot be surprised. You must know that your thesis is a very ambitious one. Ambitious and controversial."

"Yes, I realize that."

"Nevertheless, it needed to be said, and I admire your initiative. I also agree wholeheartedly with some of the points you have raised, and I say so in my article."

I thanked him gratefully, and asked him, pro forma, whether there was anything further I could do for him."

"No, thank you," he said, simply, reaching into his jacket pocket, "but I did retrieve this from Dr. Brown, and I'd like to leave it with you as a memento of my appreciation."

"My goodness! You don't mean it! How can I thank you?" I accepted the lump of charcoal with trembling fingers.

"Remember: don't let it upset your life. There are many of these where this came from, and they are all blank. You can experiment with opening it up, if you like."

"So this came from an area where no writing was found? "Exactly."

"So what was it, a kind of storage cabinet for writing materials?"

"That seems to be the most plausible hypothesis at this time. Except that all they've found there are papyrus rolls. No quills or ink bottles—or typewriter ribbons," he added with a smile. "Of course, one can't be one hundred protzent sure until the roll is actually opened . . ."

"But what if I succeed in opening it, and I find there is writing?"

"Well, that might prove a little awkward. You see," the Professor said, lowering his voice, "these were not exactly obtained through the official channels . . ."

"I can appreciate that," I nodded slowly, not sure if I really understood. "But, hypothetically, suppose I find writing: what am I to do?"

"Photograph it, mount it in a butterfly case, transcribe it, try to fill in the lacunae, type it up, and sit on it . . . the same as I did."

"Sit on it till when? . . . I beg your pardon? You found something?"

"Make sure the glass is clean before you seal it."

"Come on! I'm dying of curiosity!

"Store it in a cool, dry place, away from direct sunshine."

"Professor Heklason! This is torture!"

"Alright. Can you come to my hotel room at around 9:00 tonight? I wouldn't want the others to know."

Working on Philodemus, I had catalogued hundreds of fragmentary texts published in a large number of books and scholarly journals, each text identified by the "PHerc." (*Papyrus Herc-ulanensis*) number, and by a brief description of its contents, which often included the editor's attribution—whether certain or con-jectural—to one of the known treatises of the philosopher. These descriptions generally consisted of Greek titles like Περὶ Παρρησίας (*On Freedom of Speech*), Περὶ Κακιῶν (*On Vices*), Περὶ Θανάτου (*On Death*), Περὶ Θεῶν (*On the Gods*), etc., and several *Incerti Operis Fragmenta*, showing Philodemus's wide-ranging interests.

In those days, Philodemus was reputed to be more of a sheep than a shepherd of the Epicurean flock—a faithful exponent of the Garden and a learned exegete of its groundskeeper's philosophy, but not an original thinker. However, as more and more of his writings were unfurled into the light, Philodemus emerged, if not as an innovator, at least as a distinct and influential personality. Marcello Gigante, in particular, has shown Philodemus to have been a somewhat unorthodox element in the Epicurean world, with broad interests and an unusual openness toward other schools and competing doctrines.

Curiously, however, there was one area in which Philodemus seems to have been quite uncritically docile, and that is in the area of memory. Indeed, as I was cataloguing all these fragments, I started to become vaguely aware that not one of them contained anything resembling a theoretical discussion of memory. Now, I am far from an expert on Philodemus or Epicureanism, and I probably never would have noticed it if I had not, on my own account, been studying the structure of Lucretius's great poem, *De Rerum Natura*. The manuscript tradition has preserved that monumental tractate on Epicurean science practically intact. Lucretius, the preeminent poet of the Ciceronian age, a contemporary of Philodemus and quite possibly his pupil, had at his disposal—certainly at the *Villa Pisonis* and most likely in his own study—a complete set of the writings of Epicurus and his disciples. It had already struck me as odd that in a work of such encyclopedic scope, one that contains a succinct but integral theory of knowledge, there is no discussion of memory per se. Rather, that topic is subsumed under the general rubric of "mind". Therefore, as

I waded through the mass of Philodemiana, though I encountered from time to time the usual vocabulary of memory, such as μνήμη, μνημοσύνη, μνημονικός, etc.—the lack of a systematic discussion of memory began to assume, in my mind, the character of a phenomenon not entirely without significance.

My suspicions were reinforced when I came upon a passage—a rather famous passage—in Cicero's treatise *De Finibus* (II, 67)—in which he lambasts the Epicurean School for its cavalier treatment of history:

Quod autem patrocinium aut quae ista causa est voluptatis, quae nec testes ullos e claris viris nec laudatores poterit adhibere? Ut enim nos ex annalium monimentis testes excitamus eos, quorum omnis vita consumpta est in laboribus gloriosis, qui voluptatis nomen audire non possent, sic in vestris disputationibus historia muta est. Numquam audivi in Epicuri schola Lycurgum, Solonem, Miltiadem, Themistoclem, Epaminondam nominari, qui in ore sunt ceterorum philosophorum.

"But what kind of a case or defense can be argued for Pleasure, which boasts neither favorable witnesses nor enthusiasts among famous men? For just as we can call forth from the records of our annals witnesses whose whole lives were spent in glorious achievement— men who could not bear even to hear the word "pleasure"—so does history hold its tongue in your philosophical disputations. Indeed, never in Epicurean circles have I heard mention of Lycurgus or Solon or Miltiades or Themistocles or Epaminondas, who are always in the mouth of all the other philosophers."

History *is* memory. Virtually anything one says about the one could be said about the other. If the Epicureans had problems with the topic of memory, that was only to be expected, given their attitude toward history. Now, if it is true, as Gigante points out in an essay entitled "Philodemus and History," that Philodemus broke rank with his teachers by taking examples from historical events and personages to illustrate his ethical teachings, such anecdotal treatment of historical subjects is a far cry from historiography—the art of making coherent, human sense out of mere chronicling. For all of Philodemus's adventurousness, he still did not, so far as is known, treat of history as a theoretical subject.

The truth is, as Cicero noted, history was taboo for the Epicureans, and various reasons for this may be adduced for consideration. In the first place, the supreme goal of living, for an Epicurean, was the attainment of *Ataraxía*—a state of complete, untroubled, sustained serenity throughout life. From the perspective of *Ataraxía*, history was both meaningless and antithetical. History was war, intrigue, politics, commerce, famine and flood—constant friction, causation, danger, and uncertain outcome. Thus, to occupy oneself with history was, in one sense, to cause oneself needless distress, and in another sense, to stray from the prime directive of the Master: *Lathe biosas!*—"Live covertly."

Another possible reason is perhaps more complex, and has to do with the atomist foundations of the Epicurean doctrine. Indeed, Epicurus had constructed a complex theory of nature based on the atomist teachings of Democritus. The Epicurean universe consisted of an infinite space populated by an infinite number of basic particles, indestructible and indivisible (*átomoi*). Everything in that universe, whether physical or mental, ethereal, real or ideal, consisted of accidental combinations resulting from the collision of atoms in perpetual free fall. Different combinations manifested different properties, some being evanescent, others enduring, and still others, immortal or indestructible. Some combinations, though perishable in themselves, acquired the property of reproductive procreation and self-awareness; but all were accidental, the blind, statistical outcome of random atomic encounters. Certainly, it was possible to argue that, in the context of such a cosmology, the study of history, of cause and effect in the short-lived affairs of individuals and societies destined for disintegration, was pointless and wasteful.

On the other hand, if the Epicureans also avoided the subject of memory, then their avoidance of history might take on a somewhat different character. It has been many years since I first considered these questions, and I can't say that I ever devoted myself to resolving them, but I now believe that I have the elements of a hypothesis, and one, I must admit, that was stimulated to some degree by unexpected intervening events. I now believe that the Epicureans avoided the subject of memory (and therefore of history) because they could not explain it.

I shall try to propound this by reference to Epicurean logic. According to Epicurus, all sensory perceptions were the result of emanations from entities existing outside ourselves. Epicurus regarded these emanations as similar to the moulting of a serpent's skin. These *"simulacra,"* as Lucretius calls them, were extremely diaphanous, perceptible only to the specialized organs of perception and sensation.

Not all the *simulacra* were faithful replicas of the original entity. Epicurus distinguished between true and false perceptions. False perceptions resulted from the confusion of a multitude of emanations as they impact the organs of perception. Thus, when a person dreams of strange monsters and impossible events, it is not because such monsters exist somewhere in the universe, but because the accidental interpenetration of various emanations has produced the monstrous image in that person's mind. On the other hand, since all peoples have a notion of divine and immortal beings, Epicurus concluded that there exist such things as gods; but because every nation conceives of its gods differently, he does not venture to describe them, but concludes only that they exist, live in eternal bliss, and do not occupy themselves with human affairs—for if they did, would our perceptions of them not be virtually identical?

The shape of a theory of knowledge—inchoate, perhaps—begins to emerge from the Epicurean fog. Reality is a function of common perception: What all men perceive must be real, and the level of reality diminishes as the variances among individual perceptions increase.

Naturally, the above is only a schematic reduction, but it is immediately apparent from this outline that by such reasoning, history and memory are difficult to accommodate. An event takes place, and all who were present remember it differently. Each writes his or her own account of it, and the historian can only compare accounts and choose those parts of each that find confirmation among the others. But what about those details that are unique to each individual account and reflective of each person's unique abilities as an observer? Are they to be discarded as presumptively false? And what of those who were not present? Should they, too, not have some memory of what happened, given that a real event did take place and continues to radiate its truth upon all the organs of perception in existence? After all, all peoples are aware of the gods, but who among us has seen one?

And what about the fading of memory, what about forgetfulness? How is that to be reconciled with the endless emanations from material objects? Or is it only our organs of perception that degenerate through time? Then why do the elderly remember so well the happenings of their youth, while retaining little grasp of the events of yesterday or the day before? And if old memories are the time-hardened impressions left by ancient emanations, then why do we not remember everything from infancy? And shouldn't old impressions be obliterated, like a palimpsest, by the ceaseless superposition of new ones?

It is easy to understand why history and memory would be embarrassing to Epicurean theory, and why it would be convenient to sidestep the whole issue: memory is inconstant, therefore illusory; and history, incapable of being recovered by the illusory tool of memory. And if recoverable, doomed to be *re*-covered, scholars and all their scholarship, like the excavations at Herculaneum itself, blithely awaiting the next outbelching of ash, mud and lava—or, as Skipchick put it in one of his moments of unconscious poetic raptus,

on the Titanic, sipping gin and tonic.

Thus, why bother with the past, anyway? Seventy feet of earth is a better preservative than all the volumes of *Cronache Ercolanesi!* An Epicurean sage, bent on the attainment of *Ataraxía,* will derive more benefit from forgetting than from remembering. *Carpe diem,* says the poet Horace, a friend of the Pisos, Philodemus and others of the Epicurean circle—a phrase that might today be translated "Live in

146

the Now."

I arrived at the Stage Coach Inn on Hayakawa Street (Sessue, not S.I.) ten minutes early. Precisely at 9:00 PM, I walked up to the desk and asked the receptionist to phone up to Prof. Heklason.

"You are right on time. Please sit down." The professor offered me a chair at a table on which rested a cardboard archival box. As he maneuvered the lid off with trembling fingers, he confessed, "I couldn't sustain any more of this. I had to show someone. I had a feeling you were the one to really appreciate this." He extracted a number of 8-inch by 10-inch photographs and laid them out on the table.

"These are verses!" I said, breathlessly. Then, my eye chancing to fall upon the twelfth line, "My God!"

"Can you read it?"

"The handwriting is very clear!"

"Yes. I spent many hours with a special camera under all kinds of different lights."

"But my Greek is a bit rusty from two years of text prepping. Besides, you'll have to help me with the integrations."*

"Come, let us read it together."

- [TRANSLATION] -

O god of mystery, concealed by darkness, rememberest thou me?
Constant companion of my distant schooldays,
did we not wrestle often over books and verse
and rules of calculus and rhetoric.and metre?
Yea, thou who hoardest and dispensest knowledge,
thou who guardest the granaries of life and learning,
know that what thou suffered me to win from thee I long laid up
in store.

---

* *Integrations*: the conjectural filling in of the *lacunae* (missing words and letters) which plague the reading of ancient papyri.

Yet, life being short, that which is remembered is soon forgotten.
I have rowed my years, and, as the poet (who, then?) sings,
"What my net has caught I have sold to you."
And for good price! For thou hast left me reason, precious beyond
jewels.
Hear now my palinode and accept my repentance as an offering.
Slave, go tell the Master: I am old and have missed the mark.
For though in life I pursued the way of truth and peace
I am persuaded at the end that I have gone astray.
And you, O Memory, elusive god, now mock me wracked by time,
as, it is said, you mocked my master's master,
when in his feeble years he sensed the flight of reason from his
breast
and deeming life without philosophy more burdensome than death,
chose that.
A paradox this unequivocalest end of ends
that shamelessly swallows up a life unto itself!
Memory being first to go, paves the way for self-control,
autonomy, objective thought, and continence,
the faculties, the teeth, like scattering sheep,
and after them, like sheepdogs in a frenzy,
the legs, as gravity and chaos overcome cohesive force.
Yet by your grace and boundless generosity,
reason's chamber still leased to me remains: I think,
though indolent and scatterbrained I waste my days,
my only exercise the endless chasing after names and dates.
Whom did I encounter at such or such a time?
And whether this or that he said, or was it someone else?
Who gave it me, that memorable wine, where is that book?
What name did I confer on her—pet name—who taught me
amatory arts long put aside, alas, neglected and unused?

And where are the stars in which by night I took such limitless
                                                    delight?

Will you forgive, O God, my long neglect of you,
the casting from my mind the poignant recollection
of dear ones gone whom doctrine demurred to mourn?
Or do you but tap me triumphant on the shoulder,
as if to say, "Pardon, Sir, but will you kindly cast your eye
in my direction? Teach me now, what do you see?"
I see that you, O Memory, are One! I see Parmenides
in everlasting dance with free-falling Epikouros!
I see myself chastised among the blest
for I have sacrificed to you the bullocks of my days,
though I knew it not! And so I am rewarded!
The small boy thinks he will hate young girls forever,
the lovesick youth that he will never recover
from the love he's lost. In the flower of my manhood,
I looked too much forward to new horizons, vistas
to regret plowed fields behind that I loved best.
Now it is but memories I mourn. So much of life
is thoughtlessness. Without a key to unlock the vaults
of names and faces, tender words, the smiling gifts and gestures,
myself, too, I seem to have forgotten.
Who have I been? What were my works and days?
My deeds, good and bad, what were they, that I might account?
What? Shall I to the fire consign my tracts? The very flames
report to you my heresies, relay my errors.
Shall I sweep the continents for those I falsely taught?
Unteach my graduates, set them at this late date aright?
Have I been loved? Am I remembered? Was I of friendship
                                                    worthy?
What am I now that so much of life has fled my grasp?

149

One God I from my father learned, from my mother, many;
and so I followed him who taught no gods at all.
His Doctrine I recall—that is the irony—recall to disavow.
For what is this world if all that is be not recorded?
The Kosmos functions as an integrated whole.
The whole knows itself as one or could not function.
That knowledge-of-self sustained through time is memory.
Hence Memory is unity, is all, suppressed all banishes like ostraka.
I have offended the All-knowing, the Unforgetting.
Yet naked, shattered and abashed I stand recalled before you!
Thus have you, All-forgiving, shorn the sheep of falsehood,
Thus have you loosed the blindfold from my eyes,
Thus have you cut the moorings of my past.
Now let us launch a black ship into the bright sea . . .

* * *

When we came to the end of the text, there was a long interval of silence as we each wiped our eyes.

"That last verse!" I said. "He took it from the Iliad?"

Professor Heklason lumbered out of his chair and unstowed a bottle of Akvavit from the frigerette. We said *Prosit* with little plastic cups.

"*Nun d'age nea melaina nerussomen eis hala dian.* Verse 141. But, you see, he uses it in a different sense, doesn't he!"

"Are you sure it is his?"

"If it isn't, it is a very fine and very ancient impersonation. But why would anybody do that? It is better than most of the poems that have come down to us under his name. And how did it get into his library if it wasn't his? It's only a draft. It is unsigned, and the author is not otherwise indicated. It got into the supply cabinet because there were a lot of unused sheets left in the roll."

"You have to publish it."

"I am dying to publish it, but I can't. Once it comes out that I have been dealing in these, it will be very embarrassing, and not just for me."

"Why don't you just smuggle it back in on your next trip?"

"Hah! It is easy to take it out when it's rolled up. How do you think I would look coming in with these under glass? You can't roll them up again, you know. Pretty big scandal, I think. You have to understand: I didn't just hide these in the lining of my coat and sneak out. I am not a member of their Institute. There are other persons involved, people whose only interest is in furthering our research. The Carabinieri of the TPC are not known for upstanding comedy!"

"So why not hire a lawyer and have him ship your butterfly boxes back to the institute in Naples? Your name would never need to come out."

"They would have to be specially crated, insured and delivered by private courier. It would cost a lot of money and arouse too much curiosity. How did this get out? And then, there could be a fingerprint or a hair or some other signature. You see, I made an experiment with a liquid bandaid."

"I'm sorry?"

"Yes, you know, it comes in a little bottle, and it is for smearing over a small wound. When it dries, it sticks to the skin like glue, but very pliable. Well, I tried coating the outside of the role before unwinding it, little by little. It worked very nicely. It takes a little practice. The coat has to be very thin. I phoned up the manufacturer, and ordered a tin of the stuff without the medication. I did not speak about this to my colleagues, but it would not be difficult to trace me through my contacts with the company. Please understand: I made absolutely no attempt to cover up my hand. It was all completely spontaneous and innocent. I just did my best to keep it clean, neat and intact—preserve the writing and mount it securely. I can't afford the cost or the risk. Not only to myself. There are other people involved!"

"Then what about photographs? Couldn't you just send those back?"

"I could, I suppose, but those to whom scrolls were loaned out are few, and there are not too many experts who know how to obtain such clear imagery of the letters. The papyri themselves are almost illegible to the naked eye. Black on black, you know. Besides, I confess that it would be unbearable to see this published over someone else's name. It was a great deal of work. Many hours. Fantastic hours. I am too emotionally involved."

"I would be, too. And you are not willing to publish it under a pseudonym?"

"What satisfaction would there be in that? I would be jealous of myself! Besides, whether it appears over my name or someone else's, it's not mine to publish. I wouldn't feel right about it."

"Professor Heklason! I think you must have some Danish blood in your veins!"

"Yes, well, aren't we all a little bit Vikings! It is a Hamletian dilemma! To do justice for his father, he must shame his mother, isn't it so? Of course, on the other side, when he did make up his mind to act, there were lots of dead bodies all over the stage—including his own! At the same time, I can't sleep nights thinking that I should be the cause of this piece remaining unknown.

"You know, sometimes I ask myself, what is this all for? Why was this villa found? Why have we been digging up this library? Why have we been unrolling these lumps of coal? Speaking for a moment as an ordinary thrall—not as a papyrologist—so much of this material is banal, predictable, redundant, superfluous, dead. I'll tell you: if none of this had ever been found, it would have been no great loss to our knowledge of antiquity. Less color and detail, less charm, perhaps, less pathos, but no great loss. Keeps the humanists off the streets. A bit of glory to the humble wielders of the pickaxe. But why, why all this effort to dig, dig, dig—if not for something like *this?*" Here the Professor picked up the photos in his hand and waved them about, while saying *Sköll!* with the other hand and a sigh. "As you say in America, 'This is what it is all around!'"

"*Salute e Vita!* How did you ever get yourself into this situation? Why?"

"For the reasons that you already know. My only thought was to bring samples along with me in my journeys, to show people like that Dr. Brown you introduced me to—very nice gentleman. Hoping to find new ways of opening up the scrolls without damage and preserving them. They are all supposed to be fresh, blank rolls. You can't imagine my surprise—my exhilaration—my horror—when I found writing on this one! Try to imagine what I felt when I read the first line! You have to understand: there is no way to prove that this scroll came from the so-called 'supply room'. If this gets back to Italy, and the press gets hold of it there will be a presumption of a Mercurian—Herculean . . . *Herculanean,* really, conspiracy to engage in illegal trade involving antiquities of inestimable value."

To be honest, I did not completely believe Professor Heklason. If he had had help getting the stuff out, he should have been able to have help getting the stuff back in—and back again into his own hands with authorization to publish. Or . . . perhaps not. Heklalson knew the landscape far better than I. Still, I had a feeling that there was an aspect to this story that he was not sharing with me.

We sat in silence, again, for a long time. Then, I spoke up. "I think I have an idea. Would you be willing to trust me with a set of photos and wait three or four years?"

"Well, I would like to hear what you have in mind. But if I could see this text in print without losing my stake in it, I could die with my conscience at peace."

"Knowing that it might never be published in *Cronache Ercolanesi?*"

"I have thought, like you, that with the help of a good lawyer I could make arrangements for it to be returned to Naples, but at some future moment when I and my fellow conspirators are all comfortably tucked away under six feet of earth. Funny, isn't it? There's just no way to guarantee it. It's worth too much money."

I had an almost palpable sense that Heklason was itching to tell me how much he had sold it for, and to whom. What else could he have done with it? Anyway, I didn't want to know. So I told him about the novel I had in mind about the Archaica Project. "It's strictly confidential," I said, quite unnecessarily. "Don't breathe a word to anyone!"

We sat for a couple more hours, saying *l'Chayim* in as many languages we could think of and exchanging horror stories about papyrologists, Italian bureaucrats, antiquities smugglers and Icelandic Airlines. Finally, at around 2:00 AM, we called it and said goodbye with a hug. I had already stumbled out the door when I turned to Professor Heklason.

"One last thing I must ask you, Egil: whatever induced you to trust me with all this? With these photos? This poem? You hardly know me."

"I heard your father play many years ago in Oslo. I'll never forget it."

16

Unscrolling

As things turned out, I never wrote the Archaica novel—even though, contrary to my expectations, I had finally had a plot handed to me on a silver platter. In fact, nothing turned out the way I anticipated. Egil Heklason died two years later, and such part of his conscience as he did not bequeath to me was scattered, together with his ashes, somewhere in the Arctic Circle. If absence of evidence is evidence of absence, the other ashes—the original windings of the professor's mummified scroll—if ever found, were never published.

Meanwhile, in the more temperate zone in which Noah's Ark lay languidly at anchor, my personal affairs were also reduced to ashes and scattered to the four winds. One visible reminder of that is that whereas, thanks to my work, Phase One of the Philodemus Bibliography was now complete with over 500 entries, I was to get scant credit in the published biblio—in spite of the fact that the response from the academic community had been favorable. For some reason, my name was sandwiched between the undergraduate Sky Mileszewksy, who had put in some library orders at my request, and Clarissa Whatshername—the legendary graduate student who had provided the original Decalogue of assorted entries that I had found laid up in the old shoe box. "*Non omnia possumus omnes,*" ("Impossible to thank everyone for everything!") Strauss and Duchinsky had written in their Acknowledgments; but they did manage to thank this fictional Triumvirate "for helping us understand the sheer mass of text material Philodemus has generated." Of course, I did not know this then; I got the news later, as a sort of postcard from Nirvana.

My tour of duty on the Ark came to an end. Three years had gone by rather quickly. My contract had been twice renewed, and my grant had run its course. There had been no talk of additional funding to cover my position, and no invitation to compete for a teaching job in the adjoining Classics Department. I had done what I was hired to do.

I had mixed feelings about leaving, because despite the occasional friction, I had grown used to all the animals, and had even developed a kind of *simpatia* for Heinz and Daisy. I had grown especially fond of Sokrates and Annie and Professor Parthenopides, and it pained me, too, to say goodbye to Veronica, who seemed quite disoriented and forlorn behind a brave exterior. As we exchanged farewells and promises to stay in touch, it became apparent that something more was going on. At last, I was able to drag out of her that she had lost her scholarship. Her future in the graduate program was in doubt. I tried to reassure her with stories of the many students I knew who had managed to put themselves through graduate school working part time. I told her emphatically that she could do the same and would certainly succeed. There was little time for talk. There was a hasty and awkward hug and she turned away, leaving me deeply troubled.

At the same time, I was excited about seeking employment as a teacher of Classics. A fresh confidence about my prospects enhanced my outlook, now that I had one American institution of learning that stood between me and the ineradicable stigma of an Italian degree. I had begun the round of formal goodbyes, and at the appropriate time I knocked at Heinz's door, prepared to take my leave. Heinz invited me in, offered me a chair, and amid the usual pleasantries, I told him of my plans. Finally, I reminded him of the equivalency papers he had obtained for me, and of his promise to give them to me when I needed them.

Heinz furrowed his brow, adjusted his tinted glasses, and said, "Excuse me? Equivalency papers? I'm afraid I don't understand."

I find myself at a loss to reproduce or even reconstruct what was said in the course of the ensuing discussion. I remember the embarrassment I felt—not only for me, but for him, my inability to call him a liar to his face, my being drawn, despite myself, into his charade of denial and growing indignation, my pathetic search for some remembered detail, some mnemonic hook to catch him by, for something he would absolutely be forced to concede, something that by force of logic alone would compel him to remember, or to admit remembering. It was like begging for mercy from an executioner who has neither understanding nor appreciation of the request, nor authority to grant it, nor any interest in the matter beyond sharpening the blade. I remember snippets.

"I think you must have been dreaming."

"I have no idea what you are talking about."

"Don't try that one on me!"

"You have some nerve to come in here, etc."

It was a superb dramatic performance on his part, without shame or qualm, that could only have been fuelled by pure hatred and intense savoring of longed-for revenge.

Revenge for what? Shelumiel Yashanoshan, I am going to teach you a lesson. Shelumiel Yashanoshan, you will never work again in Classics. Shelumiel Yashanoshan, go to dentist school, go flip burgers, join the rabbinate, sell real estate. You are finished. Done. Get out.

For days afterward, in shock, sick to my stomach, I racked my brains for a reason, for a motivation, however paranoid, that bore some resemblance, however insanely distorted, to a reason. Was it that stupid birthday card I handed him? Or that I smirked at Daisy's grand research project? Or that I walked out in the middle of Heinz's grand self-serving oration on the justice and hardship of his administration? Or that Dorian Prout had slandered my dissertation in the Faculty Lounge? Or, on the other hand, that I was able to dissuade Heinz from taking a rash and harmful action against his colleague? Or that I tried to get a dear and trustworthy friend to give him a couple of hundred thousand and she didn't?

Well, all those things had happened, but my academic status

would have been settled long before. Heinz couldn't take that away by simply denying that I had asked for it. I began to question my own memory. What if I really had imagined the whole thing? What if it was all a dream? Wandering around the hallways in a stupor, I asked Janoš, didn't he remember that I had asked Heinz to have my papers evaluated? Somewhat sheepishly, I thought, Janoš didn't remember. I asked Jason. Jason didn't know anything about it. I phoned Concetta, who remembered very distinctly that Heinz and Daisy had introduced me to her as a "Ph.D.," but begged me not to involve her as Heinz had promised to get her a job teaching Italian.

"What's this all about?" they asked. I was afraid to tell them. I had to be careful. If I said too much, Heinz might turn around and charge me with slander. I phoned Hoss, who had landed an interim job at some nearby community college. Hoss remembered that he and Clarence Woodbine and I had always been introduced to "bigwig" visitors as "Our Ph.D.s," and it had always rubbed him as pretentious. But what did that prove?

With Krati I could talk. I asked him. Sokrates admitted remembering something, but he asked me to leave him out of it. He had been at JWU for nine years and was just about to complete his own Ph.D. He couldn't afford to get on Heinz's bad side. He ventured that Janoš and Jason had been close with Heinz since grad school, and their denials meant nothing.

I began to consider the opposite: what if Heinz had really forgotten? A droplet from the river of forgetfulness mixed in with that Bible-sized rainfall the previous winter? A tiny neurological tree in his brain felled by a minuscule stroke of cerebral lightning?

I myself could no longer remember with certainty which campus Strauss had said he was sending my papers to. I started a round of telephone calls to various offices at JW, at HBU, at MM, at CG (Clark Gable, not Carey Grant), the Dean of This, the Dean of That, the Provost, the Vice Presidents, the State Bureau of Education. The upshot? Humphrey Bogart had used to host a "Credentials Evaluation Service" (CES)—the only one in the entire State of Kalisperia—until five or six years prior, when it separated from the University System. It morphed into its own independent entity administered by an "International Education Research Foundation," located in Smokeville. Heinz had lied when he told me he sent my papers to HBU for evaluation. No such office then existed at Bogart or anywhere in the entire university system. Sorry, and here's lookin' at you, kid! I phoned the aforesaid International Education Research Foundation and asked them to confirm that they had received an evaluation request from the Archaica Project three years previous. They checked all their files. They had no record of any such request whatsoever.

I want to thank you, Heinrich Strauss, for teaching me—without shedding a drop of my blood—-that my trust in you, my loyalty to you, my friendship for you, my reliance on you, were folly, madness, and self-contempt. I want to thank you for teaching me this while paying my rent and my board and my gasoline, and while letting me sit in one beautiful library while helping to reconstruct another one buried in time and mud. I could have learned all this from the history of my People, from the history of my own family, from History, from the soaps; but I did not. So thank you, Heinz, thank you, thank you. And thanks to you, too, Daisy, and Edythe, and you, Janoš, and you too, Jason. And let me not forget you, Dorian Prout. Thank you for helping me understand the sheer mass of . . .

Well, as you can see, it *is* possible to thank everyone for everything!

17

Music Again

But all this, all this to what end? Was I not writing about the music of forgetting? Indeed, I was, and shall be, but the story of Noah's Ark is not quite finished yet. For about the time I was preparing to leave John Wayne and return to the family homestead in the Valley of Smokes, my father was engaged, ironically enough, to give a concert in Nirvana with the VOSCO Chamber Ensemble Gephardt Seidlitz conducting. My father was supposed to appear in the first half of the program, playing Beethoven's Fourth Piano Concerto. The venue, to everyone's surprise, was the Campus Theatre of John Wayne University!

So just a couple of months after I had left Noah's Ark, there I was, driving my mother and father down the well-worn trail back to JW. As I drove, I was possessed by a vague feeling of apprehension. Would I have to shake hands with Heinz and Daisy and Jason and Janoš and the others and have to introduce them to my mother and father? I knew Sokrates and Annie had been anticipating the concert with great excitement, and I was looking forward to seeing them again. But a symphony concert was too rarified an event for Nirvana, let alone JW. I had worked on campus for three years, and nothing like this had ever happened. I wondered whether either Beethoven or Yashanoshan would be enough to bring the natives out of their jacuzzis.

My mother and I and Maestro Seidlitz saw my father to the Green Room, where he was attended to by the stage manager, a very pleasant young man. We then walked around into the hall. The hall was empty, except for some members of the orchestra settling into their chairs, and testing their instruments and their fingers. A young couple were seated in the front-row-left, alongside of what looked

160

like two music students with music scores. As my mother and I took our seats in the middle of the auditorium, Sokrates and Annie turned around and waved to us. Sokrates gave me a questioning look and a shrug of the shoulders and I shrugged back at him. It was already 7:30, but we had to wait another ten minutes in the unfulfilled hope that an audience would still materialize. Eventually, the rest of the orchestra walked onstage and took their places. At last, Maestro Seidlitz strode to the podium, took in the scene, smiled bravely, bowed, and raised his baton.

I suppose I shall be forgiven for remembering little else about the concert except my father's performance. In truth, it feels rather odd, while writing about forgotten melodies, to be discussing a music that I remember very well. I suppose that if I had not heard my father practising it from my childhood on, and had not studied classical music myself, it would have gone the way of the Merry-go-round Waltz and the Corso Vannucci March, never to be retrieved. In compensation, I have, as I said, forgotten everything else on the program. At the conclusion of the first number, the conductor turned, bowed graciously to the exiguous but appreciative applause, and walked off.

After a brief pause, Maestro Seidlitz returned, preceded by my father, both bowing to the four people in the front-row-left and to the two music students on the right. I don't think my father could see far enough into the hall to make out my mother and me, but he gave a smile and a little nod of his majestic head in our direction. Then he sat down before the long piano—a beautiful nine-foot Steinway trucked in from Smokes—and touching the heavenly G-major chords, erased all consciousness of finite existence and filled the hall to overflowing.

Beethoven's G major piano concerto is one of his sublimest works. There is nothing else to compare it with in all the literature. It embodies all of Beethoven's mystical intentions for purifying and perfecting the world through music. The Second Movement, a measured, tersely poetic dialog between a quietly, deferentially in-quiring piano and, in answer, the restrained yet awesome power of the orchestra, has been likened to Orpheus's foredoomed tryst with

Eurydike, when the grieving poet descended into Hades to redeem her and restore her to the world of light. This oversentimental comparison has become shamelessly conventional, with some critics even referring to Beethoven's Fourth as "The Orpheus Concerto!"

To one who listens down deep, the gratuitous interpolation of Orpheus is quite out of character with the music. In the first place, to whom shall we ascribe the voice of the orchestra, to whom the piano? The solemnly booming strings are hardly appropriate to either the wraith of the dead maiden or to her lover, while the piano could just as well represent one or the other. Nor can one seriously imagine the intransigent Ruler of Hades contending with the singer for 38 bars—if not the entire piece—while Eurydike listens mutely!

My father, a man of rare culture and depth, was not shy about likening the alternate utterances of piano and orchestra to a dialog between man and God—the piano representing man, the orchestra, God—and that was how he played it. Of course, music is not semantic, and we have no way of proving what words, if any, were in Beethoven's head when he composed this movement, since it appears he left no notations in regard. Nevertheless, great music can be extremely evocative, and the clear dialogic structure of the piece moves one to wonder if Beethoven was thinking of a specific text when he wrote it.

There are several dialogs between God and man in the Torah, but only one matches the music in length, mood, and complexity of articulation. That is the conversation between God and Abraham which takes place before the destruction of Sodom and Gomorrah—in fact, the very dialog that supposedly led Skipchick to apostasy. In that conversation, Abraham pleads with the "Judge of all the earth" not to destroy the righteous with the wicked, but forbears to mention his cousin Lot—a resident of Sodom—by name. That particular text corresponds rather well, from an ideological point of view, with Beethoven's fervid belief in the redemptive power of his own music.

But there is more to it. As it turns out, one discerns a remarkable structural correspondence between the music and the Biblical text. By this, I mean that if we diagram the structure of the music and the structure of the dialog, the two structures match astonishingly well!

The Movement opens with the orchestra (strings only) pronouncing a stern introductory statement, ponderous, *forte,* unadorned, almost in *recitativo* style. Violins, violas, and bass speak in their octaves, symbolizing the unitary voice of God:

. . . Verily, the cry of Sodom and Gomorrah is great, and, verily, their sin is exceeding grievous. I will go down now, and see whether they have done altogether according to the cry of it, which is come unto Me; and if not, I will know. (Gen. 18:20-21)

This statement of the orchestra ends on a *b*—the hanging dominant of the signature key of e-minor, indicating the question with which the verses conclude, and also the undecided fate of the evil cities (Bars 1-5):

Now the piano (Abraham) answers, softly, humbly, and in sweet harmonies, a small voice before the Creator:

. . . Wilt Thou indeed sweep away the righteous with the wicked? Peradventure there are fifty righteous within the city; wilt Thou indeed sweep away and not forgive the place for the fifty righteous that are therein? That be far from Thee to do after this manner, to slay the righteous with the wicked, that so the righteous should be as the wicked; that be far from Thee; shall not the Judge of all the earth do justly?" (Gen. 18:23-25)

163

This answer of the piano ends on the tonic—not on an unresolved chord as the question mark at the end of verse 25 would seem to require; but the question is only rhetorical: one does not tell God what to do; one asks a deferential question. Thus, the sense of the phrase is clearly affirmative: "The Judge of all the earth must do justly!"—and that is what the piano's answer conveys (Bars 6-13):

Then God replies, well pleased with Abraham's request, and He grants it:

...If I find in Sodom fifty righteous within the city, then I will forgive all the place for their sake. (Gen.18:26)

In so replying, the orchestra repeats the initial pattern of its opening statement, but as the answer is favorable, the music modulates propitiously into a major key: D major (Bars 14-18):

Notice, however, that the orchestra's reply hangs on A, the unharmonized dominant of D major: the matter is not yet resolved, and God knows that Abraham has more on his mind. Indeed, it is once again Abraham's turn to speak:

. . . Behold now, I have taken upon me to speak unto the Lord, who am but dust and ashes. Peradventure there shall lack five of the fifty righteous; wilt Thou destroy all the city for lack of five? (Gen. 18:27-28)

In conveying this query, the piano now repeats in D major the pattern of its initial question, and modulates apprehensively back into the signature key of e minor (Bars 19-26):

The orchestra (God) now answers:

. . . I will not destroy it, if I find there forty and five. (Gen.18:28) (Bars 26-28):

165

It is interesting to point out here that the foregoing verse (v. 28 in Chapter 18 of Genesis) is what is called *antilabé*—the term for a verse in which a dialog break occurs. In fact, verse 28 contains both Abraham's question and God's answer. Similarly, Bar 26 in the music contains both the end of Abraham's new question and the beginning of God's new answer!

Now the piano begins an upward progression of four short phrases (each one soliciting a response from the orchestra) built on seventh chords leading from e-minor to e-minor an octave higher. This progression parallels Abraham as he conducts God dialectically through a series of four short questions—represented in the music by the four short phrases—that lead ineluctably to the answer sought by Abraham. To illustrate, I shall quote of each Biblical verse only the *ipsissima verba,* and of those only the essential part of each speech—the part reflected in Beethoven's composition:

Abraham:

... Peradventure there shall be forty found there? (Gen.18:29) (Bars 28-29):

G–d (orchestra):

". . . *I will not do it for the forty's sake.*" (Gen. 18:29) (Bars 29-31):

Abraham (piano):

. . . Peradventure there shall thirty be found there? (Gen.18:30) (Bars 31-32):

God (Orchestra) *. . . I will not do it if I find thirty there.* (Gen. 18:30) (Bars 32-33):

Abraham (piano):

. . . Peradventure there shall be twenty found there? (Gen.18:31)
(Bar 33):

God (orchestra): *. . . . I will not destroy it for the twenty's sake."* (Gen. 18:31) (Bars 33-34):

Abraham (piano):

Peradventure ten shall be found there? (Gen. 18:32) (Bars34-35):

168

But note: The orchestra has anticipated the conclusion of the piano's question! How wonderful this is! Orchestra and piano have together resolved the matter in the signature key of e minor, as God finally gives Abraham the desired answer, and the dialog is concluded:

God (orchestra):

I will not destroy it for the ten's sake." (Gen. 18:32).

Finally—and this is the most remarkable of all—the orchestra falls silent on the e minor chord, while the piano continues alone down the melodic minor scale toward the anticipated e-minor closing of the phrase (Bars 35-38):

The silence of the orchestra corresponds to the Biblical text:

And the Lord went His way, as soon as He had left off speaking to Abraham . . . . (Gen. 18:33)

The orchestra part must end there, because God "left off speaking;" and while God may descend from His heavens to converse with a man, a human being may not follow God back to His holy abode! When God "departs," He simply disappears from our ken. The piano, however, leads Abraham all the way to the end of verse 33, thus concluding the exposition section with ". . . and Abraham returned unto his place." Abraham's "place," in musical terms, is the *expected* tonic e-minor chord.

I say "expected", because, for compositional reasons, Beethoven does not in fact fulfill the expectation, but leads the music, via a deceptive cadence, into the development section. The conversation is over, but the music must go on in accordance with its own rules.

And given the collocation of this movement in the context of Genesis 18:20 ff., it would be quite strange if, after the short development, we did not hear in the stunning dissonances of the piano-solo cadenza Beethoven's rendition of the tragic denouement of this Biblical episode.

Beethoven composed his Fourth Piano Concerto in 1806, while Napoleon was fighting and winning a succession of bloody battles in which the allied armies of Prussia, Austria and Russia were badly defeated. The composer's indignation and resentment toward the occupation of Vienna by the French is well documented. On two distinct occasions he is even known to have expressed regret that he was not a master of military arts as he was of musical composition, "For then I should conquer him!"

It is easy to imagine how this anger of Beethoven's conflicted with his equally well-documented belief in Peace and Goodwill-towards-Man—in short, his love for all Humanity. Thus, it can be no surprise that Beethoven's thoughts would turn to Genesis 18:20 ff. and to the conflict between cataclysm as an instrument of Divine Justice on the one hand, and a cause of undeserved suffering on the other. Nor is it surprising that the composer would be drawn to express his musical thoughts in the style of an operatic duet, as he had just recently completed the first version (*Leonore, or the Triumph of Conjugal Love*) of his opera, *Fidelio*, and hence would still have been very much in operatic mode.

18

Intermission: What Happened at Sodom?

Of course, even Beethoven's musical translation cannot explain why Abraham left off his bargaining at ten righteous people. Without the benefit of the innumerable Commentaries preserved in the Jewish Tradition, Janoš may be excused for jumping to the wrong conclusions. Indeed, what bothered Janoš so much was the following: seeing that Abraham's nephew, Lot, has settled in Sodom with his entire household, why did Abraham leave without extracting a promise from God to save Sodom for Lot's sake? And if he realized that Sodom was doomed, why did he himself not run to rescue his nephew?

Here are the main points:

1. Abraham rests his case after successfully pleading for ten.
2. God "goes his way," seeing that Abraham is silent.
3. Abraham goes home, confident that Sodom will be spared.
4. God sends an Angel to rescue Lot.
5. The Angel warns Lot to collect his family and flee from Sodom. (According to Rashi, the great 11th-Century Commentator, Lot's family consisted of ten persons: himself, his wife, two married daughters and their husbands, two betrothed daughters still living at home, and their two fiancés.)
6. Lot's four sons-in-law (the two married and the two affianced) refuse to leave, thus sealing their fate and that of the two married daughters.

7. Lot flees Sodom with his wife and two unmarried daughters.
8. Lot seeks refuge in Zoar, one of the condemned cities of the plain. (In Jewish Tradition, Sodom and Gemorrah are just two of a cluster of five towns in the vicinity of the Dead Sea.)
9. Lot's wife dies in looking back on the destruction of Sodom.
10. God spares Lot and his two daughters, on account of Abraham.
11. After a tranquil night's sleep, Abraham returns to the site of his dialog with God, and is dismayed to see the cities of the plain on fire.

From the text itself, we see that Abraham pleads openly for neither the wicked nor for his own relations. On the surface, he pleads only for the righteous: it is for *their* sake that the city should be spared. However, our Tradition teaches (*Breishis Rabba, Lot,* 21) that Abraham went as a missionary among the wicked, seeking to draw souls away from idol worship and immorality, and lead them onward to repentance and the service of God.

It is important to underscore that *in the Jewish Tradition, the "cry of Sodom and Gemorrah" was not occasioned by "sodomy" (sexual intercourse between males) per se!* (When has this practice ever been confined to a geographical area?) The Great Sin was that the citizens of this society had cultivated an ethos of licentiousness in which excesses of every kind were not only permitted, but sanctioned (authorized) by the state and protected by law! Now according to the Midrash, Abraham's followers even included penitents from Sodom! How could Abraham not be filled with compassion for the wicked from whom he drew members of his own flock? Are the malleable youth of a state not misshapen by the perversion of its mores, deformed by the corruption of its media, its teachers and its courts?

Of course Abraham was concerned for the wicked of Sodom! Were there not, scattered among them, pure souls longing for temperance, cleanliness, honesty, wholeness and truth? But how could Father Abraham stand before Almighty God and plead for the deliverance of the *unrepentant*? And if he was troubled for the anonymous wicked, how much more was he filled with trepidation for his own nephew and his nephew's household! Yet how could he stand before the doomed cities and plead for his own flesh and blood?

Abraham has a dilemma: God has agreed to spare Sodom for the sake of ten righteous souls. Thus, the only way Lot's household can be saved along with all of Sodom is if ten righteous souls can be found among the population. *But what if they can't?* The Midrash (*Breishis Rabba,* 49: *Machanot Kehuna*) tells us that Abraham believed that Lot's family—all ten of them—were righteous. This explains why he ceased his entreaties as soon as God promised that he would spare the wicked for the sake of the ten. Abraham was confident that at least ten righteous (Lot's family) would be found in Sodom. Trusting that Sodom would be spared, Abraham returned home in peace.

On the other hand, one might ask: how could Abraham be sure that every member of Lot's household was truly righteous? Indeed, Rashi comments that Abraham actually pleaded for *less than ten.* When Abraham begged for the salvation of 45 righteous, he was really pleading for *nine*—"by combining the numbers" (*al yedei tzeyruf*), since "Sodom" really consisted of a cluster of five towns, and 45 = 5 X 9! In other words, having secured God's promise to spare the wicked for the sake of 45 righteous, Abraham intended to use arithmetic to save Sodom proper even if only nine members of Lot's family passed the test! However, Rashi concludes that God saw through Abraham's reasoning, and rejected it:

> "And for nine, *al yedei tzeyruf,* he had already requested (*kvar biqeysh*) and did not find (*velo matza*)."

Hence Abraham returned to bargaining in multiples of ten (40, *etc.*).

According to the same Rashi comment, Abraham did not venture to plead for eight, because the eight righteous members of Noah's household had not been enough to save the world from the Flood.

One could also say that the Flood was a sore point with God, Who had repented of drowning the world; and that it would have been tactless of Abraham to allude to it. Moreover, in contrast to Noah's family, Lot's (whatever his daughters had to say about it) was not needed to repopulate the world, so the comparison might not have redounded to the latter's favor. Thus, Abraham was stuck at ten, and had to pin all his hopes on Lot's family.

Now the question remains: if Abraham knew that ten is the smallest number of righteous people that would save Sodom, and if he was not sure that all ten members of Lot's household were numbered among the just, why did he go home instead of running to Sodom to warn Lot?

The answer has everything to do with the bartering of souls that has just gone on. Think about it, Skipchick! In the event that Lot's family were all righteous, Abraham, by rescuing them—*by taking them out of Sodom*—would have forfeited all hope of saving the city! And since Abraham had just risked his very life to plead for Sodom, how could he take any action which might jeopardize its survival? All he could do was go home, pray for the salvation of both the righteous and the wicked, and go to sleep, confident that God would judge mercifully.

And be assured: Abraham slept the sleep of the Just! For he was not awakened by the violent shaking of the earth or the thunder and flashing from the sky. That is why Abraham arose early the next morning and ran to the place of his meeting with God, expecting to hear a favorable verdict and, without a doubt, prepared to offer thanks. Hence Abraham's consternation when he saw the smoke and fire.

That Abraham's conduct in this matter was pleasing to God is shown by the fact that God sent an Angel to save Lot, his wife, and two of his daughters for Abraham's sake:

And it came to pass, when God destroyed the cities of the plain, that God remembered Abraham, and sent Lot out of the midst of the overthrow, when He overthrew the cities in which Lot dwelt. (Gen. 19:29)

Not only: the Angel permitted Lot to take refuge in Zoar, one of the five cities originally slated for destruction! This was a remarkable concession, for Lot had just refused the Angel's exhortation to flee to the mountain—"lest the evil attach itself to me and I die." Lot, for all that Abraham considered him a righteous man, knew he was not a Tzaddik like his uncle.* He feared that his defects would be conspicuous in the solitude of the mountain. His hope was that his merits would stand out better amid the corruption of Zoar, or that God's wrath would skip over the town because of its "small size" (Gen. 19:20). Thus, whereas God had previously denied Abraham's *tzeyruf* of nine Tzaddikim per city, He ultimately saved Zoar on account of only three persons (the fourth, Lot's wife, had perished during their flight when she paused to look back on the destruction of Sodom)—but really only for the sake of one Tzaddik—Abraham!

Well, it was clearly too late for Skippy to benefit from my Biblical readings, but if the latter had missed the significance of Gen. 19:29 (*God remembered Abraham*), Beethoven surely had not: the survival of an entire community can depend on the prayers of one righteous person—one Tzaddik! Can anyone who has read the composer's life and letters doubt that when Beethoven composed this concerto with its central message of compassion and salvation, it was with the hope and intent that composing and performing it would help purge the earthly realms of evil and corruption, and also save the innocent from destruction?

There is a great difference between understanding something with the intellect alone and comprehending it with one's entire being. Beethoven's Fourth Concerto for Piano is one of the many pieces that my father played with incomparable perception, dignity, and unsentimental yet deeply moving poetry. That night, accompanied by a superb and obviously inspired chamber orchestra, he played it magisterially, flawlessly, to a practically empty hall, played it generously and selflessly. It remains the most eerily illuminating

---

*In Jewish Tradition, the word Tzaddik has two distinct meanings: (1) a person (like Lot) whose merits outweigh his sins; and (2) a completely righteous and saintly person, who (like Abraham) is not subject to the wiles of temptation.

musical happening I have ever experienced, and one of my most precious memories. Strange that I did not fully realize it till now, but that night, he played for my mother and me alone! Perhaps it is only sentimental hindsight, but it is to that night that I ascribe the beginning of my return to the Heritage of my Fathers.

During the intermission, the entire audience of eight people went backstage to express their gratitude, good wishes, and embarrassment for the *Ataraxía* of Nirvana. However, I remember that while standing aside with Sokrates, who was still ecstatic over the performance, I was overcome by a feeling of indignation and disgust, and I remarked, perhaps with excessive bitterness, "What else would you expect from a place like Nirvana?"

"No, no, no!" replied Sokrates. "It's not what you imagine. We tried for weeks to order tickets, but the ticket office never answered the phone!"

The newlyweds, who were standing close by, confirmed. "He's right. The same thing happened to us. Thank goodness there was someone in the box office tonight. We got our tickets at the door."
I was shocked. This was too much even for JWU. "How is that possible? They paid thousands of dollars for that concert!"

"I don't know," said Sokrates, "but I called the administration office to complain, and they told me the guy who usually takes care of the ticket sales had called in sick."

"Sick for a month? And they don't call a replacement?"

There was no place to go after the concert to get something to eat, so we said goodbye and drove back to Smokey Hollow. On the way, it suddenly registered that not a single person from the Ark or Classics had shown.

At that time, I was busy teaching English for what, considering class prep time, boiled down to a dollar an hour at the Crosswind School, a private liberal arts high school, whose 12th-grade English teacher I had been called to replace. As the headmaster of this worthy institution explained, he had got my name from a mutual acquaintance after summarily firing my predecessor for his purported incompetence. The job interview took place in the headmaster's office, under the supervision of Percy Bysshe Shelley, whose blown-up portrait occupied nearly an entire wall, from which one could not fail to notice the remarkable resemblance of the poet's upper lip to the *incisivus superior* of the orifice sitting beneath it. It turned out, however, as I was to learn years later, that, contrary to the latter's representation, the neglectful instructor had not been fired at all, but merely shifted laterally to Melpomene, from whose histrionic groves he incited our mutual pupils with execrations upon the lessons of his unsuspecting rival.

The headmaster panicked when angry parents complained about the grades I was handing out. He began to pressure me to award A's and B's, so as not to spoil my students' college preferences. As my class had been accustomed—indeed instructed—to study their Hamlet without troubling themselves unnecessarily with super-annuated Shakespearian vocables—and were, most of them, incapable of writing a coherent paragraph—I refused to buckle or budge. An arctic crosswind swept over me, ultimately freezing me out of the copy room, which I found locked on the morning of final exams. Fortunately, I found an architect's firm a block away where I was graciously allowed to use the Xerox, so my students did not escape their day of judgment, nor Hamlet his vindication. The youngsters did fine, and the director expressed his gratitude by doing (no doubt superfluously) whatever is done to ensure that a person will never teach school again.

No, I did not have mind or leisure to think about the concert. A few days had passed since that unforgettable event. I was sitting at the table with my mother and father after a Friday-night dinner, nibbling on the remnants of a fruited gift basket, when it suddenly occurred to me that if two loose grapes are found at the bottom of a bowl, there is a high probability that both came from the same vine. I phoned Sokrates.

"Sokrati!"

"Louis! *Ela*! How are you?"

"Sokrati: Do you think Heinz had anything to do with it? The concert, I mean."

There was a short pause. "It is entirely possible. He supplies the whole campus."

19

Eurydike

Many months passed before I saw Sokrates again. He had been awarded his Ph.D. Annie had given up after her professor, in spite of Strelesky, had casually instructed her for the umpteenth time to rewrite her dissertation—a perfectly good one, Sokrates assured me. They had moved off campus and were now living in a rather run-down neighborhood in low-rent, "ethnic" San Andreas, where Sokrates had buried himself to finish an article he was working on before returning to Athens. I drove down for a long-overdue reunion. Their location being not far from the tiny apartment to which Veronica had removed herself after losing her scholarship, the purpose of my visit was twofold.

It was not easy to locate the Naumachou anchorage. Sokrates had told me it was across the street from a Chinese restaurant whose name he could not remember. I could see no Chinese restaurant, but as I circled round in my car, I passed a couple of times a dilapidated eatery called, according to the large wooden sign hung over the storefront, Chattanooga Choo-Choo. To a Greek, it was Chinese.

I asked about Veronica. She was not doing well, came the guttural answer. Not long after my departure from John Wayne U., Veronica received notice that she had been dismissed from the graduate program for insufficient progress in her studies and a "demonstrated lack of linguistic aptitude." Veronica had shown Sokrates the letter. I could not help thinking this, too, had something to do with the Strelesky case. After all, Strelesky had been offered out after serving only three years for murdering the professor who had led him on for twelve. The case had been a national sensation. Who (aside from Annie's thesis advisor in his deconstructionist sensory deprivation tank) could fail to get the message?

It had taken at least three years for Duchinsky and Bottom to act on Veronica's obvious deficiencies. In defense of their inertia, it must be said that Veronica was a sincere and diligent student and each year had begged, promised and pleaded to be kept on. On the other hand, if I could teach her, why couldn't they? Alas, she was lonely and depressed. All she needed was a little encouragement, and some warm companionship. As for the first, hadn't I already proven myself? And as for the second, give it a week or two. Was that too much to ask for such a lovely young girl?

I had phoned Veronica a few days before and asked her if we could come over and visit. I drove. On the way, Sokrates warned me not to be shocked.

Actually, it was not as bad as he made it sound. Veronica occupied the corner ground-floor apartment of a little house. Lots of windows, plenty of light. Veronica looked pretty, though oddly out of character, done up in a white mantilla, her hair pulled back in a tight bun and held together by a peineta. Her cheeks were artlessly and quite needlessly rouged, and now that I think of it, her scent was not patchouli but roses. I remember that because my mother had a friend who smelled the same. At first, I took this rather outlandish getup for a naive attempt to impress, but she was not playing the coquette.

The main room, or whatever it was, held enough rickety furniture to seat two, and I made do with a spare orange crate from her makeshift bookshelves. I had imagined she would be happy to see two old friends, but in her face I perceived a hopeless mixture of pleasure and embarrassment, and as if a screen over any other emotions.

To put her at her ease, I ran through briefly what they had done to me—the same people who had done this to her—and what I was doing now, and the kind of liars and crooks I had been and was now working for. I asked her how she was occupying her time. She said she was looking for a job. She didn't know what kind. Any kind.

I said, "Ronie, why don't you go back to Illinois and stay with your family a while, get yourself together, make fresh plans?"

"Oh, I could never go back," she protested with a sad, peremptory laugh. "Don't ask me. It's a long story."

I felt she was holding back lest the dam burst. It was hard to get any further with her. We asked if there was anything we could do to help. I inquired if she had thought about moving up to Smokes, where she might find more opportunities, but to her question, "Where would I stay?" I had no answer. I asked again if there was anything I could do. She said no, and she was right. I'd like to think that I offered her a loan, but I can't say that I did. I'm afraid, after all, we were intruders from an unwelcome past into an awkward present. We said goodbye and promised to keep in touch. I took her hand, wanted to kiss her rouged cheek, but she leaned slightly away, and I took the hint.

As we drove away, I said, "Sokrati, are you thinking what I'm thinking?"

"I hope not," he answered.

I never saw Veronica again. When I phoned her maybe two or three weeks later, her phone had been disconnected, and the Naumachous did not know where she had gone.

Another interval followed—maybe two or three years—during which the Naumachous and I did not see each other. I was studying for the MCA Test, and I lost touch with several friends. As their stay in Kalisperia drew to a close, however, Sokrates and Annie drove up to Smokes to visit me before flying back to Hellas. In the middle of our far-flinging conversation, I interrupted to ask if they had any news from Veronica.

"Louie! You haven't heard?"

"Heard what?"

181

"Louis, I can't be sure if it's true, but I asked about her at the university, and they told me she died."

"No!" I shouted, jumping out of my chair.

"How? What happened?"

"They told me she got sick, and died in the hospital."

That was all they told him or would tell him. Not when, not where, not how.

20

Playback

Now that I have told her story—the very little of it that I know—you must think me very callous for making no effort to find out more. Well, I agree. I can only remind you—and myself—that my professional life had recently blown up in my face, that I had been betrayed and violated by a crazy man who had just sabotaged an entire symphony concert as a warning not to pursue the administrative and legal remedies he knew I would be considering; that I was now trying to win over and teach a class of resentful 12th-graders; that I was obsessing over what to do with a life that for fifteen heart-rending years I had tortured into the mold of a classics professor without prospects; that I had begun to study for the Medical College Aptitude Test, just to help define my options.

Add to that that I believed dear Sokrates—no less a friend to Veronica than I was—had already knocked his head against a stone wall and come away with nothing; and that contacting her family would have been an extremely delicate thing to do under the circumstances. Is it any wonder that I did nothing? Could I bring her back, like Eurydike, from the world below? Come now! What would you have done?

And one more thing: I didn't want to know. Because for all those years, there has been one little thought in my brain that refused to go away; and that is that when Sokrates and I visited poor Veronica in her sordid little flat to give her a bit of friendly comfort and counsel, someone might have been watching . . .

183

But in the end, I had to know, because my pen demanded it, and my conscience, strummed by my pen, harped on it. And so, after nearly thirty years of muting it, her name once again passed between us, between Shelumiel and Sokrates, between Kalisperia and Kali Hellas.

I did not broach the subject with premeditation. I merely sent him a copy of what I had so far written, hoping to check my memory against his. Sokrates did not recall stopping to visit me at my parents' house on his way to the airport, though he did surmise that it must have been the summer of 1984. Whether to satisfy my curiosity or his, he blitzed a former colleague of his at JW—one of the few with whom he had kept in touch. This was the same Professor Marcus with whom I had shared an unwise confidence concerning Daisy's aptitude for serious research. I had asked Sokrates to keep me out of it, and he averred that he did not mention my name.

Now read Marcus's reply. Krati blitzed it over to me, and I am incorporating it into this narrative:

Yes, I remember well Veronica. She went to the Student Health and they told her she had a "yeast infection." When she died and I told this to [my wife] she said "That is crazy!! Nobody dies from a yeast infection." Then I spoke to her boyfriend, a fundamentalist like her, a fellow student in classics—a nice young man, but a weakling. She got weaker and weaker and he did nothing. It was obvious she died because of incompetent medical care, but he did nothing. Her parents were devastated, as would I [be] if my child died. He never told them how she had been misdiagnosed, so neither did I. It was a real tragedy, and it saddened me. I took her aside several years before and told her I honestly didn't think she had the ability to go into college teaching. (Dorian said, 'What the hell! She can count the men in Homer or something like that and get a Ph.D.) I urged her to consider high school teaching and try an education course. She did and liked it, got a credential and was a few weeks away from starting to teach Latin at Carver High School. I

184

had heard Mr. Grumbaugh was retiring and recommended her. She was very happy and excited. I never heard anything about a cardiac problem. But I do remember her friend told me she kept getting weaker and weaker, and he helped by shopping for her. But he didn't do anything else!!! – The whole thing enraged and saddened me. I talked to a lawyer about the matter, and he told me I had no locus standi. So I didn't pursue the matter. Her parents gave her books to the Classics Library. But "getting weaker and weaker" doesn't sound to me like a cardiac problem [. . .] I believe it was the boyfriend who told me it was a yeast infection, but I cannot be sure.

Realizing that he had forgotten to ask Prof. Marcus when Veronica died, Krati blitzed him a postscript to inquire "if Veronica died before or after I left Kalisperia." Marcus's reply is noteworthy:

Dear Sokrates,

I regret that I cannot answer your question. It is sometimes difficult for me to remember dates from my own career. However, I remember how devastated I was, and how I talked to [my wife] about it. If you had been here of course I would have talked to you about it. It bothered me intensely. I did talk to her boyfriend – at least twice. He was no help whatever . . . . If she had had a long-standing cardiac condition, he didn't know about it. But one thing was and is quite clear: Nobody dies from a yeast infection.

To which Marcus added his own postscript:

As I just wrote, I would surmise that Veronica died when you were away.

Of course, Sokrates had been "away"—living off campus—for at least two years before leaving for Greece. I distinctly remember

185

Sokrates telling me that he "inquired about her at the university." This would have been soon after learning about her death—or perhaps he learned about her death while making the inquiries; but presumably he was still "at the university" when he inquired about her. The most likely time for this to have happened would have been just before leaving Kalisperia for Athens. He wanted to say goodbye.

In the meantime, it occurred to me to search for Veronica in the vast reticulate expanse of heterogeneous data that sheath the world's fat thighs like a fishnet stocking. I was surprised at how much information I found. The following is a summary:

There is no entry for Veronica in the Social Security Death Index, but the Kalisperia Death Records shows the date of her death as October 22, 1989—more than five years later than I remembered hearing about it from Sokrates!

A Certificate of Clearance was issued to Veronica by the Kalisperia Commission on Teacher Credentialing on May 18, 1989. On August 15, 1989, the Commission issued her an emergency, long-term (ten-month), Single-Subject Kalisperia Teaching Credential in Latin, "renewable subject to the holder being admitted to a college or university program for a teaching credential in Latin." This would seem to corroborate Professor Marcus's "[urging] her to consider high school teaching and try an education course. She did and liked it."

My inquiry with the university registrar produced the following: "Veronica was enrolled from September, 1978 to December, 1981, and January, 1984 to December, 1988 in the Ph.D. program. She earned her M.A. in Spring, 1984. In Spring quarter, 1989, she enrolled in a post-baccalaureate program in education. This was her last quarter of enrollment at John Wayne."

Inconsistent with the foregoing, the Alumni Page of the JW Department of Classics website listed Veronica as having earned a Ph.D. in 1989.

I could find no information on Veronica's activities or whereabouts during the years 1982-83, except that a Veronica Agriopoulos residing in Conchacancha County, is listed as related (presumably by marriage) to a number of persons with the surname "Perez". Someone named Veronica Perez acquired a firearms permit in Chicago.

Finally, I ordered and obtained from the Conchacancha County Clerk a copy of Veronica's Death Certificate, originally dated October 23, 1989. It confirms the date of death as October 22, 1989, and bears the stamp of the Sheriff-Coroner of Conchacancha County, and the signature of a deputy. The immediate cause of death is marked "Pending investigation". The "Amendment of Medical and Health Section Data—Death" attached thereto and signed by a different deputy on February 1, 1990, reads in salient part:

INFORMATION AS IT SHOULD BE STATED:

21. DEATH WAS CAUSED BY:

(A) Hemorrhagic myocardium

(B) Intravascular coagulopathy

(C) Hemolytic anemia with thrombocytopenia secondary to probable adverse Macrodantin reaction.

25. Other significant conditions contributing to death but not related to cause given in 21: Urinary tract infection.

29. Manner of death: Accident.

33. Describe how injury occurred or events which resulted in injury: Adverse reaction to prescription medication.

The original Death Certificate indicates the "place of final disposition as _____Mortuary in Metropolis, Illinois. I contacted the mortuary by telephone and email, and they were kind enough to confirm the burial, and to send me a copy of their file, containing a couple of forms (adorned with a Superman logo) and two obituary clippings retrieved from Veronica's file. The obits, clipped *without the "folio"* (the small banner at the top of an interior page containing the newspaper name, date and page number) cite Veronica as having acquired the Ph.D. degree shortly before her death. One of clippings announces the date of burial as Saturday, November 4, 1989. One of the forms erroneously shows November 22, 1989 as the date of Veronica's death, "but every other place in the file has October 22."

Aside from hearing about Veronica's death more than five years before it officially occurred, several things disturbed me about the information I collected. I shall go through them one by one.

1.   Professor Marcus wrote, "I took Veronica aside several years before, and told her I didn't think she was qualified to teach university level Latin. I urged her to consider high school teaching and try an education course." Most plausibly, this would have been in 1980 or '81, around the time she lost her scholarship. But Marcus doesn't even refer to her expulsion in 1981. At any rate, the conversation he is referring to would have happened most likely *before, and not after,* May, 1984, when she allegedly applied for re-admission, received her M.A. in Classics and committed to pursuing the Ph.D., for by then, the die was cast, and she had crossed her Rubicon. Indeed, Marcus expressly states *"several years before"*—presumably meaning several years before she died. In other words, most probably, not long before she moved to San Andreas, where Krati and I visited her and gave her the same advice. (As opposed to Prof. Marcus, I never intimated that she was not capable of becoming a competent college-level teacher, because I saw no reason why she shouldn't.)

Yet according to both Marcus and the Kalisperia School District, Veronica didn't obtain her "emergency teaching credential" until

August of 1989, apparently after completing her introductory quarter in education. In actuality, if she really acquired her M.A. in 1984, she would have been working toward a Ph.D. in classics from 1984 onward. The Registration Office has her in the Classics Ph.D. Program until December of 1988. The most likely time for Veronica to have worked toward a teaching credential would have been from 1981 through 1984. Once she had acquired her credential, she could have pursued her Ph.D. while supporting herself through teaching high school Latin. The Kalisperia Teaching Credentialing Program is a fairly demanding two-year program of study and practice, involving part-time employment as a teaching assistant. As exaggerated as Veronica's undervaluation by the Classics faculty might have been, it would have taken a bigger capacity than hers to complete her Ph.D. dissertation while working toward a teaching credential.

2. Professor Marcus remembers a great amount of collateral detail, but declines to reconstruct or even guess the year of Veronica's passing. "I regret that I can't answer your question" strikes me as suspiciously evasive.

3. According to Marcus, neither he nor Veronica's boyfriend ever told Veronica's parents that their daughter might have died as a result of incompetent medical care. Why not? This in spite of Marcus's having consulted an attorney and been told he had no standing to sue. If Marcus was so outraged, why wouldn't he tell the parents? Clearly, *they* had standing. He attributes his decision to the boyfriend's failure to refer to the matter: "He never told them how she had been misdiagnosed, so neither did I." But assuming the boyfriend said nothing about possible medical malpractice, why should that have prevented Marcus from mentioning it? And why would the boyfriend not mention it?

4. Marcus implies that one or more family members flew to the Nirvana campus to take charge of their loved one and to seek information about the circumstances of her passing. Yet the

"Application for Disposition of Human Remains" bears the name of someone other than her parents signing on their behalf.

5. My efforts to locate an obituary in the campus newspaper *True Grit*, were futile. According to the Research Librarian, the 1989 volume was extant only in microfilm. The volume itself was missing from the JW Library collection, and the microfilm, stored at a sister campus, was labeled "non-circulating" and "not available for loan". The person in charge of the microfilm collection at the sister campus refused to let me view the film for reasons he chose not to share. The Research Librarian at JW kindly took it upon himself to scroll through the microfilm:

"I went through every issue of *True Grit* from February 1989 through June 1989, and all issues from October 1989 and [sic] November 1989. I did not find any notice of the [sic] Veronica Agriopoulos in any of those issues. I also searched the archives of the *VOS Times* database, as well as the *Daily Crow's Nest* archives database, without finding any notice there. Sorry, but I think I've exhausted my resources."

6. The librarian suggested that I search the indices of other local newspapers. I did, and found nothing. I found this extremely odd. It is unthinkable that a campus newspaper would carry no notice of the passing of a well-liked graduate student—especially in questionable circumstances—or that Veronica's death would be ignored by the local press. The only obituaries that I found were presumably from the Metropolis area, and those, as previously noted, had been mailed to me after someone clipped them without the newspaper "folios". Obviously, they could have been fabricated.

7. The Death Certificate itself raises many questions. Indeed, as I suspected, and according to the specialists I consulted, it was far more likely that Veronica died from the urinary tract infection itself than from an "adverse reaction" to Macrodantin—a medication that

is safely prescribed for millions of women every year. These doctors found the Death Certificate "very strange, to say the least." However, researching clinical reviews of this medication, I came across the following, from an official FDA (Food and Drugs Administration) website:

> "Cases of hemolytic anemia of the primaquine-sensitivity type have been induced by nitrofurantoin [the generic name for Macrodantin]. Hemolysis appears to be linked to a glucose-6-phosphate dehydrogenase deficiency in the red blood cells of the affected patients. This deficiency is found in 10 percent of Blacks and a small percentage of ethnic groups of Mediterranean and Near-Eastern origin. Hemolysis is an indication for discontinuing Macrodantin; hemolysis ceases when the drug is withdrawn."

According to the same website, Macrodantin was introduced into the market in 1953. The doctor who prescribed Macrodantin for Veronica had at least 30 years of clinical data at his disposal from which to conclude that Macrodantin might be contra-indicated for a patient of Greek origin. If Veronica's doctor made a duly considered decision to prescribe it anyway, there was clearly a catastrophic failure in post-consultation follow-up. Moreover, if "hemolysis ceases when the drug is withdrawn," as noted by the FDA, and Veronica died from hemolysis in the hospital, the obvious question is, was the drug withdrawn? If not, why not? What, if anything, was done to stop the hemolysis?

8. Inconsistencies in the mortuary documents: The Omega Society filed an "Application and Permit for Disposition of Human Remains" for the purpose of shipping Veronica's body to her home town in Illinois. According to the document, the "informant" was Veronica's brother. The document is signed by someone (neither the brother nor the boyfriend nor a Perez) "as per Agriopoulos family." The sheet contains spaces for "Date of Disposition", "Date

Shipped", "Date Received", and "Date Interred". The original of this document is the copy retained by the cemetery (its final destination), yet those spaces show blank, evidently never having been filled in. The "Application for Burial" is dated November 4, 1989 (given as the date of burial in one of the newspaper clippings). The document states: "The undersigned hereby requests the burial in _____Cemetery of Veronica Agriopoulos," but the bottom of the document is cut off, obscuring the supposed signature. The slot for "Charges to be paid by" is left blank.

9. I have already noted the inconsistency between the information provided by the registrar and the Classics Department alumni list. While going through my documentation, I realized that I had misplaced the printout of the alumni list that showed Veronica receiving a Ph.D. in 1989. Rather than hunt for the missing sheets among the dunes, drifts and mounds of unsorted paper that pollute the landscape of my study like slag along the Lackawanna River, I returned to the Classics Department's website, intending to print another copy. Veronica's name had in the meantime been altogether expunged from the list. No Ph.D. No M.A. No Veronica.

21

If I Should Die

And if I, too, should die? Because it seems clear that, whenever Veronica died, the university and who knows who or what else, did not want others to know about it. And they knew from their website tracker and my inquiries that I was looking. Amid the suppressed and muted fear I have lived with ever since and somehow inured myself to, a hallucinating scenario began to coalesce in my mind that would have explained much.

Suppose Veronica really did die in 1989, as stated on the death certificate. She had died, according to that document, of a urinary infection that was misdiagnosed or negligently treated, or left untreated until the disease had affected her heart. But if so, why the sudden suppression of Veronica's name by the Classics Department right after they got wind that someone was inquiring about her at University Registration? Why no mention of her death in *True Grit*? And why the sequestration of the 1989 volume of *True Grit* if not to hide something? Surely the possibility of a medical malpractice suit against Student Health would not have justified such extreme measures. Such measures would not have prevented the family from suing, if that was their wish. Doctors and hospitals have malpractice insurance. There must have been something more.

Now suppose instead that Veronica died shortly after Sokrates and I visited her in 1981. JWU—and more particularly, JW Classics and the Archaica Project—would have been in a state of absolute panic over their possible legal exposure (yes, the ghost in negative of

John Strelesky!)—and even more, for the negative publicity—the public relations, financial, and professional repercussions—that threatened to engulf them, for ousting from their graduate program and concomitant financial support, a student whom they all personally knew to be totally dependent on them, one who, very arguably, was not without determination, ability and promise, one whose expulsion was apparently opposed by Dorian Prout and without a doubt would have been vociferously contested by that good soul, Parthenopides. It was known that Veronica had not been in touch with her family for many years. Is it outrageous to conjecture that someone might have devised a plan to hush everything up? For all we know, the "Veronica Agriopoulos" allegedly "readmitted" in 1984 and "enrolled" in the Classics Ph.D. Program was a *myortvyjye dushi*—a "Dead Soul", as in Gogol's famous play!

As for her obsequies, any Coroner's Office has procedures for burying unidentifiable victims. If officials are willing, it is no difficult thing to attach a false name to a nameless corpse.

Whatever the original plan, something must have happened, after a number of years, that caused it to fall apart. An inquiry from a dying parent into the whereabouts of their wayward daughter? An aunt's legacy left in her name? An investigation by the Student Loan Administration? Whatever it was, it sent those responsible for the cover-up scurrying to find a way to postdate Veronica's death. It had to be made to look recent. An opportunity had to be fabricated to notify the family and interested entities. An explanation had to be found for keeping this Born-Again Dead Soul on a Ph.D. track. Veronica's teaching credentials would have had to be post-dated or fabricated from scratch. Strings would have to be pulled. A false Death Certificate would be issued in place of the original. Another corpse—a Jane Doe—would be shipped to Illinois for burial in Veronica's stead. Fake enrollment, fake degrees, fake teaching credentials.

The Board of Governors of JWU and its sister universities are State-appointed officials, and may be presumed to have close ties with the Kalisperia Department of Education. The Governor of the

194

State of Kalisperia is the Chairman of that Board. There is an ominous pyramid of authority sitting on that campus, and all of it answerable in some degree to the same "Higher Authority" that allowed Heinrich Strauss to fly in and out of Mexico like a trip to the *tienda de abarrotes.* As for the boyfriend, it would have been easy to shut him up: he was in line for a Ph.D. in Classics. I identified him and located him and thought of contacting him directly, but discarded that option as futile and dangerous: he was implicated, and I had to regard him as one of Strauss's flunkies.

Unfortunately for the fakers, however, the bureaucrat who was instructed to doctor the Death Certificate did not sufficiently research the *causa mortis* listed in Paragraph 21(C) of the document. Or maybe he did, and blew a dog whistle that only a shlemiel with ears for music could hear?

Hemolytic anemia with thrombocytopenia secondary to probable adverse Macrodantin reaction.

With Veronica's Greek name on the same paper, the certificate remains *prima facie* evidence (*i.e.,* sufficient to file a claim) of "medical mal". If not for that oversight, and the unexplained removal of Veronica's name from the list of Classics Ph.D. and M.A. conferees, my inquiries might have ended there, but a mop, a bucket and a bottle of bleach always arouse suspicion when found in odd places.

My suspicions opened up a whole Pandora's can of red herrings—the Perez firearm, the Perez relatives, the Spanish *disfraz,* the rouged cheeks—who can say what the poor girl went through in the days or years following her expulsion? Indeed, from her departure from Metropolis, Illinois? But I digress. The hypothesis I have chosen to pursue cannot be summarily dismissed. It is sufficient to explain and reconcile the inconsistencies in Veronica's records, Professor Marcus's fakir's walk over the dying embers of his memory, the sequestration of the 1989 volume of *True Grit,* and my own best recollection.

Of course, there were other, more innocent ways of explaining all the discrepancies. Incompetence, carelessness, coincidence, compassion. Perhaps the M.A. and the Ph.D. were motivated by nothing more than a well-meant desire to honor Veronica's memory? Perhaps Veronica found herself a job in 1981, pulled herself together, enrolled in a community college, mastered her Latin, got herself readmitted to JWU in 1984, and really did die in 1989? Perhaps it wasn't a case of medical malpractice at all. Could Veronica have died because she refused further medical assistance? Could someone have persuaded her—re-Born-Again-Christian that she was—to rely on prayer? Was that why her fundamentalist boyfriend—seconded by Marcus—said nothing to her parents about misdiagnosis?

In fairness, I must also ask myself: was there something, long forgotten, that could have induced me to look up Veronica five or six years later—in 1989 or '90, perhaps—so many years after our last farewell? Could it have been another, more recent chair I jumped out of—a chair in my private study, perhaps, while talking long-distance to Sokrates?

Yes, it was possible. My memory began to shift from one chair to the other, from one year to the other. Both hypothetical chairs were consistent with the hard fossils of my recollection: she had died, I found out about it some years after the fact, and the news shocked and shook me. But what reason could I have had, so many years later, in 1989 or '90, for inquiring about Veronica in the first place? By then, I had already become a Torah-observant Jew, was perhaps already happily married. I remembered Veronica as a naïve young woman with whom I had little in common and with whom I had wisely avoided getting involved.

Well, there *was* a reason. I remembered an incident—and it still burns within me—I believe it happened during the time I was helping Veronica with her Latin. We had walked over to Don Corleone's Campus Pizza Parlor for a cup of coffee and something to eat. We were talking of loneliness and sharing our respective lonelinesses with each other. "I envy you, Ms Agriopoulos," I was saying, using her Greek last name with deliberation. "You come from a noble culture, a great and unique civilization that has managed to keep its pride in itself intact through the centuries. You have your own customs, your common language, literature, music, dance and mythology, and it's all alive and thriving. You share this with others who share your origins. You can talk to them. You can go home. You can find yourself. I can't. I'm alone. I can't effectively identify with the American heritage I was born into, because it has been repudiated by my generation, and they've replaced it with radical kitsch, and because anyway I haven't really melted into the pot, have I? Sometimes I wish I were a Greek, a Chinaman—something that would bind me others, to a people, a society, a culture . . ."

Hardly were the words out of my mouth, I blushed with shame I *had* a culture. I *had* a people, I *had* a heritage—a great, inestimable Heritage, and I had done nothing to accept it, to explore it, to appraise it, let alone appreciate or embrace it. That conversation had sat inside me for years, and it weighed on me. I had said nothing to retract this careless slander of myself, my People, my Heritage. I had said nothing to explain why my face had suddenly lit up in shameful conflagration. Now I wanted to set the record straight. I wanted to right myself in her eyes and mine. I wanted to talk to her, tell her about my experience, my return to my Heritage and my Faith. That made perfect sense to me.

But not everything that makes sense is fact. Many things happen that do not make sense. There *was* another chair, another reason to jump out of it, another death. And it was, indeed, during a phone call to Sokrates from my study. The year could well have been 1989. My father had recently died, and it was natural that my thoughts should turn at some point to Euphemios, who had treated me with paternal solicitude during my worst troubles at JW. "How is Parthenopides?" I asked, remembering the pink cherub's face and the sky-blue mug. "I haven't heard anything about him in years. Do you have any news of him?"

"Louis, Parthenopides passed away a long time ago. I thought you knew!"

I did not know. With all that Krati was going through to establish himself in his new career, he had neglected to tell me. So had my former bosses. Poor Euphemios died in 1985. Pheemy was teaching a seminar on "Poetry as a Reflection of National Culture" when he contracted a cold. The cold turned into bronchitis, the bronchitis into pneumonia, and the pneumonia killed him. At least that is the version I heard either from Krati or from an obituary posted on the noosphere by the Classics Department. If it was from the latter, it was replaced later on by another which did not mention the cause of death. The obituary published in the *Smoke and Mirror* and the *Crow's Nest* likewise omits the cause of his death. Yet another version, told to Krati by a close friend of the professor, was that his lady love found him on the bathroom floor. This faithful paramour, to whom Pheemy had apparently left nothing, disappeared without trace, possibly returning to her country of origin. During the years that followed, the friend had also died, so where he got his version could not be ascertained.

I knew Parthenopides well enough to feel certain that he would never have gone along with a plan to cover up Veronica's demise. Culture is a word that has many meanings. *Ariston Ton Hydor*. Water is best. Coffee will do. But that is beside the point.

While mulling over these half-baked conclusions, and the additional questions they raise, I received a blitz that froze the blood in my veins. Here it is, verbatim:

"Dear Mr. Yashanoshan:

"Being a classical scholar, you are often groping for words, names, phrases, and texts. And people—your potential colleagues, associates and correspondents in far places who ought to be in your professional network. We at *Argiope.com* are developing a web of associative links that can instantly provide pathways to answers and contacts even before the question or need has been properly formulated. For instance, clicking on the name Ovid in the below list will bring to your screen our patented "spidergram" containing all the main topics of research into the subject of Ovid. Clicking on any one of those topics will evoke another spidergram with further subtopical classifications, and so on, down to the dictionary meaning of each word comprising the Ovidian corpus, and the location of that word in all the Ovidian texts in which that word appears, as well as bibliographies of all published work in which those texts are cited. Participants involved in current research on Ovid are invited to submit their information. For a simple demonstration of how the system works, click on the following link and follow the instructions. We are sure you will want to join our growing number of subscribers to this fantastic research and writing aid.

—Your friends at Argiope.co, *"the writing spider"*

What caught my attention, of course, was the blitz address of the sender: verena@argiope.co. It was simply too close to be ignored. I clicked on the link provided in the body of the message, and was taken to a list of Latin words (harvested from Ovid) beginning with "L" arranged in alphabetical order. Near the top of the screen the word "languor" pulsated energetically. Obligingly, I clicked on it, whereupon, in jarring repudiation of the described system, a page of Latin text materialized followed by an English translation:

Languor enim causis non apparentibus haeret;
adiuvor et nulla fessa medentis ope.
quam tibi nunc gracilem vix haec rescribere quamque
pallida vix cubito membra levare putas?
nunc timor accedit, ne quis nisi conscia nutrix
colloquii nobis sentiat esse vices.
ante fores sedet haec quid agamque rogantibus intus,
ut possim tuto scribere, "dormit," ait.
mox, ubi, secreti longi causa optima, somnus
credibilis tarda desinit esse mora,
iamque venire videt quos non admittere durum est,
excreat et ficta dat mihi signa nota.

sicut erant, properans verba inperfecta relinquo,
et tegitur trepido littera coepta sinu.
Inde meos digitos iterum repetita fatigat;
quantus sit nobis adspicis ipse labor.
quo peream si dignus eras, ut vera loquamur;
sed melior iusto quamque mereris ego.

"The languor that clings to me is due to invisible causes. Exhausted as I am, no medicine can help me. Can you imagine how thin I am, and how I am hardly able to raise my pallid body on my elbow to write this reply? Now I grow more fearful that someone other than my caretaker (who knows all) may perceive that we are corresponding. She sits by the door, and to those who inquire what am I doing within, she replies, "She sleeps," that I may write in safety. Thus, when slumber—the most plausible explanation for my long cloistering, ceases to be believable—and now she sees approaching those whom it is hard to keep from entering—she clears her throat, giving me the prearranged sign. In haste, I leave my unfinished words just as they were, and the letter I started is hidden in my palpitating bosom. Retrieved again from thence, it fatigues my fingers. You behold how heavy this task is for me. But—if only you were worthy—let me perish thereby, that we might speak truly. But I am a better friend to you than is right, or than you deserve."

The text was from Ovid's *Heroides,* Chapter XXI—Cydippe's letter to Acontius—her reply to the very letter I had studied with Veronica! Given the context, I had no difficulty interpreting the special meaning the sender reserved for these verses:

"For reasons I cannot disclose, I am living under an assumed identity and under strict surveillance. Those who are searching for me are told that I am dead. By contacting you, I am endangering myself, and possibly you.as well. I have tried other ways of responding to you, but had to give them up lest I be discovered. I would tell you more, at the risk of my very life, if you were only worthy of it, but you are not, and in writing this much I am kinder than warranted by your behavior."

By my "behavior", I could not tell whether the sender was referring to my rejection of her so many years ago, or to my persistent inquiries into the time and manner of her purported death, or to both. It all depended on who the sender was.

Only three people could have known that this letter of Cydippe's held special significance for me: Sokrates had read an early draft of my memoir, but his English wasn't good enough for the spiel spun by the "writing spider." That left Veronica herself, and Daisy, who had sent her to me in the first place! Of course, either Daisy and Veronica could have told Heinz. Whoever it was, it seemed clear to me that I was being warned to back off. It was either Veronica's life that I was endangering, or my own.

Well, you may say that this is all the product of an overwrought imagination, a good treatment for a Hollywood script, a good plot for the movies. You may say that it is ridiculous to suppose that all this skullduggery could have emanated from inside a small and very third-rate classics department. But if you reflect on the stakes, the persons, the infrastructures; if you consider their characters, their connections and their liabilities, you will see that it is not ridiculous at all. As for me, this is still all very real, and I have given copies of all my documentation to those I trust for safekeeping in case anything were to happen . . .

22

Man of La Concha

I never saw Heinz or Daisy or Jason or Edythe or Janoš or any of that gang again. And poor Pheemy, my only friend in American Academe, was dead. Sometimes I think it was his only way out of all the domestic tangles he had got himself into.

As for Heinz Strauss, creating the Archaica Project was a remarkable feat, but I am not sure whether a praiseworthy one. Aside from the contradictory interests inherent in a project designed to preserve static data in a constantly evolving medium, the Ark—not unlike the original Ark of four thousand years ago, had just enough space (*read:* economic resources) to digitize only those editions of ancient text deemed by a putative majority of contemporary critics to be the most authoritative. By this process of "natural selection", the Archaica Project willfully, if reluctantly, consigned many significant variant textual traditions and insightful reconstructions to presumptive drowning in the seas of time.

While this eventuality has to some extent been mitigated, thanks to various technological advances and the ongoing electronic scanning of many thousands of disintegrating books, the availability of innumerable authors and texts in machine-readable form has led to a proliferation of machine-based research. The trend, characterized by an avalanche of computer-generated concordances and "frequency" analyses (how often a certain author uses a certain word or phrase or phoneme) both fostered and condoned a concomitant decline in the publishing of thoughtful, imaginative work. The scholars' lament—occasionally in print—that "all the major discoveries have been made" became a justification and an excuse.

Nevertheless, thanks ultimately to Strauss's efforts, perhaps there will be time for the West to recover its bearings and rediscover its great classical heritage before one or the other disintegrates beyond repair. It took someone like ol' 57 Varieties to do the job—to network the globe and wheedle and lie and bluff and bluster and cajole his way through the apathy, the ignorance, and the narrow-minded invidiousness of the most ingrown, inbred and crabby of all academic fields. I liked and respected Heinz for abhorring the stereotype and actively avoiding it.

Ironically, however, Strauss lacked the high-mindedness that was the essence of the legacy he worked so hard to preserve. I never once saw him ecstatic over a verse of Homer or of Virgil, but I know how much he enjoyed his designer house, his computer toys, his Caddy, his guns, his loudspeakers, his ham radio equipment, his fine, casual weeds and his fine, casual wines. He was a politikant, an intriguant who fell into a good cause and turned it into a great career.

Strauss must have had high Federal connections. Nothing else could explain the drugs, the freedom and candor displayed in regard to that subject, or the severity of the scolding I got for worrying about what others were smoking. Nothing else could have explained the extreme measures taken to keep Veronica's death—or perhaps Veronica herself—out of the public eye.

There was a lot more at stake here than bad publicity. I once shared with Heinz the story of a curious encounter I had, toward the end of my Italian sojourn, with a certain professor from the University of Hyperborea. The fellow was chaperoning a herd of yokels studying at the Istituto di Lingua e Cultura Italiana for their semester abroad. After a brief acquaintance, the man—a Pole, by name and accent—offered to have me take over his job so he could return Stateside for "medical treatments." He had me write up my bio "for the dean," and then vanished. Nothing came of the offer, and nobody knew anything about it at the Istituto, or at Hicksville U., where the dean had never heard of me. As for the professor, added the dean, he couldn't be reached, since he had very regrettably "died." Obviously, the bio I had written under false pretenses disappeared. Heinz casually seconded my hypothesis that the man was a CIA operative. "Yeah, in those days, it was not uncommon for Government to enlist college faculty to keep tabs on Americans studying abroad."

In those days?

Heinz must have known what he was talking about, but he was not being candid. A few hours' mousing through excerpts from the *Church Committee Report* and the peripheral literature concerning intelligence operations on university campuses throughout the Country were enough to convince me that if there was any paranoia involved, it was not mine. To be sure, I don't know whether Heinz's trafficking activities were authorized by his handlers, or merely tolerated; but I am certain that the Agency had no reasonable motive or interest to destroy my academic career. At best, Strauss was a rogue agent who abused for his own ends his license to recruit and to spy. Like him, there must have been a thousand others, heady with the power that had been wantonly dropped into their hands. I scraped by; but how many good people's lives, careers, reputations, have they destroyed?

One has to ask: what was it about the Ark that would have cemented the quiet patronage of the Feds? Their passion for Ancient Greek lyric poetry? The Archaica Project fostered the evolution of very sophisticated new software that availed itself, moreover, of experimental hardware being developed by one of the more prominent computer companies in the country. Clearly, any practical advances in the field of digital data storage and retrieval would be of interest to the various intelligence communities working under Government auspices. The software and organization of labor developed by and for the Archaica Project was cutting edge. Clearly the Feds were warily testing that blade against their fingernail like ritual slaughterers.

Still, I found it impossible to explain why Strauss did to me what he did. I harbored no reason or desire to do him ill. He caused me a great deal of harm. At my groveling entreaty, he eventually wrote me a letter of recommendation, but it contained one or two subtle turns of phrase which made me chary of using it. I was afraid to name him as a reference, but I had no alternative if I was to remain in Classics. I did not remain in Classics. I was never again called for an interview.

As a test, I applied for and obtained a listing in the teachers' pool of the Kalisperia Community College system, making sure to name Heinz as my most important reference. I have forgotten how much time I let pass, but, after a few years without a response, I presented myself at the Smokes office of the KCCS and asked to see my file. Predictably, I was told that the file was confidential, and that I could not see it.

"But it's my file!" I protested. Nothing doing. I called for the head clerk, asked to speak to him privately and explained my situation candidly in a little side room. The man was sympathetic. He retrieved the file, looked through it, but refused apologetically to divulge its contents. A phone rang outside and he excused himself, saying he "had to get that." The file lay on the table in front of me. I am sure now that he left it there on purpose to give me the opportunity to examine it, but I was unable to move a finger. Imagine that! I just sat there frozen, staring at it. I guess I was terrified that it might be some kind of trap.

Not long after that, I applied and, thanks to some string pulling by Rachel Wago, was accepted into medical school. It was a long, hard haul, and I forgot about Heinz and his cronies and John Wayne and Nirvana and Egil Heklason and Philodemus's poem. I also forgot most of my Greek and my Latin. Veronica lingered in my mind like an evanescent melody.

When my father died, a few years after my Nirvana experience, I was astounded, amid my abysmal grief, to receive a letter of condolence from Heinz Strauss. "I know what it means to lose a father," he wrote! It was the last straw. It must have been around that time that two people came to me during sleep and said to me in the blurred, conceptual words of a dream, "Your case against Professor Strauss has come before the Court, and he has been found wanting. What is the punishment you ask for him?"

"Death," I murmured, thinking less of my own pain than of the indignity inflicted on my father that night at JWU. Then, as they turned to leave, I called out to them. "Wait!" I said. "Don't kill him!

He fed me and housed me and paid my bills for three years."

Not much later, I got a phone call from Hoss Cartwright. He told me, among other things, that a while back Heinz Strauss had been hit by a truck as he was crossing the street. Seriously injured, he had nevertheless survived and recovered.

Reliving my travails on the Ark in order to write them, I regretted my access of misericordia. So what that John Wayne sent me a check every month that was gone days before the next one came? So what that Strauss gave me three years of the only steady employment I have ever known in my chosen field? Classics had been my love, my muse, my mistress. I had spent years in straitened exile to court and conquer her. I had shivered autumn nights in a drafty convent to win her. I had sloshed in my slippers through midwinter snow and slush to cold-shower in outdoor stalls to melt her heart. I had suffered agonies of loneliness and doubt while translating sheepslaughtering *Aias*. Thanks to ol' Heinz, I spent the rest of my working life struggling to maintain my station in a career for which I was not constitutionally fitted and my equilibrium under the staggering load of neuroses and insecurities retrieved from the dark caves of my patients' formidable subconsciouses. I dealt, too, with years of attenuated terror—fear of being watched, of being followed, of being assassinated. And Heinz knew, as he lied to me through his hateful teeth, that if I ever saw him drowning I would throw him a rope.

I never saw him drown. As I was ruminating over the final corrections to my manuscript, a letter arrived from an acquaintance from whom I would have sooner expected a carrier pigeon. It contained an obit from the *Daily Smoke and Mirror*. It said:

"Heinrich Strauss, 72: Creator of JWU's Archaica Project."

Lung Cancer. The obituary added little about Noah's life that I have not already relayed in these pages. However, from the day I left the Ark, Heinz's fate and that of his companions had remained a Terra Incognita into which I had no desire to venture on what would have been a very ill-advised safari. Thus, I was surprised (and yet not very) to read:

> A man who had spent his life immersed in Greek and Latin letters took an unusual career detour after retiring in 1998: He became a reserve officer for the Porto Madeira Police Department, patrolling the streets and enforcing the letter of the law. A ham radio enthusiast, Strauss got involved with the Porto Madeira Police by assisting the agency with its emergency response efforts, said his wife Daisy, who also volunteers with the department.

So they had finally tied the knot! When? On his deathbed? Posthumously? Or when they left Bohemia for the button-down world of cops and robbers and parking tickets? Or was it all a crock?

> After retiring from the university, he enrolled in the Concha County Sheriff's Academy in 2001 and graduated at age 67, by far the oldest member of his class. He served as a reserve officer for the Porto Madeira Police Department until September of 2005, when he was diagnosed with cancer.

It had taken him a good couple of years to die. The article, dated September __, 2007, is graced by a posed snapshot of Heinz and Daisy standing white-haired beside their patrol car. Heinz, holstered, uniformed and badged, fearsome behind tinted glasses, Daisy, partly shielded by the open door, grinning idiotically in police-issue shirt and tie, reaching for something at her hip that was hidden by the rearview mirror. Heinz had fudged his age to get into the police academy—or perhaps for other reasons—for at his bracket I can't understand why five or six years would matter one way or the other. I remember very well that "Big Five-0" birthday party in 1978 or '79. That would make him 77 or 78 at death, not 72. But Strauss had made a gut gesheft of trading in time, had he not?

It took me a few years to figure it out, but as gratuitous as were the things that Heinrich Strauss did to me, they were not without his special brand of exasperated logic. My skirmish with academia had so discomfited me that many years were to pass before I remembered that I had shown a distinct talent for classics, a genuine flair for research, and an organized, systematic approach to scholarship. This, Heinz and Daisy would have seen at once. It was more than just my command of the necessary languages: they could see that I possessed the basic skills needed to tackle Philodemus—an undertaking whose complexity the Ark was as yet unequipped to deal with. In their scholarly mediocrity, Heinz and Daisy saw me as a ripe apple with "Philodemus" inscribed around its edible equator in golden letters: a windfall, a godsend! Had I not been assured that my Italian credentials were equivalent to a Ph.D., I might, they feared, leave the Ark to enroll in a graduate studies program. Had I not had the stuffing beaten out of me, all this would have been obvious to me long ago.

That was why they hired Concetta, whose Italian proved largely superfluous. They needed to assure themselves that my participation was not all that essential to the Philodemus project; that if I chose to leave, it would be with their blessing; that they could replace me with Concetta. But Concetta, for all her Tuscan charm, was a scatterbrain for whom the Philodemus bibliography remained something arcanely quaint. Heinz never even bothered to have me train her as a backup! Sure, she could have carried on where I left off, but there was no need. The job was done.

As surreal a tack as Heinz's life took in retirement, what he did was in essence no different from my own fantastic face-about. How does a Jew, born, raised and educated in a secular and "free-thinking" environment, find himself suddenly at home and at one with a Community of "Ultra-Orthodox" Jews?

I like to flatter myself that I came to the realization (and it didn't happen overnight) that one who aspires to justness has no place in the world unless he makes a place for himself among the just. I believe this holds true even if we admit that the human condition compels us to tweak the definition of "the just" to little more than honest men and women who band together to help each other behave correctly and who constantly work on themselves in order to improve. Simple souls who gather around the truly accomplished among us in order to learn from their example and follow it.

Apart from a true Tzaddik, there is nothing that lives that is not influenced by its worldly, day-to-day environment. I like to flatter myself that I had sufficient self-perception to recognize myself in others and see in myself the incipient signs of moral decay that I despised in others; that I saw my true face turning into a mask which concealed traits and tendencies that were foreign and repugnant to my nature—an alien pod that had already twirled its tendrils around my innermost being and affected my behavior, my speech and my thinking; that I saw that the refinements of art, literature, music and intellectual pursuits were not sufficient to defend an ordinary soul from the inroads of vulgarity, sensuality and spiritual atrophy; that, on the contrary, I saw how such intellectual and esthetic refinements not only increased the appetite for their opposites in physical gratification, but also served ignobly to rationalize, dissemble, disguise and even dignify the very same baseness in myself that I scorned in others.

I did see all this. I saw it in the Villa dei Papiri, I saw it in the Ark, and I saw it in myself. It became necessary to choose between the path of my righteous ancestors—the path of Torah and holiness on the one hand—and the path of decadence and ruination on the other. It became imperative to exchange the environment of Sodom, not for the wilderness of the hermit or the seclusion of a monastery, but, like Joseph Knecht—the hero of Hesse's *Magister Ludi*, who renounced a castrated utopia to wade into the seas of turbulent humanity—for the suffering and imperfect school of men and women whose merits outweigh their demerits, whose spiritual and material labors bring justice and decency into the world and into their own lives.

It occurred to me that if there was such a school, if such a people existed—a people in the world but not confined to it—then they would be the most contemned and ridiculed, the most misrepresented, misunderstood and hated of all peoples. It occurred to me that if the teaching and example and society of this people could restore me to my true self, then it would be worthwhile, despite everything, to become one of them. My only problem was, I didn't know how. And then I remembered: I didn't have to *become*. I already *was*. All that I needed was a little work. A great deal of work, as it turned out.

Nevertheless, I fear the truth is both simpler and less flattering. Like Heinz, I found myself without a job, without a network of support, fearful of the future, fearful of the enemies I had made and the wrongs I had done. Like Heinz, I had sought refuge among my own kind. Like Heinz, I threw away the mask and reconciled myself to the spirit within me.

With suchlike thoughts, I dropped the obit into my desk drawer. I was late for Minyan. As I headed out the front door and clicked the clicker, a crow flew over my head, cawing, and dropped a memento on my left shoulder.

"Nevermore, you sonofabitch!" quoth I aloud as I wiped the mess with a kleenex. Then, quite suddenly, I exploded in a fit of laughter that melded with his from already halfway down the block.

23

The River Pauses

There is one Narrative for all humanity, but it changes accent according to who is speaking. My Biblical great grandfather Zimri, a prince of Shimon renowned for his song (*zemirah*), led a Moabite princess to his tent in full sight of the assembled People and in the presence of an outraged, onlooking God. Intent upon his pleasure, Zimri failed to look behind him. Both he and she died in the act, spitted through on the spear of a righteous and zealous man who was rewarded with the priesthood.

Orpheus, another musical luminary (*Ohr Peh*, Hebrew for "Light of the Mouth"), a priest of Dionysus and founder of erotic mystery cults, never consummated his wedding. The chaste Eurydike, fleeing the lust of an enflamed satyr, trod on a deadly snake. Rejecting fate and braving the river Lethe, Orpheus followed her into Hades where with plaintive song he extracted permission to retrieve her from death—on the sole condition that he not look behind him. However, as his bride followed him up, he, anxious, looked over his shoulder, losing her forever to wander in the gloaming.

Though Zimri and his whore princess were returned to daylight spitted through from the dark shame of his tent, Zimri's death saved Israel from destruction by halting the plague unleashed by God's anger. Having fully atoned for his terrible sin, Zimri is remembered honorably, though briefly, as Shelumiel, the Israelite prince who had brought Tribal offerings into the newly inaugurated *Mishkan*—the

Holy Tabernacle.

Distraught and contrite after his failed mission to the underworld, "Mouthlight" entered the service of Apollo—the sun god—to impart the mysteries he had gleaned from the infernal darkness. With such presumption, the novice priest offended his previous patron, Dionysus, the mystery-god of drunken ribaldry and unbridled lust. The latter sicced upon the faithless servant his ecstatic female acolytes, the Maenads. These burst in on the poet as he preached, and hacked him to pieces. The severed head, by the way, kept on singing, until Apollo, his patience exhausted, told it to shut up—but only after it had floated to the shores of Lesbos—the Greek isle of lyric poetry and Sapphic love.

Both versions of this ur-narrative have to do with repentance, yet the one stands strictly in relation to the other as positive to negative.

How is this inversion to be explained? Here is a diagram:

1.   The kingdom of Moab sends a Moabite harlot to seduce Zimri into sexual immorality.

Eurydike, Orpheus's virgin bride, pursued by an enflamed satyr, dies bitten by a snake, symbol of sexual immorality.

2.   Zimri, accompanied by his whore, wades through a flowing crowd of Israelites, and enters his tent to commit fornication. The sight of vast throngs of his brethren streaming to assemble before Moses should have reminded Zimri of himself, his princely status and his consecrated purpose, but in spite of the remonstrances of his fellows, it did not. The unholy union is consummated.

Orpheus, unaccompanied, enters the world of the dead in order to retrieve his betrothed, a woman of chastity. Their union is never consummated. Crossing the river Lethe should have wiped the poet's memory clean of every vestige, but it did not.

3. Zimri, absorbed in his lust, fails to look behind him, thus allowing both himself and his whore to be killed in one stroke by a man who will be rewarded with the priesthood: one stroke, two victims.

Orpheus, transgressing the sole condition enabling his descent into Hades, looks behind him, inadvertently bringing irreversible death to his dead bride: one victim, two strokes. He subsequently confers on himself the priesthood of Apollo.

4. Zimri's sin is "cured" *ante factum* by Shelumiel-Zimri's bringing Tribal gifts into the Holy Tabernacle.

Orpheus's transgression is "cured" *post factum* by his bringing the "New Mysteries" into the temple of Apollo.

5. Zimri's conduct offended God, Who sent a plague to destroy the Israelite camp.

Orpheus's conduct offended Dionysus, who has Orpheus torn limb from limb.

6. Zimri ("My Song") lives on in the memory of Shelumiel's gift.

Orpheus (Light of the Mouth) lives on in the tradition of lyric song rooted in in the Island of Lesbos.

The social context in which Zimri's fall took place was one of strict law and a divinely imposed code of sexual morality. As a descendent of Adam, he shared the appetites and lusts of all humanity; but as a son of Israel and a pupil of Moses, he had inherited all the tools a man needs to avert temptation and live by the straight and narrow. Zimri forfeited the opportunity to repent by neglecting to look back over his shoulder at the pious and law-abiding society in which he was raised. In so doing, he surrendered his own soul to an evil woman sent from a hostile camp expressly to destroy him and his People through moral corruption.

Conversely, *Ohr Peh* lived in a time and place of licentious lawlessness, but his love for the chaste Eurydike ("Strait Justice" or, in Hebrew, *Tzaddeket*) was genuine and pure, the institution of marriage moral and honorable. The venom that killed her—and threatened the sanctity of marriage—was the inescapable immorality of the very society in which both she and he were raised. Orpheus's severed head, presaged so dramatically in the Bronzino portrait last seen in Ugo Marinelli's underground workshop, represents the dystony, so familiar to the creative psyche, between the inspired head and the lusting heart.

When a pure soul is wounded through the example of its immediate surroundings, the wounds can be sown up. Such a soul can be saved from ruin. But *Teshuvah*—"Return," the Hebrew word for repentance—only works if the subject is scrupulous not to look back. Orpheus lost more than his bride when he turned to dwell on his past: his dismemberment by the handmaids of Dionysus confirms the inefficacy of his repentance. Lot's wife, Iris ("rainbow" in Greek), also looked back with regret for the free and easy life of the doomed cities. Her ambivalence changed her into a pillar (phallus) of salt—salt: the drawer of forbidden blood—in just retribution for her laxity in the laws of intercourse and kashering meat. Like Eurydike, the Greek Iris, too, is depicted on Greek vases (5th Century BCE) as lust-bait of satyrs; like Orpheus, she, too attempted to disrupt the licentious rites of Dionysus.

The Christian savior has taught, "Resist not evil" (Matthew 5:39). But this meant much more than "turn the other cheek." To a Jew schooled in the holy Tradition, it meant, "Don't try to wrestle with evil; just turn away from it and do good." Jewish Teaching rejects as pagan the Greek idea that human beings must have a safety valve for their animal instincts, a periodic fire for a controlled burn, a safety net for a controlled fall. The base animal is an indefatigable seducer. The safety valve quickly turns into a fuse-hole, the controlled burn into a conflagration, the safety net into a playing field. The Torah teaches that by focusing on deeds of *Chessed* ("Lovingkindness"), by nurturing compassionate and respectful consideration for others—both humans and animals—by occupying our minds with God's wisdom and awesomeness, by studying and practising His Laws, we weaken and disarm the animal aspects of our psyche while strengthening the divine.

Jesus, too, supposedly taught that same lesson, but his followers did not always understand him aright.

24

The River Is Dragged

Assuming that Heinz is not still alive and sunning himself on some private Mexican beach, it seems ironic that his shade should have climbed unaccompanied out of the fire to pursue me in Smokes. For he had many years before contrived a message that he must have planned to send me under contingencies that happily never developed. The message reached me, nonetheless, in a circuitous way that even he could not have prearranged.

I was treating a young man, a graduate student on a break from one of the football colleges in the Midwest. "Brock", as I shall call him here, presented with a type of obsessive-compulsive neurosis associated with the pornographic material with which the noosphere is rife, thanks to the exertions of its untouchable purveyors. Without going deep into Brock's background, I will say that he manifested symptoms of guilt, shame and low self-esteem arising from his inability to steer his normal sexual interest into healthier channels. The intensity of his quest for self-understanding was noteworthy. In fact, though I warned him that his stated budget was far short of what a full course of therapy would cost, Brock insisted he wanted to pursue it as long as the money held out.

I must digress briefly to elaborate that a child growing up in contemporary western society is daily assaulted practically from infancy by images, writings, and public conduct calculated to draw him or her into a world of ever-thickening darkness—and not by seedy characters whispering *hssst* in dark corners, as in Victorian London—but by publications openly displayed on newsstands, in liquor stores and supermarkets, by movies, television, billboards, and the noosphere, with the full sanction of society and the law. I mean the same law that ultimately and hypocritically protects the vilest pornography on the controversial theory that it provides a redemptive "safety valve" for those psycho-sexual pressures that might otherwise explode into violence.

The machinery behind such insidious complicity is of course essentially commercial, though naturally there are those who attempt to defend it on ideological grounds. In fact, however, as Janoš had pointed out, virtually no cultural significance attaches to mere visual representations of sexual activity, whose only "redeeming" function is to advertise and sell *itself* as a meretricious commodity—hardly an adequate First-Amendment shield for a commerce with such negative ramifications!

The effect of such regulatory laxity, apart from the direct economic benefit to the parasites and mobsters who run the industry, is to inculcate habits and behaviors that evolve, if left unchecked, toward a demeaned life, an imperiled and degraded citizenry, and ultimately, to a diseased, lawless and violent society. The descent is facilitated by the physiology of the brain, which is mapped out in such a way as to promote procreation irrespective of context, manner, or moral or legal restraints; and by public policy, which smiles on the cash and tax revenues generated by the trade. Hence the necessary interposition of religious laws of sexual morality as sentinels of civilized society—that same civilized society which under the triple and frivolously waved flags of "Freedom of Speech", "Free Enterprise", and "Separation of Powers", seeks unremittingly to dismantle them.

During our introductory session, it became evident that "Brock" was especially troubled by one short video which he referred to several times, ultimately requesting that I view it and discuss it with him.

Declining repeatedly, in deference to established professional norms, his pleas to view the material, I encouraged my client to verbalize the reasons for his special discomfort with this particular specimen. Finally, I was able to coax from him that he feared that the arousal he felt in response to viewing the action was a manifestation of dangerous, if not criminal, tendencies.

"More likely," I said, "it is a manifestation of your obsessive need to revisit something that you witnessed as a small child and that you buried in your subconscious mind."

"Come on, Sherlock! How would you know what I saw yesterday or as a small child?"

"I don't, but you do, and I think you have come here to ask me to help you find it."

"Why would I ask you to do that?"

"Because when you remember it and understand it, you will gradually lose interest in your video and others like it, and eventually in pornography altogether, and be able to get on with your life and hopefully enjoy it."

"But you haven't even watched the video!"

Finally, unable to overcome his determination, I conceded that if Brock would provide me with the link, I would view the material privately in my office, and discuss it with him when I had had the opportunity to think about its contents. I made my promise contingent on one condition. "In return," I told the young man, "I want you to read a certain short story that I find very pertinent to your situation. Will you do that?"

"What short story is that?"

"I gather that you have read Arthur Conan Doyle?"

"In college I took an elective course in detective fiction. We read a couple of Sherlock Holmes stories. I thought they were great."

"Have you read 'The Man with the Twisted Lip'? No? I'd like you to read it and think about it," I said, as I pulled my dog-eared copy of *The Sherlock Holmes Reader* off the shelf. "Here. Take it home and keep it. I'm going to discuss it with you and ask you to tell me how you think it relates to your case."

"Is this some kind of test?"

"Don't worry," I said, smiling, "I won't be grading you. I have something in mind. Besides, you want to have a discussion about your video, and I want to discuss the story. Fair is fair."

To be honest, I would never have acceded to Brock's request, for true healing begins with the patient learning to verbalize his deepest anxieties, rather than merely displaying what triggers them. Brock was setting himself up for a detour. However, his reluctance to put his distress into words had been extreme. He had viewed the material, found it reprehensible and shocking, yet violently exciting. He wanted to know how to deal with this unbidden response, what it meant, and how to quash it. I hoped that knowing I had seen what he was referring to might help him overcome his inability to speak about it.

There was another reason why I wrote down the link. I had already formed from Brock's tentative and halting description of its contents the suspicion that I had already seen this video myself, as an 8 mm. film, a long time ago, when as a youth and young man I stumbled into a condition not qualitatively dissimilar to his, and from which I had thankfully recovered under a self-imposed regime of my own experimental design—a regime inspired by the very story I had just prescribed to my young client. The flashback awakened a vague feeling that there was something unresolved about that dreadful experience that I still needed to confront.

Sherlock Holmes fans may remember "The Man with the Twisted Lip" as perhaps the most psychologically layered of all the tales written by Conan Doyle. The action begins as Dr. Watson, Holmes's trusted friend and chronicler, makes his way to an opium den to retrieve an errant patient from the jaws of addiction and restore him to his frantic wife, who had earlier solicited the doctor's help. As Watson leaves the den with his unresisting ward, he feels a tug at the skirt of his coat and turns to discover none other than the wily Holmes spying out the premises in the disguise of an inveterate opium addict.

The circumstance that has brought the dignified Holmes to such a disreputable locale turns out to be a mirror image of the first encounter: another wife, equally distraught, has engaged Holmes to rescue her own missing husband, whom she has last seen from the street gesticulating at a window located over the very same opium den. Sensing her husband to be in some sort of danger, she rushes up the stairway, only to be blocked by the ruffian den master. The wife summons the police, who, happening by at that very moment, accompany the woman upstairs to the only room on the upper floor.

They find it empty save for its sole occupant, a crippled beggar. If it was really her husband that the woman saw from below, he could only have disappeared through a second window opposite the one facing the street. This second window overlooks the flooded banks of the swollen Thames.

We know that the river Thames flows through Holmes's London, but Doyle suppresses the name, referring to it only as *the river.* Finding the husband's clothes in a pile by the window, the police conclude that the poor man either jumped or was dumped into the water.

Only one person can know what really happened—the beggar (owner of the disfigured lip in the story's title), who lodges in the very room where the victim was last seen and his clothes found. Known to have been home when the tragedy unfolded, yet denying any knowledge of the matter, the beggar is consequently arrested and charged with murder. Meanwhile, the victim's coat is fished from the water, but his body is never found. Therein lies the mystery.

Even Holmes is stumped, but after an all-night session in his own apartment, alternately dreaming upon a luxurious pile of cushions and cogitating in the opiate manner of an oriental pasha, he realizes that the jailed suspect can be none other than the woman's husband. Indeed, as it turns out, this unfortunate, unbeknownst to family and friends, has been spending his work-days in the street in beggarly disguise!

How did this once respectably bourgeois civil servant get himself wrapped up in a double life of shame and deception? The explanation for this remarkable twist (the "lip" of the gentleman's disguise) is no less curious than the plot itself. It transpires that years before, as a tyro journalist, he had been assigned to write an article on the beggars of London, and profited so successfully from the experiment, that later, under financial duress, he turned to mendicancy on a professional basis! Of this change, however, he assiduously neglected to inform his family and friends.

How this story relates to my treatment of Brock will presently emerge, but first I must discuss the offending video.

The link provided by my young client transported me, through a gauntlet of salacious ads, offers and solicitations, to the expected video. My suspicion was confirmed as soon as it started to run: the staging, the plot, and the young woman were unmistakable: a couple is shown in a lawyer's office, where they are finalizing the terms for their divorce. From the dialog, which is in German, it is evident that the husband has just been forced into a settlement that he regards as egregiously unfair. Moreover, as they leave the office, the woman bids the humiliated husband auf wiedersehen with a gross insult.

In the next scene, the divorced husband approaches a group of lounging construction workers, whose assistance he hires in the cause of revenge. They are to do to her physically what she has done to him emotionally and financially. Per his instructions, they abduct the woman and drive her to a deserted warehouse, where the ex-husband views the proceedings from behind a stack of cardboard boxes. From the man's unsuccessful attempts at arousing himself, the viewer is perhaps intended to surmise the ostensible cause of the divorce.

My young client appeared the following week, punctual, eager, and nervous.

"Did you watch the video?" he asked, bypassing the customary civilities.

"I did, but I want to discuss the story I gave you, first. Have you read it?"

"I read it three times, but I don't see how it is relevant."

"Well, let's see if it is or isn't. What do you think the story is about?"

"I need us to talk about the video."

"And I promise you, we will. Many tens of thousands of people have seen this video, and, disturbing as it is, they are most likely not a danger to society. Neither are you. Got that? Now, what about 'The Man with the Twisted Lip'?"

"Well, this woman asks Sherlock Holmes to . . ."

"No. I don't want you to retell me the story. What is the subject of the story, generally?"

Brock thought for a minute. "I guess it's about addiction—how this guy disguises himself as a disgusting beggar, and then becomes

221

addicted to it."

"So it's not just about addiction, is it? What's the other important word you mentioned?"

A long pause. "Disguise?"

"Yes. Right. So it's about addiction and disguise, isn't it? In fact, how does the story begin?"

"Well, Dr. Watson discovers Holmes disguised as an opium addict."

"Right, but let's forget their names for a moment and just stick to their generic roles. How does the doctor make this discovery?"

"Holmes . . . sorry, the man disguised as an opium addict tugs at the 'skirt' of his jacket—I guess that means he gets his attention—and Holmes is not really an addict."

"Well, ironically, he is, actually, but we'll get to that later. The 'skirt' means the bottom edge of the jacket, and, sticking to their functional roles, we have a respectable man playing the part of an opium addict and trying to attract the attention of a doctor. Is that relevant?"

"Oh, I see! You mean like me calling you and asking for an appointment?"

"Exactly."

"But I'm not an opium addict."

"Hold on. Now, shift to the next panel. The distraught wife begs the famous detective to find her missing husband, who, she has reason to believe, is in danger. Looking once more at the functional roles, what is this panel about?"

"Another plea for help?"

"Yes, but different from the first panel, isn't it? In what way?"

"This time the plea is coming from the man's wife. In the first panel, it's the detective—I mean, the false addict himself—who tugs at the doctor's coat."

"Right. And what does the wife represent?"

"I guess she loves her husband and is worried about him."

"And what does she do about it?"

"Well, she engages Holmes—the private eye—to find him."

"Yes, but what did she do before that?"

"She tries to rescue him herself. She goes inside the building where she thinks she saw her husband at the window."

"And?"

"Her way is barred by this evil Lascar fellow. I did look that up, by the way. Lascars were foreign sailors employed by the British Navy. What do you suppose Doyle meant by putting a Lascar in the role of an evil oppressor? Was he some kind of racist?"

"Lascar is a Hindu or Persian word meaning 'army.' Maybe Doyle wanted to suggest that the wife's attempt to save the endangered husband was blocked by an army of evil forces that thrive on the exploitation of addicts. Did you notice that Lascar is an anagram of 'rascal?' The Lascars were recruited from the British Colonies. Doyle was writing at the high point of the British Empire, but I don't think that Lascar is used here to convey a racial message.

"But let's get back to our analysis of the story. Can we say then that the Lascar represents dark psychological forces that threaten the open and loving relationship between a man and a woman? Do you think that this analogy can apply to you?"

"I'm not sure. How, exactly?"

"Let's see. Do you have a girlfriend? No? Do you think you might have one if you did not allow yourself to become, shall we say, distracted?"

"OK, I see what you mean."

"And can we say, also, that the distraught wife represents a part of your own mind—some would say your 'soul,' your 'conscience,' your 'guardian angel'—who, finding herself unable to rescue you by herself, prompted you to seek the help of a therapist?"

"Yes. OK. That fits."

"And that she is much distressed over your current state?"

"Yes. I get it."

"Great! Now let's move on to the next panel. We have moved upstairs into the room of the beggar with the twisted lip. We find him dressed in his habitual rags. Nothing is left of the endangered husband but a pile of his gentleman clothes. Is the husband alive or dead?"

"At this point, we don't know. It could be either-or. Like

Schrödinger's cat."

"Right. (Laughing.) So how does this cat relate to you?"

"Well, I suppose that if I recover from this addiction, the cat will be found alive, and if I don't, well . . ."

"Remember, we're not talking about a physical death here—you'll be just fine. Now what about the beggar with the twisted lip? Is he a killer?"

"No. He is just a sell-out who has demeaned himself for easy profit."

"Actually, that is for the final panel. But meantime, yes, he is a harmless beggar whose only friends are the occasional passers-by who absolve themselves of their indifference by dropping a few spare coins into his hat. You understand that 'easy profit' doesn't necessarily mean money, don't you?"

"I'm not sure what you mean."

"I mean when you want to be with a woman, and you settle for a bit of visual stimulation, and the stimulation provides you with the relief you feel you need. That's profit of some sort, isn't it? And since it is easier and quicker than dating and courtship, or building a reputation among the ladies as a charming and desirable companion, it becomes a habit. But how does this particular habit leave you feeling?"

"Pretty awful. I mean, that's why I'm here, isn't it?"

"Unfulfilled? Anxious? Lonely? Miserable? Isn't that like the well-bred gentleman who chooses easy profit over self-respect?"

"Yes. I see that."

"In fact, doesn't the man say at the end that he would rather die than have his family know the truth? Can you relate to that?"

"Yes. I guess so."

"But *he* knows the truth, doesn't he?"

"Obviously."

"And, knowing the truth, how can he be happy?"

"But his wife and children love him, don't they?"

"Yes, they do. But whom do they love? Is it the real him? Do they love the beggar with the twisted lip, or do they love someone disguised as a well-bred gentleman?"

"Wait a minute. You're switching things around! I thought the beggar with the lip was the disguise. Are you saying now that the man in the fine clothes is the real disguise? Which is which?

"Exactly! Isn't that the question? Isn't that the very question the gentleman must be asking himself every time he goes home?"

"See, that's where I get confused. I don't understand, really, how I am supposed to be like some guy going around disguised as a beggar. I am just looking for a way out of my neurosis, as you call it."

"Which brings us back to the first panel, doesn't it? What was the very civilized Holmes doing in an opium den disguised as a beggar? Remember, Holmes is on the trail of the vanished husband, but as Sherlock Holmes fans well know, he has his own addiction, right?"

"Opium?"

"He shoots cocaine. So what do you think he could be thinking about? What would you be thinking about in his position?"

"*Who am I?* and *do I really belong here?*"

"Very good! And who are you?"

"I was hoping you would tell me."

"No. It won't help if I tell you. I want *you* to tell *me*."

Our hour was about up, so I said, "Let's start from there next week."

"What about the video? Aren't we going to talk about it?"

"We will, at the right time. Let's get a handle on it before we take the lid off that pot. Remember my last question. Who are you? I want you to think about that. It's not an easy question. Prepare your best answer for our next appointment. And then we'll discuss the video."

I did not see Brock. again. He called a few days later to cancel his appointment, alleging his inability to pay. I did not quite believe him, although he had raised this issue during his first appointment. I asked him if there wasn't another reason.

"Look," he replied, "I budgeted a certain amount for this therapy, and half of it is gone. If I need to talk about books, I can join a book club for free."

"Well, you must do as you see fit, but what I've given you is not literary criticism. You made it clear from the start that your budget was not enough to sustain a full course of therapy, so I've given you a formula for self-healing. Don't underestimate it, because that's what that story is. It is your mantra. And don't hesitate to call me if you change your mind."

Holmes, as noted, was an addict himself, and although opium was not his particular cup of tea, the famous seven-percent solution found its way into Holmes's virtual veins whenever their owner was too long deprived of the stimulus of an unsolved crime. Thus, Holmes's espionage of the opium den is in a sense a pretext for some serious Holmesian introspection. With all due respect for the great detective's imperturbable focus, there is no way the wily logician could have sat there for hours without giving intermittent thought to his own condition—which is precisely what I was hoping to inspire in Brock during his visits to his own personal den.

Doyle never overtly reveals the origins of Holmes's dependency, but the author deliberately affords us glimpses into the bleakness of his character's emotional life—a barrenness only partially alleviated by his sincere, if stilted, friendship with Dr. Watson. It is a touching father-son, relationship, but one that can only render more salient the ghastly loneliness of the great sleuth-after-truth! "Watson!" What son indeed? What love? What life?

I hoped that my patient would get the message and start searching for the early causes of his particular neurosis. Freud, as is known, would have suspected an early traumatic encounter with a "primal scene". I always regretted that I did not take the opportunity to discuss this with my young patient, but I knew that I had given him the tools for discovering it on his own, and this would give him more powerful insight than if I led him by the hand.

In retrospect, it was also unfortunate that Brock and I never got around to analyzing the guilty video. The fault was entirely mine, for in my attachment to orderly progression I underestimated the immediacy of the young man's need for reassurance. Moreover, allowing the patient to view the forbidden images and analyze them in the company of a therapist can narrow the gateway to the private realm where the patient takes refuge in illicit fantasy. This disrupts the addictive cycle, and that is what I was hoping "The Man with the Twisted Lip" would convey to my anguished patient.

Nevertheless, preparing for the unrealized appointment opened an unexpected door to a great deal of personal retrospection and introspection. While the video was substantially similar to the film I remembered, certain discrepancies immediately convinced me that it was not an exact copy. In the first place, the present version was several minutes shorter than the one I remembered, some original scenes having been cut—including footage of the goings-on inside the car during the automobile ride. Second, I remembered the woman wearing a green dress, not the yellow one she wore in the version I had just revisited. Finally, I remembered quite well the face of the man who played the ex-husband in the original film: it was a mature, jowled face, with a groomed mat of silver-gray hair. My impression at the time was that the face belonged to the mogul who produced this film and, no doubt, others like it. The face in the video was not the same face. It was a younger head, cropped flat on top and ornamented with a Prussian moustache, eyes shaded by tinted glasses—a face and figure I knew very well. Same build, same coloring, same language, same voice. It even had a slight lisp.

Yes, I had seen that video before, as an 8-mm reel secreted on the closet floor of my naugahyde, Driftwood Cove hide-away, where I had for a while submerged it, along with a few magazines of a broadly similar nature (I referred to them, earlier, as "articles"). I had first seen it in a series of still shots on the cover of a sex rag openly displayed on various news kiosks strewn about the town of Perugia, and when I came across the film version during one of my midnight forays into the DMZs of La Concha, I purchased it out of brazen, prurient curiosity, viewed it in agitated horror, and destroyed it in disgust, fear and shame shortly afterwards. But apparently not before Heinz, armed with his secret-agent mentality, latex gloves, and skeleton key, had rifled through my closet. He would have found the reel. "I <u>watch</u> people," Heinz had written in his thank-you note for the magnolia, underlining "watch."

Not like a 'boss,' but like someone who is concerned, and who cares. Very few of the crew members know it, but I am aware of what goes on in all of them, and what makes all of them tick. I've been watching you tick, too.

I remembered that Heinz had more than once absented himself from the Ark, rumor having it that he was off to Europe for two or three weeks to confer with various classics professors. I did not keep track of his comings and goings. The web version of the film is dated the same year I left the Ark, but I had acquired the 8-mm version earlier than that, and I had seen the still shots of it in Italy some years before that. Had Heinz remade the whole film, or simply inserted himself into a re-edited version?

Strauss would not have needed to reshoot the whole script, and no, nothing in the web version—besides the presumed Strauss exposing and fondling himself among the cartons—shows him personally engaged in any of the "action". The only part of the video where he is clearly, unmistakably shown together with other actors is at the beginning, where he appears with the woman at the attorney's office. Was it the same actress, or a look-alike? But there is nothing in the video to tip off the first-time viewer that Strauss was not a part of the original production. Except that, if he was, wouldn't he have let his hair grow or shaved his moustache—done something to disguise himself for the camera? And if it wasn't he, waving his floppy thing at the viewer, but, say, a diabolical twin, wouldn't the real Heinz have had himself made over for reputation's sake? All he needed was a wave and a shave to be virtually unrecognizable.

The biggest problem with placing Heinz in the original film is this: if I recognized him now, wouldn't I have recognized him then? I saw Heinz practically every day. He was my boss, a respected scholar. Could I have so totally willed him, blocked him out of the film that I spliced in another face in my own brain? But if he was in the original film, he knew that I had seen it! Would he have risked goading me to revenge by destroying my academic career? I could have done the same to him!

But if he wasn't in the original, then he had inserted himself at a later time, and had done so deliberately for some specific purpose. Such as? And why was the original version not in the noosphere?

Whereas, if he was in the original, what could have been his purpose *then*? Just to enjoy himself? But he could have done that and stayed off camera!

Then, there was the matter of funding. What with Strauss's unconventional connections, he certainly had the resources to undertake unconventional projects. But he would have derived particular pleasure from having me, of all people, provide him with a respectable source. He knew that through my father's celebrity I would have access to philanthropic wellsprings. Was it for the remake that he had solicited "extra" funds for an "underfunded" project? Was it for this I had brought him to Dr. Wago?

Thinking back the torrent of unsavory inferences, I have to ask: Was Heinrich Strauss even a government agent? Was he simply a kindynophile, a danger addict, a psychopath who enjoyed thumbing his nose at the universe, secure in his own imagined invulnerability or aroused by his fear of exposure?

Strauss anticipated, in spite of the menace implied in the empty concert hall, that I would be consulting an attorney about the trick he had played on me with my credentials. He knew there was liability hanging over his head for the prank he had pulled with the symphony concert. He was walking a tightrope. He knew that a lawsuit would threaten the survival of his pet project, as well as collaterally expose his dubious connections. Perhaps by then Veronica was already dead; or maybe in training as a government operative; or in protective sequestration. What was one to think? Strauss needed a tool that he could use as leverage, in case I actually filed suit—a crowbar to pry me away from the legal snoops he wouldn't want sniffing around his operation. It wasn't blackmail he was after. He wanted a weapon that would persuade me, my co-plaintiffs, our lawyers, and himself, that he was untouchable, that he was from *Mission Impossible* and *Fantasy Island* combined, that he was the Godfather and 007 all rolled into one. Or that I was deranged, and that I would be an *autogol* witness if placed on the stand. He had his remake of *Community Property* tucked quietly away in his desk drawer, ready for delivery at a moment's notice—perhaps to be slid between my bed sheets like a severed canary's head. "Careful, Louis, don't sing!" It was a bluff, of course, but he knew I wouldn't call it.

Strauss's precautions were exaggerated. The lawyers I consulted advised me that the cost of the contemplated lawsuit—including, as it would have had to, the university as a defendant—was prohibitive, that any witnesses would be hostile or reluctant, that the harm to me from Strauss's refusal to have my credentials evaluated was hard to prove and the damages speculative, that it would be easy for Strauss to deny—his word against mine—that I had ever approached him with a request to establish my academic equivalency. As for the Chamber Ensemble—the conductor and the soloist—they had all been duly paid and would want nothing to do with a public airing of the Campus Theatre fiasco.

There was a rumor many years ago that a huge warehouse of master reels of the genre and type discussed above was destroyed in a huge fire that was started to avoid an anticipated police raid. The conflagration, reminiscent, in the negative, of the burning of the great library at Alexandria, would have left Heinz's remake a providential replacement for lost master footage of a profitable collector's item. That would explain its appearance on the web as the only extant version.

25

The River Speaks

Yet something about my hypothesis did not convince me. In fact, there was no hypothesis, because there were too many of them, too many alternatives, and no compelling reason to prefer one over the other. I became obsessed with finding a thread that would stitch everything together—obsessed to the point of exhaustion. Until, thanks to my psychiatric training, I realized that if I had been another person, I would have told me to make an appointment with a therapist.

Instead, I dreamed another dream. I woke from a deep sleep in the middle of Hampstead Heath, and made my way in a thick fog and a state of grief to the nearest tube station. Descending deep into the earth, I took the Northern Line to Charing Cross, changed to the Bakerloo and got out at Baker Street. I walked directly, as though I knew the way, to No. 221, and heretically descended the stairs to unit "B", which in my dream I assumed stood for "Basement". Hearing the melancholy strains of a violin playing a strangely familiar waltz motif, I was loath to knock, but no need, as the door opened and a rather dowdy housekeeper ushered me into the presence of a tall, thin man whose name you already know.

"Excuse my informality, Rabbi," said my host, as he bent over his violin case, showing me his rear end. "I like to play a tune or two before client intake. It calms my nerves and clears my head."

Suppressing an obvious riposte, I said, "We observant Jews all look like rabbis, Mr. Holmes . . ."

"But you're not. I can see that. No offense. I see it from your Greek fishing cap."

"You can see my cap with your . . . back turned?"

"I see your reflection in the mirror stitched into the lining of my violin case. No, good sir, we will not be needing my brother to solve your case."

"So you can read my thoughts in that little mirror?"

"You have made four erroneous assumptions, sir: one, that I have not read the papers you sent me; two, that I mistook you for clergy; three, that I am not aware of Jewish etiquette, and four, that I have no manners. I read your cover letter, as well as the documents it covered. Your lay affiliation is as obvious from the contents of your head as from its covering. Forgive me," said Holmes, turning around, and extending his hand, but withdrawing it before I could seize it. "My seeming discourtesy is but a stratagem to draw you out. I can tell more about a client with my backside than most detectives can with their Uncle Ned. You are a 6-O (i)-w in the Schlangenwurzel Catalogue of Personality Types. There's no need to patronize me. You've expressed your diffidence in my abilities rather well, in spite of your natural reticence."

"How so? Surely you don't deduce that I've come here to offend!"

"No, but you overestimate the difficulty of your case, and you underestimate the ease with which I can solve it."

"Really? Then have you solved the mystery from where you sit?" Holmes had in fact seated himself in the armchair facing mine, and bade me be seated.

"Mysteries exist only in literature. In life, there are no mysteries, only puzzles from which one or two pieces are missing to untrained eyes."

"How interesting! I would have thought quite the reverse!"

"You are a mystic. I am more practical. In your case, you already possess all the pieces . . . I beg your pardon! *Lupus in fabula!* The devil if it isn't Mycroft! Mrs Hudson, please show my brother in, and bring us some tea. I believe he grows more telepathic—not to say energetic—every day! Mycroft! What a pleasant surprise! Your timing evinces growing psychic powers! My client prefers your services to mine."

The dig was softened by a faint but benign smile.

"Gentlemen!" I protested weakly, as I rose to my feet. "You are both deservedly famous. Perhaps," I said, addressing the newcomer, who ignored my extended hand, "I was projecting my own frustrations upon your esteemed brother's abilities." And, turning to the latter, "I apologize for seeming to slight you. You are known for your ingenious investigative techniques, your brother for his armchair solutions." And again to the visitor, "However, your esteemed brother was just telling me that I already possess all the pieces to my puzzle."

"Very likely," replied the oracular presence as he sank his corpulent mass deep into a waiting armchair. "It is quite common to overlook the missing component simply because it is not made of the same material. *Dixine bene*, Sherlock? Not every jigsaw is all of wood."

"*Bene bonaque dixisti, frater.* But what brings you here?"

"I have an important question that only a Jew can answer. But the question can wait."

"Then take a moment, my dear Mycroft, and read this fellow's manuscript. It is only a couple of hundred pages. Meanwhile, I shall entertain Mister He-Didn't-Say-Who with a few not impertinent remarks of a prefatory nature. First, I take it that since you did not send in a calling card you are no longer sure who you are?"

"I think I have had as many as five names, but at the moment, I can't seem remember even one of them. But you read my papers, you said?"

"You have not slept well for a long time. Prolonged distress can erode one's memory as well as one's health. Perhaps, notwithstanding your doubts, I can restore both."

"Apropos, where is your friend, Dr. Watson?"

"Dr. Watson, I am afraid, has misplaced his jezail bullet. As he never leaves home without it, he is at present confined to his lodgings, where I trust his wife is helping him look for it. No doubt he'll drop in as soon as he settles on its location. Or perhaps not . . . But as I was intimating a moment ago, in our province, it is a mark of the amateur to overlook the obvious. You were well on the road to solving your puzzle. You have talent, imagination, logic, and intuition; but, like a true 6-O (i)-w, you are too preoccupied with your own pride and person to snatch the key that dangles before your very eyes. There are two elements to these crimes—for I do consider it a criminal matter—that you have failed to consider."

"Please go on."

"Two persons, in fact. Are you done, then, Mycroft? Good! Then you can follow along."

"Dear boy! I have been following your every word!"

"The human species, however abnormal in the individual specimen, does not act without motivation. The actions of your nemesis, bizarre as they might seem, were not without his own brand of tainted logic. They certainly bear the telltale signs of his mental condition. Now suppose we add to the *dramatis personae* of this sordid little skit the character of a woman, probably young, doubtless one of his pupils at the university, or perhaps simply one of the several he supplied with drugs. There was an affair. She became possessive, and he informed her of his intention to break it off. She resorted to threats. She would inform his wife. She would expose his drug activities. The usual folderol. The scandal would rock the entire Archaica Project to its nautical ribs, possibly terminate his academic career.

"Terrified, panicked, the professor pretended to relent, thinking to buy time to find a way out. The exit he found was grotesque and insane, but perfectly consistent with the type you have described. Too cagey to ward off the woman directly, he contacted an acquaintance of his in the Vaterland, a film-maker specializing in a certain genre of disreputable entertainment. To this contact, he proposed a plot and a joint venture. We know that the film was made, and we are certain that Strauss had a signal part in its making. His appearance in it was purposeful. It bore a message—his kind of message: 'If you fiddle with me, I'll faddle with you and fivefold. This is who I am, and this is what I can do with total impunity.' He had it delivered, probably with an invoice implying that she had ordered it.

"Your friend Strauss was an excellent judge of human psychology. The lady reconsidered, and probably left town posthaste.

The rest you know."

"But the yellow dress!" I protested. "The silver-haired executive! Surely, you can't totally eliminate the possibility that Strauss tampered with the original film?"

"Come, come! It is much easier to edit one's own memory than to splice new footage into an old film. Admitted: the original filming may well have required more than one take of two or three scenes. The dress would not have survived more than one shoot. You may well be correct that the version you saw contained a green dress. But they all contained Strauss. The silver-haired executive was, as you yourself suspect, an artifact of your own brain that you constructed to replace the likeness of the man you considered your benefactor."

"But if your hypothesis is correct," I interposed, "why did Strauss not grow a beard and a shag?"

"Because, on screen or off, to be recognized was the very point! He had to appear to his former paramour in his customary guise, had he not? How else would she understand that the message was from him and for her, and that he feared nothing and no one? Moreover, a change of style would have created identity problems for him at airport customs, where his appearance must have been well known—or, more importantly, with the people he traded with. He had reason enough to feel safe behind his moustache and tinted glasses. You know the expression, 'honor among thieves'? There is also discretion among perverts. And then, there was the specter of a libel suit against anyone so incautious as to name him: how to prove that it was not a look-alike?

"Perhaps his biggest concern should have been his government connections; but they probably knew about his cinematographic digression anyway, and what were they going to do about it? They certainly knew about his drug trade, and probably facilitated it. He had one on them, too, didn't he! Their files are bursting with unsavory information on millions of people, many of whom work for the government. Do you imagine that people who spy on their fellow citizens go flitting about with harps and haloes? Anyway, you have already pointed out that walking this sort of tightrope gave him a thrill. Such flamboyance is typical of megalomania, which he seems to have possessed to an extraordinary degree.

"So far, so good. But if megalomaniacs get a thrill out of risk taking, they also do not enjoy much peace of mind, do they? Not four years after he defuses one crisis, here you come traipsing into his life with another one—your copy of the very film! Boomerang! By his own thinly-veiled admission, he breaks into your apartment—as he seems to have done with all his charges—and discovers it hidden away in your closet. He is shocked and dismayed. Then you go to him with your request for certification of your status as a Ph.D.! Your request was perfectly correct, by the way. They told you quite baldly that you were a Ph.D., and you sought official confirmation. Naturally, having lied to you about it, he feared that you would try to extort something from him in writing! Indeed, in your farewell interview with him, he came right out and accused you of doing just that! You knew as well as he that he couldn't declare you a Ph.D. any more than he could declare you a Chinaman; but he saw you as a naïf, swaddled in a roseate vision of the world. I believe he calls you a 'Romantic' in his letter.

"You then had the poor judgement to hand him an obscene card for his alleged fiftieth birthday. You were applying for membership in their vulgar little club, but your joke misfired. We have seen how he dealt with threats, real or imagined. Your suspicion that the symphony concert was rigged is quite on the nail. I am certain of it. He warned you off as he warned off his mistress. It is a measure of his power that he was able to solicit university funding for this enterprise and yet blow it all to pieces with no accountability whatsoever.

"But there is something more. He destroyed your academic career. How did he manage that?"

"I have come to you, Mr. Holmes, with that very question. I do not know the answer."

"Well, say you felt obliged to destroy mine: how would you go about it?"

"I suppose there are only two ways: to besmirch either your competence or your moral fitness."

"Exactly. And your competence had already been amply demonstrated. Your scholarly reputation would have survived the setback of their degradation of your biblio credit, would it not?"

"I suppose so, if given half the chance."

"That leaves moral fitness, does it not?"

"I would have to agree."

"Tell me. Mr. Five-Names-Or-None: you have aliases; do you have a criminal record?"

"Certainly not!"

"Then were you ever accused of a crime? Rumors, perhaps? Talk?"

"Now that you mention it, there was something . . . when I taught at that friggin—pardon me!—the Crosswind school—that was soon after I left JWU—and ran into so many problems. Some students approached me on the playground to interview me for the school paper. During our conversation one of them asked if it was true that I had raped one of the women teachers. I laughed incredulously and said no, of course not. I didn't give it much thought. I took it for pure malicious gossip, of the kind that typically circulates among high-school students about their teachers. In fact, there was another ridiculous rumor that I was having an affair with the head of the English Department, an elderly woman. It probably started because the two of us occasionally took coffee together at a nearby café during lunch break. It was all too ridiculous."

"So there was talk. Talk is like snow crystals. It eventually melts away, but it forms around a tiny kernel of truth. Was there ever a complaint filed against you?"

"Not that I am aware of."

"You had submitted your resumé with Heinz's name in it to the principal of the Breakwind school?"

"Crosswind. Yes, of course. But I am sure you understand. I have not had many affairs. They were few, short-lived and far between. I am not the forward type. I have not been very successful in that department. People ask me why. They say I am good looking, attractive . . ."

"You are a quaint and gentlemanly relic, my dear sir. You would have done well enough in my time. Women of your generation and onward are surface dwellers. The telly, the silver screen, Elvis, the

Beatles, Ken & Barbie, Conan—the Barbarian, not Doyle. They fear depth. They do not read souls. They wish to be entertained. You are a closed book to them. You do not unleash their hormones."

"Of course, now and then . . ."

"Of course, now and then you do. But to those you titillate, you are a hot pot without a handle."

"Well, but I don't see how it is relevant."

"Trust me: 'Tis. Ah! Here's our tea! Thank you, Mrs. Hudson."

"There you are Mr. 'Olmes. The one in the middle is just the way you like it—not too 'ot, not too cold. I've brought your favorite Peak Freens, too."

"What would I do without you?"

"Same as anyways, Mr. 'Olmes. Will that be all?"

"Yes, Mrs. Hudson. Thank you. Please help yourself, Rabbi, and continue with your story."

"Just tea, thank you. For the blessing only. I'm not much in the mood for anything right now . . . *Baruch* . . ."

The tea was scalding. I put it down to let it cool.

"There was one young woman I dated for a short time at JW. I think she was a graduate student, a divorcee—her ex had been a minister, a preacher of some sort. She was a nice, clean girl, quite pretty in an ordinary way, attractive figure, a bit thinner than I usually go for. Her nose had been fixed. I remember, when she spoke, she always sounded as though she were getting over a cold."

"No doubt she told you she had a septoplasty."

"Yes, as a matter of fact, she did mention that she had had surgery for a deviated septum! How did you guess?"

"The vanity of a pretty girl. She would not have confessed to a nose job had she really had one. The septoplasty tells us something else. Go on."

"We went out a few times. Her name was Fiona. She showed me her room, introduced me to her landlady. Everything nice, neat and proper. Fiona and I quickly became quite affectionate with each other. We held hands, necked in the car, but she gave excuses when I invited her up to my apartment. Then, one Saturday morning, I drove up to Smokes to visit my family. Fiona went with me. Before we left, she asked me, "Where will I sleep?" and I told her, "In my room, with me." She made no objection, but I remember, when it was time to go to bed, she said she had a headache and needed to be alone. So I slept on the sofa in the next room. The den—my father's study. However, the next morning, I went to my room to check on her."

"Had she locked the door?"

"No. It was unlocked. She said she was fine. So I slipped into bed next to her, and we made love."

"Did she say anything? Did she protest?"

"No. Not at all. Well, she did feign surprise, she said—rather coyly, I thought—'What are you doing?' And I answered, 'Making love to you.'"

"In those words."

"Yes. And she seemed quite comfortable. It was very nice. I took precautions, of course. I don't remember at all what we did during the rest of the day. Maybe the art museum. We had breakfast together with my mother and father. We drove back to Nirvana that afternoon, and I dropped her off at her landlady's."

"What happened then?"

"I believe we had a date a few nights later. I wanted to take her to my apartment. But she said no, and backed away when I wanted to kiss her. I said, 'Fiona, what's the matter?' and she said, 'You raped me.'"

"And what did you do?"

"I was flabbergasted. You could have knocked me over with a feather. I thought for a moment, and then I said quietly, 'Well, then go to the police and file a complaint.' And I turned around and walked away."

"And did she? What happened next?"

"At first I was frightened, but then of course I realized that she had no case. Time passed, and nothing came of it. I never saw her again. Not even from a distance."

"I would wager that she filed a complaint with the Campus Police or with the Vice-Chancellor's office. Of course, no action was taken. But the complaint was there. Strauss now had a weapon in his pocket.

And he was ready to use it if you threatened him in any way."

"My God! Are you suggesting that I was set up?"

"Tell me: how did you meet Fiona? Who initiated the contact, you or she?"

"I did. Wait a minute! I was having lunch in the cafeteria with my colleagues from the Ark. Janoš, Edythe, Sky, Jason, and I think maybe Daisy and one or two others. That didn't happen very often— maybe twice during my whole three years at JW. Jason was sitting across from me. 'Louis!' he whispered, with a big wink. 'You see that cute blonde sitting at the table over there? By golly, I think you've made a conquest! She's sitting there all alone, and she's been looking at you sideways for the last several minutes!' Of course all my co-workers were aware of my chronic celibacy. After some egging on from my companions, I got up and went over to Fiona's table."

"My dear Louis—I see you've remembered at least one of your names! You are aware, no doubt, that nasal congestion is sometimes an indication of regular cocaine use?"

"No, I was not aware. You mean . . . ?"

"I do. I think Fiona and Cocamama were well acquainted. I should know. But at least I had the sense to use a needle. Where do you think she got her coke?"

"I begin to understand! I suppose I should thank God that she didn't extort money from my father!"

"Hold your thanks until you are sure she didn't. What would your father have done if he'd received a phone call or a letter from her attorney?"

"Good Heavens! My father was a most unworldly man! He would have been devastated. I suppose he would have called a friend of his to ask for advice."

"Any particular friend?"

"Well, yes. He had an old friend, a confidant—still from Vienna. The man had made a huge fortune in Hollywood. He had a genuine love and boundless admiration for my father. I guess he would have told my father, 'Yasha, don't worry about it. I'll take care of it. I know how to deal with such people. Leave it to me.'"

"And you don't know what happened?"

"No. My father never said a word to me. No one did. If money changed hands, he would not have been told."

"A loving father, and a worthy friend!"

"A son should give only *nachas* to his father. My God! What have I done?" I started to cry. I was dreaming, asleep, but I remember that I cried.

"So my conjecture rings true?"

"It would explain the loss of a close and precious friendship—the son of that man. I was dropped without explanation. The whole family shunned me. Openly. Cut me socially. Not a word of explanation. I wrote a letter. Unanswered. I don't suppose you know what that does to you."

"I have been called to cases for less. You meant no harm. You liked the girl, and you thought she liked you. Pop! Into bed! That's how it was in those inebriate, post-war days. You were raised in the murky tide pools of your times. These days, of course, everyone sticks to the straight and narrow.

"Now, you say that you continued to leave Strauss's name on your resume. The headmaster bloke as well. Am I correct? A foolish decision."

"Yes, perhaps it was foolish, but what was I to do? I had to have something to show for experience. Expunging their names would have meant conceding that their behavior towards me was justified. All I could do was hope that no one would contact them or that they would do the honorable thing."

"A reasonable hope on a different planet. What transpired next?"

"I went to two or three JWU officials to complain about Strauss's behavior—his refusal to hand over my equivalency papers. One of them, a woman—I think she was Assistant Dean of Something or Other—Students, I think—said, 'We've had complaints about him before,' and, 'There's more than one way to skin a cat.' She advised me to go back to him and plead for a letter of recommendation. It felt more like being skinned than skinning, but I did it."

"And of course your complaints went back to Strauss, who took the weapon out of his pocket—and used it every time he got a phone call from one of your prospective employers. Mycroft, do you agree with my reasoning?"

"My dear brother! I could have done no better. But there are some interesting points that you have passed over—no doubt for the sake of expediency, but I think they are worth mentioning."

"By all means, let's hear them!"

"I say, though, do you think you might ask Mrs. 'Udson to inject a bit of 'eat into this 'ere tea? I've left my skates at 'ome."

There was a long pause while the elder Holmes waited in a brown study for the requested BTUs to be poured into his rosy, and the younger chewed his lip to suppress the incongruous image of his bulky sibling turning pirouettes inside a tea cup.

"Mr. Yashanoshan, I find certain elements of your story extremely intriguing. Strauss's association with the police. His alteration of his age. His ham radio set. Did you see it, by the way?"

"I don't remember if he showed it to me, but there is a photo of it posted on the noosphere."

"Who posted it?"

"I believe the Police Department, in tribute to his service."

"Aha! He included it in his application package. Describe it to me, please."

"It's quite a stack, really. It looked very sophisticated. I know nothing about such things."

"He obviously used it for more than assisting the Police. It would have been very useful for scheduling his field trips.

"Tell me. You say he celebrated his fiftieth birthday in 1978 or 9. That would place his birth around 1928 or '29. Yet his obituary gives his birth year as 1934. What do you make of that?"

"At first, I assumed that it was to squeeze him into the Police Academy, but it seems rather pointless. It turns out there was no upper age limit for reservists. The obituary says he was graduated from the Academy in 2001. That would make him 67 years old by their count. That's over the hill whatever year you start counting, but he could have applied at ninety!"

"Quite so, but at 64 or 65, it is still possible for a man in excellent physical condition to pass the rather grueling physical training portion of the exam. According to you, however, he would have been above 70, and was probably hobbling around after his tête-à-tête with the truck. I do not say it is impossible, but his real age would have drawn attention to the preferential treatment he clearly received. Strauss had been assisting the police for years. I suppose he got his training years earlier. Who knows what credentials he had from the Feds! My own theory is that his Academy training was purely pro forma. Have you thought of another reason?"

"Well, he was born in Germany; whether in 1928 or '34, that would have put him in Hitler Youth during his teen years. He might have felt uncomfortable about that, but he didn't try to hide it. At least not as long as I was on the Ark. It was talked about."

"What if something developed that would have made him less comfortable?"

"Such as?"

"Such as networking with Nazi émigrés. Of course, that coin has two sides. If he was working as a mole for your knights on white horses, then he would have left his past alone. It would have been an asset. But what if he still had a sentimental attachment for the Old Order? To have been only eleven when the war ended suggests that one was too young to have compromising connections.

"Of course, that is all speculation, but the man had all the attributes of a double agent. Whatever he did had a double aspect. The loving preservation of ancient Greek literature versus the development of secret new software of great interest to the Government. Producing an innocuous film to promote the Ark, and a horrifying one to scare off an importunate woman. The bene-factor who gave you your first crack at academia, versus the scoundrel who destroyed your academic career. The sedate and sober, single-minded scholar versus the campus joy boy. The paternal shepherd of his flock versus the snoop with a skeleton key. The amateur policeman and the drug smuggler. He must have had fairly close connections with the German demimonde to co-produce that piece of filth. The matter calls for further investigation, but I have a hunch that what we have seen is just the tip of the iceberg. I think it is safe to assume that Herr Strauss made very full and ambiguous use of his 'ham' and his 'stack'. Let me not mince words: that he sent you condolences on hearing of your father's death shows a ferocious hatred and contempt the likes of which I have only observed in dyed-in-the-wool Jew haters."

"But Daisy—his lawfully wedded or common-law wife—was a Jew!"

"*Et voilà!* Another fine example."

"What about the girl, Veronica?"

"We shall return to her later. But apropos wife, I wanted to ask you, Sherlock: Why do you assume that the target of Herr Strauss's cinematographic masterpiece was a disgruntled paramour, and not his own wife? Is it not obvious from the preamble of the video that if it contained a warning, it was not to overmulct him at law? I thought your client made it clear that Strauss was divorced."

"Aha! Dear Mycroft, I was wondering when you would come around to that. I confess that I had my doubts. My reasons, in brief, are that I have been given no evidence that Strauss was married more than once, and as you know, I avoid unfounded assumptions. Edythe is the only former Mrs. Strauss we know about. Certainly there was no other wife around when that Bunny person—the heiress—got things rolling. Edythe seems quite chummy with her former spouse, whose loyal employee she has remained. Is it likely that he would have produced that revolting reel for her? It is far more probable that the divorce was occasioned by an escapade of the kind I have postulated. The divorce scene in the lawyer's office contains all the gunpowder needed for a powerful shot across the lady's piratical bows. She could not have been so literal as to have missed the point."

"She would have got the point alright, Sherlock, but where was it pointing? I think an *hetaera* would have found it confusing to watch someone portraying her lover's wife being subjected to a treatment she herself might have wished upon her. No, dear *frater minor*. Women have always fogged over that diamantine brain of yours. You've gone astray. Shocking as it may seem, the movie—the original or the patch job—it doesn't really matter which—was made for none other than Edythe. Her divorce from Herr Heinrich must have reached a pitch of acrimony that threatened to unravel all that he had worked for and dreamt of. Strauss was no poet. He had no patience for metaphor. Divorce meant divorce."

"Then what do you make of his playing with himself in front of the camera? Was that not a metaphor for 'Begone, Megaera, you don't ring my Little Ben anymore!'?"

"No, Sherlock. I think it meant quite literally, 'I am disarmed by the camera eye.' Strauss did not perform well under scrutiny. The scene may have been scripted differently, but he was, after all, no professional."

"Mycroft! You have once again demonstrated your peerless acumen. I humbly defer to your superior reasoning. But explain to me then Edythe's permanence on the Ark! Would she not have fled, like the mistress in my hypothesis?"

"Strauss's personality was that of a Mafia don. He could be ruthless, but once you kissed his *annulus*, he was your friend and protector. He liked to control people, situations, surroundings. He kept close watch on Edythe, married her off to his assistant, and gave her a position subordinate to his own and Jason's. But he also granted her supervisory authority, guaranteed her security and treated her with kindness and respect.

"Still, the strain on Edythe must have been close to unbearable. She is said to have been an extraordinarily beautiful woman at the Ark's inauguration, but just three or four years later, when your client first met her, she was already dowdy, pasty and bloated. Sigmund— I mean Doctor Freud—would have said this was her subconscious working to distance her from sexual assault. You describe her, Mr. Yashanoshan, as high-pitched and high-strung. It is a wonder the string did not snap under the strain."

"But you're saying that he made her a virtual prisoner!" I objected.

"Indeed I am! And Jason, too. You remember their failed rebellion, their pathetic attempt to break away? The naked photo in the X-rated tabloid—do you really believe they were hoping for discretion? Edythe was a good pupil. She learned something from her ex. A more desperate ploy—conscious or subconscious—is hard to imagine. But it wasn't their ad in the classifieds that sent Strauss scurrying for impromptu funds. You don't imagine that you were the only campus denizen who had seen that hideous film, do you? If anything could have sunk the Archaica Project, that was it! Your campus editor fellow may have been a cad and a scoundrel, but he was no blackmailer. Except for that one little detail, your analysis of the crisis was spot on."

"And what about Veronica?"

"Alas, she is alive or dead, like the cat i' the adage. How, when, or why, we do not precisely know, but it is clear that whatever happened, the university still does not want anyone to learn about it. I'd like to think Strauss rescued her from villainy and calumny and sent her away to a charmed new life on some Pacific island, but I don't believe it. Her expulsion was callous, pretentious, and unwarranted. It would not have been carried out without Strauss's acquiescence. It may very well have led to her demise. The Death Certificate seems genuine, at least as to the *causa mortis*. But it is *too* genuine! It is one of the few *causae* that cannot be tagged as a foreseeable consequence of her expulsion. Without foreseeability, there is no liability for negligent homicide. That fact inclines me to believe that the death certificate was falsified. Ironically, the ploy overlooked the victim's Hellenic ancestry. Thus, if she really died because of a yeast infection, there is malpractice lurking somewhere. And if she died for some other reason, there is far worse.

"If I could wave a wand, I'd have her grave dug up, and the box opened. You might get a hold of her family DNA. Perhaps she gave you a lock of her hair? Our old friend Lestrade could arrange all that."

"There's no need, Mycroft," interrupted the younger brother. "Don't wake up Lestrade! The girl is dead and in her grave at Metropolis. Your flights of fancy are spectacular, dear brother, but in soaring you sometimes lose sight of the lay of the land. Your theory about Neo-Nazi networking is certainly plausible, but, as you said, it is pure speculation. There are no facts to support it. I prefer gum shoes to wax wings. As our client intuited, the girl died at least five years before the date shown in the official record. The murderer must have dumped her body and run. It wouldn't have taken more than a day or two for someone to discover the body, but considerably longer to identify it. Once they knew who she was, she would have been interred under a false name, to be exhumed if the family ever inquired about her. Scandal! Why invite trouble? In 1989, when the inquiries came, the authorities would have retrieved her own corpse rather than that of a substitute and sent it on to Illinois."

"But Sherlock! How can you be sure that the girl is dead?"

"My dear brother! There is no other way to make sense of Strauss's five-year rejuvenation. It is the missing piece, the key to the whole puzzle."

"I don't understand," I interjected. "How does it fit in?"

"You remembered correctly," continued Sherlock. "You learned of her death in 1984, when your friend Sokrates came to bid you farewell. But she died not long after your visit—probably from a violent beating. It was not the first time she had been beaten. Indeed, you remarked the excessive rouge on her cheeks, which you at first took for a coquettish affectation, and then, reluctantly, as a sign of her latter occupation. It was neither, I assure you! The white mantilla—a precious memento from her bygone life—she threw it on quite literally as a veil over her present one. The poor girl must have been dying of shame before her two sympathetic friends. Her 'protector' evidently mistook you for paying clients. He took her driver's license. and left her by a country roadside—you indicated that there was farmland in the vicinity. There was no one to file a missing persons report. Her landlord was no doubt relieved to be rid of the pair of them, scupper the rent! The young woman was estranged from her family and secretive about her life. The passage of three years between her death and Strauss's statement tells us the Police had problems identifying the body. Who was she? For all you, Naumachou, or anybody knew, Veronica simply moved away and changed her name.

"But if nobody suspected foul play, how could they identify her body?"

"Mycroft, I defer to your superior imaginative arts. I suspect it had something to do with her books, but I can see the wheels already turning beneath that formidable brow, and I shall venture no further."

"You are too modest, Sherlock. I see by your smile that you have

247

fully grasped the matter. Yes, of course Veronica left books behind in her protector's apartment. Some of them were textbooks from the university bookstore. The landlord would have donated them to the university library. Among Veronica's books—I am quite certain of it—was a Septuagint, a Greek Bible with Greek text. Obviously, it took a while, but someone from Archaica or Classics must have come across it while browsing the stacks. They would have found it very alarming to see Veronica's name written on the flyleaf. They remembered Veronica. She would never have parted with it. They notified the Police, who sat them down with a pile of photographs of unidentified female corpses. The photos of Veronica, shocking as they were after a fatal beating and a night in a cabbage field, would not have been hard to recognize."

"Precisely! Thank you Mycroft! How could I have overlooked that? Of course! The girl had originally enrolled in Classics to study the Scriptures 'in the original Greek!' I have allowed myself to be led astray by her latter pursuit of the higher degrees! Forgive me, Mr. Yashanoshan! Dr. Watson confiscated my syringe, and I fear I am but the shadow of myself without it.

"Now, if I may continue, when the Police finally took Strauss's statement, it would have focused on Veronica's academic performance and the deliberations over her dismissal. However, Strauss gave his age truthfully as 55 or 56. The case was closed and sealed on Strauss's petition. Indeed, the shock did not prevent him from orchestrating and implementing a cover-up with the full cooperation of the Classics Department and University Admin.

"Later, when unexpected developments forced the authorities to reopen the file, postdate her demise and falsify its cause, Strauss's recycled deposition still had him at the same age in 1989 as it was in 1984. When he realized the anomaly, he fretted that, if noticed, the contradiction would open him and his accomplices up to a charge of perjury and a host of other offenses. An investigation into Strauss's extracurricular activities would surely follow. Of course, the chance of the file being scrutinized was small, but the stakes were enormous! What if you or perhaps someone else filed a complaint against him? What if someone blew the whistle on the autopsy and the cover-up?"

"And what if the family wanted to view her body before interment?" interjected Mycroft.

"Highly unlikely, Mycroft! Remember, twelve days passed between the faux death certificate and the reburial. That would be enough time to justify shipping an unembalmed corpse in a sealed casket. No doubt the university was happy to foot that bill, but five years had already passed since her first burial. It was too late to embalm her."

"But the death certificate itself . . ."

"Yes, I know. It is suspicious on its face, but only as it pertains to medical malpractice. If it had come to that, the university would have gladly settled with the family rather than undergo pretrial discovery. The 1989 volume of *True Grit* had already been sequestered because it contained no mention of Veronica's death or her Ph.D. candidacy. I don't know if Strauss felt any younger after postdating himself, but he could certainly feel safer. He did not like to leave loose ends."

"But what about his birth certificate? His passport?"

"All he would have had to do is report to his handlers that there was uncomfortable talk on campus about his past membership in Hitler Youth and they would have provided him with revised documents. As for his original birth certificate, it was safely tucked away in some Nazi archive back home in the Reich. I find it rather amusing that Strauss died born-again, don't you?"

Holmes chuckled as he contemplated the toes of his worn slippers. "Forgive me, Mycroft, but I can just see you raising hue and cry for Veronica's grave to be opened! And what do they find? Veronica! A bit disheveled, perhaps, after two burials and thirty-odd years, but Veronica, no less. End of story! You must understand, dear sir: my esteemed brother once nearly got a client of mine killed by publishing an ad in the Classifieds requesting information on the very ruffians who had threatened my client's life! Remember, Mycroft? That Greek Interpreter fellow?"

"You have never let me forget it! But what makes you so sure that it was Veronica's body that they sent back to Metropolis?"

"It was the one decent thing they could still do," replied the detective matter-of-factly. "The miscreants could now look at themselves in the mirror."

Holmes paused thoughtfully, then, turning to me, "You haven't yet leafed through volumes 1981 through 1984 of *True Grit*. I wouldn't rush into it, though, if I were you, sir. You don't know to what lengths your adversaries might be willing to go to protect their interests. Corrupt institutions are more dangerous than corrupt individuals. It is right and good that you have remembered your friend, but you can't bring her back. In fact, my solemn advice to you, old fellow, is put all this behind you and get on with your life."

It was touching to see Mycroft beaming with pride at his brother's performance, but the great detective's words rang somewhat hollow in my ears.

"I aim to," I replied, wondering how much of my life there remained to get on with.

"Well then, it appears that the matter is concluded. I regret that closure cannot under the circumstances procure for you the compensation you undoubtedly deserve. It appears you have been severely punished for a youthful folly. Perhaps . . ."

"Apropos compensation, Mr. Holmes . . ."

"A thousand Victorian pounds or nothing! Tut, tut, there's no need. You've stirred my congealed blood. Mycroft removed a small clot or two. That's reward enough.

"Now then, Mycroft, ask the Jew your question, and let us depart."

Depart? I wondered. But this is *your* home!

"Well then, by your leave," began the senior Holmes, "Good sir: in my former capacity as Portfolio without Ministry, I had the honor to be invited one Friday evening—and, may I say, in some very distinguished company!—to Mrs. Meir's table . . ."

"Mrs. Meir?"

"Golda Meir—your namesake, Sherlock, sort of—I always thought you two would have made a good match. I'll tell you, old chap, had you married her, you would have seen a lot more of me!"

"Mycroft, you know very well that I am as sexual as a parsnip."

250

"I can vouch for that!" The ill-suppressed grumble issued from the kitchen.

"You used to grow them, I believe."

"Sherlock, you grow shy potatoes in the presence of feminine grace. Our nanny must have done something to you. Golda would have set you right! — Sir, he is jesting about the parsnips. It is a family joke. But on that memorable occasion, Mrs. Meir served something absolutely delicious called a . . . a 'Ge- . . . Gefilte Fish'? I'd never tasted anything like it. Her own recipe! I begged her to give it me. It was quite divine, but she flatly refused. Said it was a state secret. I've never had anything so heavenly before or since. I am told, however, unlikely as it may seem, that you Jews habitually partake of this delicacy on Sabbaths and Festivals. Could you . . . would you . . . might you be so kind as to procure me the recipe?"

"*The* recipe, dear sir? *The* recipe? There are a thousand recipes for gefilte fish! It is an art like music and dance and painting. Many have tried, but few have succeeded."

"Get me just one from one of those who have succeeded, good sir, and I shall be eternally indebted to you!"

"Then the indebtedness will be mutual," I said, "and a gefilte fish shall be our witness!"

With this sententious nonsense on my lips, I gently awoke. My wife was cooking the Shabbos meal, and the fragrance was from Heaven.

26

Nigun

And now I must borrow a term from that great crucible of American culture, that grail of enlightenment and humanity, champion of the intellect and defender of ethics, historical truth, and gentle custom, and *cut* to a place and a time sixty miles and light years from Conchacancha County and its hot tubs, its rolling surf, its tennis courts and digitized time capsules . . .

It was a Shabbos night and there had been a happy event. I was walking up Riverside Avenue on my way to a Shalom Zachar to welcome the arrival of a Jewish boy-baby, when I heard the muffled sound of choral singing coming from an open doorway. It was one of the many synagogues that stand in rows along that busy thoroughfare, like sentinels, and one I subsequently became quite familiar with, except that my memory of it as it was that night does not correspond to its present condition, which I am quite sure is just the same as it was then. I stopped short to listen, straining to hear. Drawn irresistibly toward the music, which reached me in brief snatches between the rumblings of passing vehicles, I passed through the entrance and up the stairs, emerging into a dark and narrow hallway at the end of which was a smaller dining room, used for prayer and study, off the main banquet hall. Except that I remember it at the opposite end of the hallway instead of where I know it is really located. The doorway to this chamber was open and ablaze with light and song. The study tables had been joined together in a great "U" and covered with white cloth so as to form two large banquet tables stretching all the way down the center of the room and joined at the

252

head by a shorter row of tables.

Framed in the doorway, at the far end of the room, at the conjunction of the two long rows of tables, seated at the very middle between two of his attendants, was the figure of a white-robed rabbi with a long, reddish-brown beard and a tall fur hat—a spoddek. A Chassid who was sitting at the table closest to the entrance turned to me and gestured to an empty chair squeezed in beside his, but I stood hesitant. I had been to more than one Tish, and I was quite familiar with such proceedings, but there was something intimidating about this particular scene, as though I had been invited to walk into a different world. The Chassid rose from his seat and walked toward the open door, gesturing for me to enter.

"Why you standing outside?" he queried in mixed Yiddish and broken English. "Kim h'rein un zitz! Iz a empty chair." He pulled me inside, sat me down beside him, and reached for a plate, a piece of kugel and a leg of roast chicken, which he set before me.

"Thank you! Who is the Tzaddik?"

"This the Molodianer Rebbe," answered the Chassid. "You not see him before? He not give Brochos. He sing. You sit, you eat, you hear, you ask Hashem Brochos what you need. It go up to Shamayim with the nigun." The Chassid laughed quietly to himself.

"Molodia?" I said. "My mother was born in Molodia!" I had already eaten my Shabbos dinner, and the music was food enough for me; but knowing that there is merit in eating at the table of a Tzaddik, I said the blessings *Mezonos* and *Shehakol.*

Around the tables sat, squeezed-in tight, a curious assortment of Jews—black hats, streimels, spoddeks, kapelitches, golf caps, and just plain yarmulkes, men in capotes, and bekishes and business suits as well as three or four shnorrers and students in street clothes. At the Rebbe's right hand, at a right angle, sat a row of five or six Chassidim in white capotes—the Rebbe's choristers. They and the Rebbe were the source of the music I heard outside on the street.

To be sure, we all joined in when we weren't busy chewing, and nobody sang out of tune, but it was clear that the white-clad men on the left and the radiant apparition at the head of the table were accomplished vocalists in the middle of a concert performance. I was surprised to discover how challenging it can be to eat good food, listen to rapturous music, and talk to God, all at the same time.

Not long after I sat down, there was a pause in the singing, and the Rebbe reached his hands into a large basket of fruits, took two or three pieces for his own plate and then distributed the remainder to his Chassidim, who passed it around the table in smaller baskets. Another *nigun* took flight, even more beautiful than the last. This continued for some time, with many strange and wonderful nigunim following suit. Finally, and much to my disappointment, the singing came to a close, and the Cup of Blessing was placed before the Rebbe, who passed it to the Chassid whom the Rebbe designated to lead the Grace, and the bentshing began.

To my happy surprise, as soon as the concluding blessing over the wine was said, the Rebbe stood up, held out his hands, which were immediately taken by the Chassidim at his side, and launched into yet another nigun. At this, everyone stood up, joined hands and commenced to walk—it was more like dancing—a stately circling around the hall, in step and in time to the music, one-two, one-two, a march.

Now, all the tunes I had heard sung at the table were beautiful and distinctive, unlike any other nigunim I had heard before, but this particular nigun was special—in a minor key, yet full of convivial happiness and confident trust in Providence, with all the parts—melody, rhythm and structure—fitting together with such a sense of rightness and satisfaction that we could have danced around the tables for hours on end without tiring.

The one thought that kept talking to me, whispering in my ear, was a verse from Psalms, *You have lifted me from the dungheap and placed me among nobles.* Becoming strictly observant and attaching myself to a Rebbe had not made my life any easier. I had lost friends and forfeited the respect of many people whose esteem, rightly or wrongly, had meant something to me. My wonderful humanistic education meant nothing here. I had seen many doors close shut that I had assumed would remain open. I was still beset by many problems and anxieties—my mother's deteriorating health, difficulties finding a compatible mate, obstacles in the way of establishing myself professionally. Yet that night, I felt positively victorious. I had fallen among the wicked and survived to do good. Against my will, I had cultivated darkness and despair and had seen the crop blasted by light and hope. I had lost my way in a savage wood and found myself whole and my way open before me. I had turned back the river and crossed over dry land. I had found light, purpose, the path of my saintly ancestors. I had planted myself in the society of the just. I had known almost nothing about my Heritage, yet here I was, a Jew among Jews, a Chassid among Chassidim, a brother among brothers.

You have lifted me from the dungheap and planted me among nobles.

It was hard to talk to the One Above about my needs, because in that moment I had none. Everything I needed was in that moment given me. The music, the dance, the company of other Jews—strangers to me, yet brothers, friends, family. All I really needed was to remember this nigun forever.

I don't know how many times we marched around the table, how many times we sang the beautiful melody over and over again before the human ring disbanded and the Molodianer Rebbe, accompanied by his choir and Chassidim, filed out of the hall, still singing, in a lingering flash of white.

Straining to catch the last notes as they floated up the stairs, I knew I would remember them forever.

There is no need to tell you, my friends. By the time I got home, humming frantically all the way, I couldn't remember a note.

Several years have passed since that Shabbos night, and the Molodianer has not returned to the Valley of Smokes. The memory of that Shabbos night has never left me, nor has my longing for the sweet sounds of that elusive Song. Over the course of those years, I asked several people who I thought might have attended that Tish, but none of them knew what I was talking about. I found a cassette of Molodianer Nigunim and bought it, but the March was not among them.

Nor have I ever come across those other forgotten melodies—the jaunty tune the brass band played that desperate night in Perugia, marching like a spectral apparition out of the fog, nor the calliope waltz that accompanied the solitary carousel on that dark, deserted beach.

On the other hand, among the music that I do remember, I consider myself fortunate—indeed, blessed—to have heard Beethoven's Fourth Piano Concerto played by my father. And perhaps I have even remembered something about its second movement that nobody else knows.

27

Mandelbaum

There is one final chapter to this story, and it is the element that inspired me to begin it. Some years ago, I had a little guest house built in our back garden so that my mother could live out her last years in my care. That arrangement did not please her, so another one had to be found. Meanwhile, the guest house ended up as a storage room for the many items that my wife and I were unable to integrate into our joint lives. After several years of discussing the obvious fact that the space could be more profitably used as a rental, we cleared out the storage and made it ready for occupancy. Word got out before we had time to place an ad, and my wife received an inquiry in rudimentary English from a "Mr." Mandelbaum.

"Mandelbaum the Rabbi?" I asked.

"He didn't say Rabbi. At least I don't think he did," replied my wife.

"If it's the rabbi, we must get him. It would be a great honor!" Rabbi Mandelbaum was known in our Community as a big Chocham and a Tzaddik, and though I did not really know him personally, and could not remember how or where I had met him, I had some personal acquaintance with the sweetness of his character. Whenever our paths crossed he would always greet me warmly, sometimes stopping to share with me some Torah thought in a nervous, express-train Yiddish that I could have only understood via telepathy.

"Mr." Mandelbaum proved indeed to be the rabbi, and in due time he moved into our guest house with a load of holy books and used furniture that violated all the fire codes and barely left him room to turn around in. Naturally, we invited him to join us for dinner the very next Shabbos, and were surprised and delighted when he accepted.

Rabbi Mandelbaum proved to be a most precious acquisition to our Shabbos table, which I am happy to say he often attended. His stories, his Torah expositions (Droshos), his displays of Halachic knowledge, his personal reminiscences were a fascination and a delight. He had an unpretentious yet beautiful voice, and his repertory of nigunim was inexhaustible. Every tune the Rabbi sang was prefaced by an announcement of its meaning, the branch of Chassidus to which it belonged, and often the Rebbe or Chassid who composed it. That first Shabbos night, he sang nigunim from Bobov, Vizhnitz, Lubavitch, and Boyan. When to this string of musical pearls he added a little jewel from Molodia, I told Rabbi Mandelbaum about my experience with the Molodianer Rebbe some thirteen years before, how we had danced around the Tish to a wonderful, joy-giving melody. I told him how frustrated I had been not being able to remember it.

"Was it this one?" the Rabbi smiled, and immediately launched into song.

"Yes! That's *it*!" I shouted, incredulous, jumping out of my chair in my excitement. "That's it! That's the one! How do you know this nigun? How did you know that was the one I was speaking of?"

"I was there," said the Rabbi, laughing quietly. "I was at that Tish."

"But that was many years ago!"

"Nu, nu . . ."

"Yes, now I remember! You *were* there. Yes, yes! It was you! Of course! You were the one I sat next to! You invited me in and made me sit next to you!"

No doubt you are thinking, "How wonderful! Now the shlemiel will be able to sing his nigun whenever he needs to hear it!" The truth is, my friends, I was never able to memorize it, those simple, magical notes! Perhaps they belong to a sphere that I have not yet been granted clearance to enter unaccompanied. For a time, Rabbi Mandelbaum would sing it for me whenever I asked him to, and then I would join in; but he has long since returned to his home in the Land of our Fathers.

No doubt, you are also wondering, what became of the other scroll—the one that Egil Heklason gave me?

I am still trying to remember where I hid it . . .

NOTES

NOTES

NOTES

Other Works by Peter Gimpel

POIKILOPAIDIA: Collected Poems (1960 – 2020)

Green Beetle Diaries: a Haiku Novel (forthcoming)

Professor Gansa's Dream, or Science as a Naked Lightbulb:
a Jewish Reply in 75 "Stanzos" to Carl Sagan's *Science as a Candle in the Dark*

The Carnevalis of Eusebius Asch: a Polymorphic Romance
of Image and Dialectic

Other Works Published by Red Heifer Press

Tell It Not: 17 Stories by Deborah Freeman

TANAIS: Kyklonio & Tanaïs: Two Poem Cycles by Iossif Ventura
Commemorating the Destruction of the Jewish Community of Crete.
(Greek, with English version)

Until Your People Pass Over: The Story of Our Lives,
by Moishe & Yetta Feiner

Sobol Says (Two Minutes of Torah): Bereishis, by Ephraim Sobol

Luminous Orange: Haiku by Alexander Forbes

After the Moon a Blue Ocean: Haiku by Alexander Forbes

Concert Paraphrase of the Song of the Soldiers of the Sea:
For the Piano, by Jakob Gimpel (Sheet Music)

If I Could Sleep. Novel by Alex Stone

Light in the Closet: Torah, Homosexuality and Power to Change,
by Arthur Goldberg

13 Ways of Looking at Images: The Logic of Visualization in Literature
& Society, by Mervyn Nicholson

Red Heifer Press

Publishers of Torah/Judaica, Survivor Memoirs,
the Humanities, Arts & Sciences,
Belles Lettres, Poetry & Literary Fiction

www.ingramcontent.com/pod-product-compliance
Lightning Source LLC
Chambersburg PA
CBHW020400120726
47904CB00002B/639